White

I0611300

Dorf

Dorf

Copyright 2007 by David White

ISBN 978-0-6151-9617-6


Cover Artwork by Shakeil Greeley

*To my friends and family,*

*don't worry, that includes dogs as well, Bravo*

The Dwarven race has existed ever since the world was created. They were forged by the very energies that the world was born from, sculpted by the gods and animated by the air. From the dawn of time, they have lived beside humans and had lived with them as equals for many centuries. Though only half as large as human beings, the dwarves were treated with the same respect that humans gave to each other. But it would not last.

When the three-thousandth anniversary of the recording of time approached, some dwarves began to exhibit strange, foreign, yet useful powers. They could move the wind to meet their desires, fortify their own natural abilities for combat, and could hold fire in their hands as if it was merely a clump of dirt. These dwarves had been given a gift.

For decades, the dwarves used their powers to fulfill their own interests, sometimes at the expense of others. They quickly became superior in combat and renowned in every part of their home country, Arcoiris. Dwarves would often hold contests in which only they could win, simply to show their power over the humans. Although not necessarily dominating the country, the dwarves were eager to become the more prominent beings in the land. Yet they were outnumbered greatly by the humans, which turned out to be their downfall.

Around the year three-thousand two-hundred, men and women in Arcoiris began to emulate the dwarves, and to learn their powers. Through extensive research and experiments, a handful of men learned how to perform other feats that were new and strange to their society. They learned that if they focused their minds properly, they could produce magical effects such as conjuring a flame, manipulating the wind, and other actions that were impossible for humans to accomplish. These men became the first wizards of their country.

The wizards first thought that their magic could rival the dwarves. No longer were they so easily bested in fights, no longer were they left out of contests involving nearly impossible tasks. And no longer was the Dwarven race the undisputed all-powerful race in the world.

Yet, when the wizards next observed the dwarves carefully, they found out that their powers were still superior to theirs. The wizards' spells themselves had not changed, just their method of casting them. Meanwhile, the dwarves were still able to effortlessly use their powers infinitely and to further show signs of their great power. Finally, the wizards were brought back on track; they knew that they would need to learn the dwarves' powers if they truly wished to prove humanity to be the more powerful race.

The wizards began using their magic to capture dwarves and  to furiously question them about their powers. They would go to their homes, round them up in the street, or do whatever they felt to be necessary for their victory. But when questioned about their powers, the dwarves could not provide explanations. They insisted that their powers were purely instinctive, and that they did not know whether or not humans were capable of using them. Now desperate for answers, the wizards interrogated dwarves and killed them if they did not provide them with methods of gaining their powers. Though the dwarves had significant powers, the wizards would take them by surprise, outnumber them, and terrify them until they died.

The wizards soon authorized a formal hunt for any dwarves in Arcoiris, persuading their fellow humans to join them in the quest for power. They offered ridiculously high bounties for each dwarf captured, organized hunting parties, and passed several decrees restricting the movement of dwarves throughout the country. Naturally, the dwarves fled in multitudes, but most of them would be captured and killed. In more than one instance, the wizards would kill the dwarves who resisted them the least, claiming their powers to be of little or no use to them.

The Dwarf Hunts lasted for two decades, then came to a close when a new order of wizards and sorceresses was founded. They scorned the violence of the previous wizards, and gave up their inherited hold on the country immediately. They abolished all laws against dwarves and gave them equal status as humans in a desperate attempt to undo the past, but the damage was already done. The few dwarves who had survived were hiding outside of any civilized area of the country, not entirely trusting the new wizards or the subjects of the newly crowned King.

But over the next millennium, the dwarves slowly died out and became nothing more than distant memories within Arcoiris. Yet one family of dwarves managed to survive the persecution and injustice thrust upon them, managed to exist well into the four-thousandth year of recorded history. And the entire Dwarven lineage, the years of prosperity and the years of destruction, have led up to this moment, and to this young hero.

# The Beginning

Nathaniel Dorf woke up to the most annoying noise in the world: angry chickens who wanted to be fed. Nathaniel turned over under his comfortable blanket and looked at his silver watch. The time was six o'clock in the morning. *The chickens were on time today* thought Nathaniel. Unfortunately, the farmer doesn't wake up until eight.

Nathaniel Dorf had to wake up each morning by six o' clock to get to the local tavern, The Golden Tavern, on time to tend to his customers from behind a counter. Nathaniel had long pondered the best way of waking up, and even went as far as testing them during the winter holidays. He tried telling the Night Watch when to wake him up, but they tricked him and woke him up six minutes after he fell asleep. He tried telling his parrot, Herbert, when to wake him up, but Herbert had a mind of his own and decided to let him sleep for half of the day before allowing him to discover the parrot holding a house party in his cottage. Each time, Nathaniel thought *this has to be the worst way to wake up*, when it had hit him: he needed to choose the worst way to wake up so he could never fall asleep. After sleeping in the town barn for one night, the chickens became used to his schedule, and worked as the best waking-up device in history. Unfortunately, Herbert was *very* skilled at mimicking voices and animal noises.

"Bawk! Bawk!" Herbert would yell on several occasions, making a dead-on impression of the farmer's chickens. Nathaniel would often turn his slingshot on the parrot, but Herbert was a fast-moving bird who could fly out of the reach of a longbow let alone a slingshot aimed by someone three feet tall.

Nathaniel Dorf was a dwarf. He stood three feet tall, had feet as large as an adult male's, and was the only bartender in all of Arcoiris who used a stool like his customers. Nathaniel was twenty years of age, young by any race's standards, but was no larger than a human seven-year-old.

Nathaniel swung his legs out of his warm bed and grabbed his watch from his old wooded night table. His watch, gleaming and bright with polished silver, was the single most valuable object in his possession. The watch not only looked nice, but had a one-hundred an twenty-five year history behind it. The watch had been passed down to each generation of Dorfs and had never needed to go to a shop for repair. The black hands always turned and swung at the right time and at the right place. Nathaniel always knew what time it was when he had his watch on.

Anywhere else in the world, a watch that does not need repair seems useless, because getting a watch fixed takes little and little money. In Kumaiyan, the small town that Nathaniel lived in, most people would sell the clothing off their backs for that watch. Not as if it would be enough.

No man or woman capable of repairing a watch lived in town. Of course, that can be attributed not to the ineptitudes of the townspeople, but to the small population in town. Only three-hundred men, women, children, and one dwarf lived in Kumaiyan. Yes, travelers came through the town on many occasions but very few repairmen traveled through that part of the woods.

Kumaiyan was situated in the middle of a gigantic forest, known as The Maze. The Maze, however, was very easy to find your way through for it had a neat dirt path carved through it, but it was a long path and Kumaiyan provided rest and shelter for weary travelers.

Kumaiyan was south of the capital city, Vikelad, and north of the southern border town, Geroed. People going to and fro the two large cities had little choice but to stay in Kumaiyan, for the other small villages were located further to the east and west of the cities. Traders would often stop in Vikelad to sell valuable objects and trinkets, move south to Kumaiyan to see which of their lower-priced objects could fetch a nice pile of gold, and move south again to Geroed to purchase what would become valuable jewels, pots, and other signs of wealth for single coins. Several merchants fell out of the good books of Geroedians; the Geroedians, a proud, hard-working people did not like being cheated. Their warriors sent many merchants into hiding, up north, or into graves.

As Nathaniel pulled his light brown pants up to his waist and tied them off with a large, dark brown string, Herbert came flying in through his cottage window holding a roll of parchment. Herbert dropped the parchment onto Nathaniel's bed, then rested on his perch over it. Nathaniel looked up at Herbert.

"Thanks, Herbert," said Nathaniel curtly. He was still peeved at the parrot's latest attempt to sabotage his work day. Nathaniel had woken up on time, gotten dressed up for the tavern, eaten a half-loaf of bread and fruit at his cottage table next to his bed, and opened his cottage door to leave when everything went wrong. His shoes, made of brown leather, had been tied together while he was eating breakfast. Because of this, Nathaniel had fallen over to land face-first in a nicely placed bucket of beer. His hair, blond and growing down past his ears, was drenched and smelled like beer. And to top it off, Nathaniel had finally entered The Golden Tavern, explained his bizarre appearance to his customers and assistants, and began to walk behind his counter to his stool only to find that he had misplaced his pants. Nathaniel's boss, Ralf, would have kicked him out of the bar and fired him from his job, but he was too busy laughing his head off and painting a picture of Nathaniel to take any action against the young dwarf.

"You're lucky I didn't decide to plant a surprise under your pillow last night with that attitude," replied Herbert as Nathaniel immediately lifted his pillow and closely examined the stainless blanket beneath. "I said I didn't."

Nathaniel turned to where the parchment lay on his bed. He picked it up and unrolled the first six inches, about the first half, of the piece.

"Hmm....not much here. This says that a few more bears have been seen by the merchants.....no deaths, by the way. Let's see....oh! A new article on the tavern!" exclaimed Nathaniel. Herbert flew down to rest on Nathaniel's shoulder as the dwarf began to read.

"Traveling through the seemingly endless Maze? Need to give your legs a hard-earned break? Do you just need to find a place to sit down and enjoy yourself? Then come to The Golden

Tavern, where you never have a reason to be anywhere else!" read Nathaniel aloud. "And that's from the capital!"

"Oh, did they have the picture of the drunken dwarf?" asked Herbert enthusiastically. Nathaniel glared at him. "Joking, joking....I wonder if they never even got it." Nathaniel strode to his round table. The table, made out of wood like every other part of the house, was large enough to fit four human-sized people with chairs for people of both human and dwarf height. Nathaniel held the hope that one day another dwarf would waltz into town and have a cup of tea with him.

But that was a very unlikely event. No other city or town in the country had ever heard of the rumor of another dwarf. The dwarves were thought to be nearly extinct. Nathaniel Dorf was the exception to that. Although his parents had both been human, his father's father had been a dwarf and passed the Dwarven blood down to him. It was believed that the dwarves simply died out, ironically their life expectancy was vastly greater than humans. Nathaniel Dorf was proud of his heritage and the townspeople respected his heritage, but life was still difficult when you can only reach the top shelf of your own house on your tip-toes when your flying parrot friend feels like he is being treated like a slave.

Nathaniel had to make many adjustments to his life that humans didn't need to make. As it was mentioned before, he was the only bartender to use a stool. Nathaniel also needed

Herbert to fetch items from the top shelves at the market because he could not reach them. Nathaniel had built a small stool for himself with metal hinges that he could carry on his back to take with him when he went out. The door to Nathaniel's house was where a grown human's waist would be. Nathaniel could participate in the town duels every End Day, but had a distinct disadvantage due to his height.

Nathaniel poured himself a cup of tea and sat down at his chair. Nathaniel has always liked tea, and it was nearly impossible for him to start the day without it. Nathaniel took a sip of the hot liquid. It warmed his mouth, giving him a pleasant sensation. Even though it was springtime, the weather was still a little chilly in the morning. Also, dwarves enjoyed the heat, and disliked the cold. Every second that Nathaniel could spend being warm was better than a second being cold.

Herbert flew down from his perch and landed on the table a foot away from Nathaniel's cup of tea. Herbert was a green parrot with a yellow beak and yellow markings, and had several strange qualities. For one, he could speak on his own. Secondly, he was as intelligent as any human, an odd attribute for any bird. Thirdly, Herbert sported two black, circular markings around his eyes that very much represented glasses. Whether or not he was born with them Nathaniel did not know. Nathaniel had not met Herbert until two years ago.

It had been a dark, gloomy night. Nathaniel had been seeing off the rest of his customers at the tavern and locking up the building when he heard a strange knock on the door. Believing it to be a drunk who simply wanted another mug, Nathaniel opened the door, ready to kindly tell the man that the tavern was closed for the night, when a green mass soared through the door and struck him on the head. After much swearing and swatting, He had managed to find himself face-to-face with the green parrot. Nathaniel had tried to simply shoo the parrot out of the tavern, but the parrot kept flying further and further into the bar with a happy expression on its face. Finally, the parrot had flown onto one of the barstools. Nathaniel, seeing an opportunity to catch the parrot, closed the door and slowly made his way towards the bird. When he was a foot away from victory, the parrot turned around to face him and said in a very human-like voice:

"How 'bout a pint?" The two stared at each other, Nathaniel in disbelief and the parrot with pleading. After several long seconds, Nathaniel broke down laughing and in minutes the two were speaking to each other and becoming the best of friends. For hours and hours they talked, drank, and even sang a little. When the time grew very late, Nathaniel, although slightly inebriated, allowed Herbert to rest on his shoulder for the walk to his cottage. When Nathaniel had woken up the next morning, he found Herbert sitting at his table reading the daily newsletter.

Thus a routine had been arranged: Herbert, who always managed to wake up at the crack of dawn, would fetch the newsletter from the town square and return to the cottage where Nathaniel and Herbert would eat their breakfast.

"Hey, Dorf," said Herbert after he landed on the table. Like most of the townspeople, Herbert did not call him Nathaniel, Nathan, or even Nate, but his last name, Dorf. "Remember that night we met? It had been a dark, gloomy-"

"Yes, yes I do Herb, thank you very much," said Nathaniel, who remembered that night perfectly well. "Speaking of which, are you coming to the tavern with me today? We're going to need someone to entertain the crowd."

"Yes, I'll do it. What do you want me to start off with? The dumb parrot, the flying beerman, the disappearing drinks?" replied Herbert.

"Well, as long as you don't make our customers' drinks disappear. We want to keep them nice and happy. Kumaiyan hasn't had a mean drunk in ages."

"Oh, I don't know about that. Remember that dwarf who got pretty bent out of shape? He was terrible!" said Herbert. Herbert suddenly flew up, for a well-aimed stone from Nathaniel's slingshot had nearly shattered his skull. "Hey, I was joking! Everybody loves that one!" Nathaniel stowed his slingshot back in his pocket. It was bad enough, being joked about because of his height, but being made a mockery of at the place that he worked was worse. Nathaniel glowered at Herbert and finished his tea. As he reached for his bread, he addressed the parrot.

"Hey, Herbert! You ever hear the one about the dead parrot?"

# The Three Travelers

Nathaniel exited his cottage after finishing his breakfast. Herbert sat perched on his left shoulder, and his stool was tied to his back. Nathaniel walked down the dirt pathway that led away from his home and turned right into the town center.

Kumaiyan was a small town, but by no means was it quiet. The center of town was lined with wooden two-story buildings and shops. Merchants and their apprentices stood outside and called pedestrians into their stores. People gathered in the town square to discuss the reports in the daily newsletter. Nathaniel strode through the center of town, shorter than every other adult but as tall as the small children. Nathaniel walked to a two-story wooden building with a sign that read: *The Golden Tavern*. Nathaniel reached the doorknob with some difficulty, turned, and pulled the door open. He then dashed into the tavern before the massive oak door could swing back at him.

Even though it was a tavern, The Golden Tavern was one of the best places in town to stop by. The walls of the tavern were decorated with portraits of past Kings, knights, and wizards of Arcoiris. Torches were mounted on walls, ready to be lit in the later hours of the day. The many tables to the left of the bar were round and equipped with four chairs on each. The bar, obviously to the right of the tables, consisted of a high counter and ten barstools clustered around it. The counter was painted a bright red, and hadn't faded one bit in the three years that Nathaniel had worked there. Today, the only person at the bar this early was Ralf.

Ralf was the head bartender at the tavern. He was a tall man (yes, even by human standards), with a bushy black beard and a hearty laugh. His hands were the size of small plates. The top of his head was bald, showing his tanned skin. Ralf wore a white apron to shield himself from the many spills and swigs of drunken singers. However, on several occasions the stains turned out to be his own, as he would often join in with the customers and sing merrily. Ralf was about forty years of age.

Ralf was also the captain of the town militia. About five years ago, a group of twenty men met in the bar to discuss the rebellion going on in Arcoiris. A large group of rebels from the east was gaining power and decided to take on the country for reasons unknown to even most of them. The rebels were reckless, destructive, and brutal. They would sweep through towns at lightning-fast paces, killing many and burning everything in their way. The only condition that a village would be spared from the hand of death was joining the rebellion. After about a year, the rebellion was larger than anyone had ever anticipated. Nearly half of Arcoiris was on their side. A giant civil war was prone to breakout at any moment. So, Ralf and his twenty men formed a local militia to combat any threat to Kumaiyan, and to assist the capital if threatened. The militia trained night and day for a month, and by the end of their first two months had accumulated seventy members. Fortunately, the rebellion leader, a powerful sorcerer, fled the country and the rebels became unorganized and quickly defeated. The war never reached the small town, but the militia was kept in place in case of future threats.

Nathaniel was part of the militia too. Ralf knew he was useful in scouting and was a good shot with a bow. Only trouble was, Nathaniel was so small that it was very hard for him to mount a horse. Yes, he needed to use his stool for that.

"'Morning Dorf!" cried Ralf from the bar.

"Hey, Ralf," said Nathaniel. "You read the newsletter?"

"Yea, mighty good piece that was. You think the bears are gonna slow business down?"

"I hope not. Might even be able to trade for a few skins while they're here," replied Nathaniel optimistically.

"Eh, I wonder what made them come here all of a sudden?" said Ralf as he polished a glass with a cloth. "You don't think a wizard's around, do ya?"

"Well, Ralf, I thought all of the wizards were either in towers or at their assigned cities."

"Yes," said Ralf, "but what if they weren't under assignment?"

"What do you mean?"

"Well," said Ralf, lowering his voice, "there have been rumors that the King's crown has gone missing. And of course, you know his ol' wizard was guarding it? Well, he deduced that some wizard must've broken the spell holding it in place and made off with it. He says there is a wizard on the loose. Might even conjure up a few bodyguards while he is in hiding."

"But why would someone take the King's crown? He doesn't seriously expect to be able to sell it, does he?"

"No, I've got no idea why anyone would take it. But be on the lookout for this wizard. I might call you in for scouting duty tonight." said Ralf.

"Seriously? Ralf, you really think this could be involved with a rumor about the King? And plus, the capital is over one-hundred miles from here! How could a wizard get here that quickly?"

"Now, I have a good answer to that. Wizards can teleport to places they've already been. A flash of light and -crack! Your wizard moves to another city in seconds," said Ralf.

"Already been.....but that means the wizard would have to have been here before!"

"Exactly....we may have to start askin' travelers a few questions. But enough, help me set up the bar, will ya? An' Herb, start practicing your routine. I swear, if any glass ends up in my head today...." Jon made a cutting motion with his index finger and neck.

Nathaniel and Ralf busied themselves by getting the bar ready for customers. Nathaniel unpacked his stool and set it up at his place behind the bar. He had to walk to each table and flip the chairs over and under the tables (hard work when you're as tall as them). Nathaniel had to sweep the floor, a futile task for it grew dirty within seconds of customers arriving. By eight o'clock, the tavern was ready to serve its customers.

Business in the morning was slow. People rarely entered The tavern earlier than three o'clock, but there were a few travelers who came into the bar the minute after Nathaniel and Ralf finished their preparations. Three of them walked in first.

The first traveler to sit down on a stool was tall and muscular. He wore a white collared shirt with short sleeves that revealed his strength and mass. Attached to his brown leather belt was an ax, presumably to cut wood. The traveler also had a bow hung over his shoulder, which he did not remove after sitting down. He had a short, blond beard and a stony face. The traveler put a coin on the counter and asked for a beer.

The second traveler was short and slightly heavy. He was bald except for a thin ring of dark hair around the sides of his head. He wore black pants and a white shirt. Over his white shirt was a brown fur vest, probably made from a bear. Nathaniel registered this and looked to Ralf, who did not look back. The second traveler put a coin on the counter too and ordered a beer.

The third traveler was a woman. She was taller than the second traveler but not quite as tall as the first. She wore a leather-padded top exposing her arms and lower stomach. Her black hair was tied back in a bun. She wore a hard expression like the first traveler. The third traveler made no attempt to hide the long, jagged knife attached to her waist. She sat down on a stool, placed a coin on the counter and asked for a beer.

Now, seeing as Nathaniel had chose to size up his customers rather than get their drinks, the first traveler coughed loudly into his hand. Nathaniel swept his hand across the counter and collected the coins, put them in the tavern's lock box, and hopped of his stool to fetch the drinks. Nathaniel entered the back room of the bar, filled three mugs with beer, placed them on a tray, and walked back into the main part of the tavern holding the three beers. He placed the tray on the counter with a little difficulty, then hopped back up on his stool. The three travelers took their drinks and downed them surprisingly quickly. In fact, the tall man and the woman had finished their beers in one long sip. Nathaniel waited for them to drop more coins on the counter, then went into the back room to refill the mugs. When he returned and placed the mugs on the counter, the small traveler was speaking.

"....and so, there wasn't much choice of places to go," said the small man in a high, squeaky voice, "so we decided to sprint to the nearest clearing to surround it."

"How did you finish it?" asked the woman. Her voice was surprisingly soft considering her hard expression.

"We didn't," said the small man. He looked slightly crestfallen at the statement. "Three of us ran, two of us made it out of the Maze, one of us is sitting here sipping a mug of drink."

"That's awful!" shouted the woman. "How did they find you so quickly?"

"Smelled him, by the looks of it," replied the tall man blankly. The woman glanced at him, then turned to the small man to hear his reply. Nathaniel felt his head turn with hers.

"I'm not sure. We-we heard someone ye-yelling and the next thing we knew four of them were chasing us. Jeb thought it was a warning, and I rightly agree. I think they picked up on our trail days ago. They were just waiting for the right time," said the small man.

"These bears, they have given people much trouble lately! What do you think is going on?" the woman turned to the tall man.

"I have a theory," he said in a deep voice, "but you might not like it."

"Please, share it with us!" exclaimed the woman. "I would love to hear what ever you have to say!"

"All right then, I'll just be out with it. Talitenkus is back in the country, and he's stirring up trouble," said the tall man. The two other travelers looked back and forth at each other. Nathaniel was waiting to hear that it was all just a joke. With a rush of relief, the sound of laughter filled the room. Then, with the force of an imaginary fist crushing his relief, he noticed that the tall man was not laughing. He glared at the other two travelers until they fell silent.

"But you cannot be serious?" said the woman. "Why would he return, after three and a half years of exile? I'm sure the other wizards, few though they are, would have picked up on it and found him!"

"Talitenkus the Sorcerer never fled this country. He has been hiding in the Maze for a few years, deciding what his next plan of attack is," said the tall man. "I'll bet that he's training the bears in the Maze as his new warriors." The small man looked bewildered.

"Plan of attack? Sir, the rebellion is over! Our Kingdom is whole again! All rebel officers have been tried and punished appropriately! Did you really think that Talitenkus would still have his army after the war was over?" asked the small man.

# The Request

"Well, this is all very helpful," said the  woman, "but how do you suppose something can be done to stop it?"

"If we can find Talitenkus, we can end the war. No one has to die except him, but he deserves it anyway," said the hunter. "In the meantime, the King's wizards seem to have many more 'important' things to do instead."

"On a more *realistic* note, did you happen to hear about the King's crown? It's gone missing!" exclaimed the woman. So the rumors weren't just the mad ravings of Ralf. Other people had heard similar stories.

"No!" said the small man. "How could anyone steal that? They would have to get through all of the wizards' spells, the King's guard, the army. That's gotta be the most difficult thing to even get a finger on!"

"Apparently, it isn't. There was no struggle, no alerts, no suspicious behavior. The King woke up, reached for his crown, and it was missing," finished the woman.

"How badly does the King want it back?" asked the hunter.

"What, like how much he would pay? Probably hundreds of thousands of coins for whoever finds it!" said the small man.

"Yes, if he didn't lock you up for possessing it in the first place. I think that whoever returns the crown, thief or not, will be hanged. After all, the evidence against them would be the crown," said the woman. Nathaniel listened intently, eager to hear more of the travelers' news. "Naturally, several bounty hunters have begun searching. They are being tracked by crystal ball to make sure that they didn't just return to their homes and come back to the King with it. But, he can't track everybody like that, so I wouldn't want to be the one to return it, whether or not I found it." There was a loud thumping noise, and Nathaniel turned to see another one of the townspeople sprawled on the ground in the front of the tavern. Colin, the town's news writer, got up to his feet. He was about twenty years of age and shorter than both the woman and hunter, but towered over the small traveler. He wore a green shirt with a collar and four pockets, one for each of his quills. His hair was dark, contrasting to his pale skin. Colin walked to the bar, sat next to the hunter, and smiled at Nathaniel.

"Hey! Dorf! Sorry about the noise, I tripped over some kind of a green rock- hey!" shouted Colin, as he saw Herbert getting up and flying away from where Colin had fallen. "Did he trip me?"

"You know, you can talk to him also," said Nathaniel. At this remark, the three travelers turned to look at Herbert, who had rested on Nathaniel's right shoulder.

"Yeah, Colin, I've known you for nearly a year. You know perfectly well I can talk!" said Herbert. The woman looked from Nathaniel to Herbert, as if seeing them for the first time.

"A talking-smart parrot? That's amazing! Did you get a wizard to do him?" asked the woman. Herbert stiffly shook his head. He was often offended when a person attributed his intelligence to a wizard or spell.

"No, I'm just a smart bird. Gotta problem?" the woman quickly shook her head, and turned to Nathaniel.

"Are you, are you a dwarf?" she asked.

"Yep," was Nathaniel's reply. He was used to people asking him about his height. He wasn't however, comfortable with it being made a joke of.

"He's so little!" exclaimed the hunter. "I could probably pick him up in one arm and cradle him like a baby!"

"Oh, no, you wouldn't want to do that," said Colin. "He's a dead shot with a slingshot, like the one in his pocket right now. Am I right, Dorf?" Nathaniel merely glared at Colin.

"Ah, I'm just kidding with you!" said the hunter. "The name's Renol. Been a hunter in these parts for nearly six years. I'd shake your hand, but that last deer I took down was kind of hard to cut open, if you get my drift," said Renol, indicating a red stain in his palm. Nathaniel, Herbert, and the two other travelers grimaced in unison. "By the way, didn't catch the names of you two," he said, turning to the woman and the small man.

"I'm called April," said the woman. "I'm an escort for other travelers."

"My name's Soris," said the small man, in a surprisingly deep voice. "I'm a merchant, mostly trade in wines and drinks."

"And your name must be Dorf?" asked April.

"No, actually it's Nathaniel. Dorf is the last name," said Nathaniel. "And my parrot is named Herbert." Herbert flapped his wings as everyone turned to look at him.

"So, Nathaniel, what's your story?" asked Renol.

"Well, not very interesting really, but there's not much work for a dwarf anywhere. So, a few years ago, I started working here, and I love it. It's where my friends are, where I met all of my friends, even where I met Herbert. See, it was a dark, gloomy night-"

"All right, all right, we met each other here," said Herbert, cutting across Nathaniel's speech.

"Mr. Renol, we in Kumaiyan enjoy our privacy," said Colin, "and you'll have to do a lot better than that to earn my friendship."

"How about I start with a round of beers for all of us?" asked Renol. Colin suddenly grabbed his hand and shook it vigorously, disregarding the blood stain.

"Done," he said as Renol shook his hand off.

Just as Nathaniel walked into the back room to grab the drinks, Ralf came rushing past him gripping a long sword in one hand and a wooden shield bound to his left arm.

"Dorf, run home and grab your bow. We've got intruders."

# The Missing Crown

"Intruders?" asked Nathaniel.

---

"No time Dorf, no time! I've got to get the militia in formation. Grab your weapon and come back here within ten minutes!" ordered Ralf as he ran out of the tavern. Nathaniel stood there for a second, shocked, then woke up and ran into the bar. Herbert was laughing with the other four at the counter. When they saw Nathaniel's expression, their laughter died.

"What's the matter, Dorf?" asked Soris. Like everybody else, he had settled in to call him by his last name.

"We've got intruders. Probably in military form by the sound of it. Ralf's getting the militia ready. Herb, fly ahead and see how many of them there are. Colin, get inside. You three," he pointed at the travelers, "if you've got weapons, get outside and draw them. I'm off to arm myself." With that, Nathaniel dashed out of The tavern and ran through the street towards his cottage.

On all sides of him, people were gathering towards the north end of town, some of them holding weapons. Nathaniel began to take Renol's story very seriously. Nathaniel reached his home, unlocked the door, and grabbed the bow hanging on the coat rack next to the door. The bow was already strung, part of Nathaniel's morning routine. Nathaniel walked to his bed, and pulled his quiver full of two dozen arrows out from under it. He slung his quiver over his back and turned around and leapt out of the cottage.

As he reached the north entrance to town, Nathaniel saw what the commotion was. Ralf and ten other men had formed a line to block five armored men on black horses from advancing into the town. Ralf was in a ready position with his sword held over his shield. Two of the men trained arrows on the front horsemen. Nathaniel caught a glimpse of Renol holding a bow and arrow aimed at the horseman in front, while April was holding a knife in the front line.

Nathaniel turned his attention to the horsemen. They were all dressed in identical golden suits of armor. They wore helmets resembling masks of the same still faced person. They all had silver long swords sheathed at their sides and round, golden shields bound to their left arms. Each horseman made no response to the "warm" welcome by the townspeople.

It was a woman, Gretchen, who walked forward to meet the newcomers. She was a young woman, dressed in plain white and black garments. Her long blond hair was tied back into a ponytail to prevent it from getting in her way while working.

"Hello, welcome to Kumaiyan," said Gretchen.

"Yes, woman, we know where we are," came the gruff response from the lead horseman. "And, unlike yourself, we know why."

"Excuse me, I should have known to give you my proper name first," began Gretchen sarcastically. "After all, you can't just go around calling every woman in sight 'woman', can you?"

The mounted soldier made no comment on this, but his silence suggested that he was rather taken aback by Gretchen's attitude and toughness. After several long seconds, he managed to speak again, but this time to the whole crowd.

"We have been sent here by the King, King Percy Krellin, to investigate the theft of his crown. Every minor settlement within two-hundred miles of the capital is being searched over the course of the next week. We expect full cooperation with the civilians and military men while we conduct our search.

"Be warned. Anyone found guilty in the theft will be taken to the capital for further questioning. However, any attempts to disrupt our search or simply get in our way, could result in arrest and possible fines. I suggest that the....the army that was sent here to lower their weapons and return to their homes. No one will be fighting here." This resulted in much muttering and disagreement throughout the crowd. No one seemed to take the news well at all. Becoming involved in politics was never a big part of living in Kumaiyan. After a few minutes, Ralf walked up to the knights and turned around to face the crowd.

"Silence! Silence! We don't seem to have any other choice, do we? Each of you will return to your homes immediately.

However ," he turned to the knights, "if any of our citizens are injured or harmed in any way, you will be giving us a declaration of open combat. We have the right to arm ourselves."

"That may be true," said the lead knight, "but we will not attack unless provoked." At the last word, the villagers dispersed to their homes. Everyone was panicking, trying to run to their homes as quickly as possible. Nathaniel stayed behind to allow Ralf to reach him through the moving crowd. Ralf reached Nathaniel and bent over and spoke quietly.

"Dorf, you get home and comply just as we do. But, keep your sword nearby and don't let them draw their weapons without letting someone else know. I'm not sure if they're really here to search for the crown to give it to the King, or to take it. Herbert, you need to fly straight to me if there's a problem. They don't know you can talk, so they won't try and stop you. Look, tonight I'm putting you on scouting duty in town. We're going to have the Night Watch out tonight watching the horsemen. I'm also going to have the rest of the militia meet at the tavern and a few of their homes. I don't trust these folks, but they sure as hell better trust us." With that, Ralf sped off towards the tavern.

Nathaniel ran home as fast as possible. It was no trouble, for the streets were empty already. Nathaniel reached the cottage door and whipped his key out of his pocket. He unlocked the door, entered his home and slammed it shut behind it. Herbert flew off of his shoulder and rested on his perch above the bed.

"What do we do now?" asked Herbert. Nathaniel strode to a cabinet beside his table and opened it. He pushed aside several fruits and other food items and pulled his dueling sword out of the cabinet. The sword was about one and a half feet in length with a slightly curved blade made out of steel. The handle was made of steel also, but colored gold. Nathaniel closed the cabinet and put his sword through his pant string.

"For now, we're going to wait. If they come, we do what they say. Get near the window when they come, however," said Nathaniel. He sat down on his small stool and filled a glass with water from a pitcher. He took a sip, then sighed. It was going to be one long, boring day.

Three hours passed. No soldiers had come to Nathaniel's cottage. No sounds were heard except for the occasional galloping of horses throughout the streets. Nathaniel sat at his table, half asleep and half awake, glancing at his watch every few minutes. Herbert was completely asleep, having dozed off an hour into the siege. Oddly enough, the parrot was snoring loudly as a human would. Nathaniel was sure that Herbert learned how to do this just to imitate him.

The dwarf was sure that no one in town had been arrested with the possession of the crown. No one in town had recently visited the capital for starters. Also, people in town knew what was going on most of the time thanks to writers such as Colin Mitchell. Nathaniel along with the rest of the townspeople would have known if one of their own had stolen a piece of bread from the bakery, let alone a valuable object from the King. The only possible suspects were the travelers going through the town that day. Nathaniel assumed that these travelers had gone to the tavern when told to return to their homes.

Nathaniel had never been trapped in his own cottage since the times of the rebellion. All of the townspeople who were non-militia were told to get inside whenever a threat of an attack was picked up. Eventually, Nathaniel joined the militia and did not have to stay inside but would be out in the streets or outside of the town with the militia.

Once it seemed that the hands on his watch couldn't move quickly enough, Nathaniel got up from his chair and pushed it under the table. Just as he was ready to leave the house and take a nice walk around town, there was a loud banging noise at the door. Nathaniel knew what this meant. The soldiers had arrived.

Nathaniel had no choice. He pulled the knob on his door and pulled it open to allow the soldiers in. Three soldiers stood in the doorway. The lead soldier did not wear a mask like the others, but was recognizable as a soldier because of his golden battle armor. His hair was short, cut around his ears, and black. His skin was tan and smooth. His eyes were large and blue, staring down at Nathaniel.

"Let us in," said the lead soldier. His tone was cold. Nathaniel, thoroughly frightened, hurriedly backed towards his cottage table. The three soldiers stepped into the cottage, and the two masked ones sat down on chairs at either side of Nathaniel.

"Thank you for inviting us to sit," said the unmasked soldier, "but I prefer to stand, *dwarf*." Nathaniel could not help but pick up on the disgust in the word *dwarf*. The unmasked soldier turned and surveyed the cottage, waving his hands through the air and muttering under his breath. Yellow sparks flew from them and settled around the room. They moved like birds, flying from chairs to the bed, even around Herbert. Herbert, startled by the activity, woke up and flapped his wings in an attempt to scare away the sparks. The soldier continued the rather impressive show for a few minutes, then flicked his wrist. The sparks shot into his palms and vanished. The soldier looked around the room one more time, then pointed his index finger at Nathaniel. Nathaniel swallowed loudly.

"Name," the unmasked soldier said.

"Nathaniel Dorf," said Nathaniel.

"Occupation," said the soldier.

"Bartender," said Nathaniel.

"Race."

"Dwarf."

"Mister Dorf, have you ever visited the capital city?"

"No sir, I have not," replied Nathaniel.

"How many locks are on the King's door?"

"How should I know? I have never been!"

"You will give me an answer, dwarf!" yelled the soldier. He jerked his finger up and down in Nathaniel's direction.

"Fine, twenty-six?" asked Nathaniel sarcastically.

"I noticed you were out in the street, with a bow earlier," began the soldier, "for the greeting. What do you know about the town Rebellion force?" Nathaniel was startled by the question. There was no Rebellion in Kumaiyan.

"It is not a rebel group," said Nathaniel, "it's our town militia. We formed it in case either side chose to attack us during the war."

"Why is your town trying to overthrow the King?"

"We are not trying to overthrow him. We have enough training and soldiers to protect ourselves, not to lead a war. We don't have any reason to fight him."

"Do you know of any townspeople who are involved in criminal activity at the present time?"

"No."

"Have you ever committed, witnessed, or assisted in a crime?"

"No."

"Do you believe that the King can sometimes make the wrong decision on major points of importance?"

"Everyone can make mistakes, but I've been happy with how the country has been doing so far."

"Have you ever given anyone information that could set them on the trail of the King of his valuables?"

"No, I only give directions to travelers, not bandits. I ask everybody about their business, and everyone gives me a straight answer."

"I have already interrogated the travelers in the taverns and inns. Do you know any of them from meetings prior to today?"

"No."

Nathaniel looked the soldier right in the eyes when he said it. He heard the helmets of the other two soldiers clang loudly as they turned to look at the unmasked soldier. The unmasked soldier stared at Nathaniel, as if to see past the words.

"Do you have knowledge pertaining to the use of magic?"

"I know that a wizard, like yourself, waves his hands around and things happen, but not anything else."

"Nothing else? Be careful, dwarf."

"I do not know anything else about magic."

"How does one conjure a snake?"

"I don't know!"

"Do not use that tone with me. What instruments can be used to use magical power?"

"I do not know."

"What is my name?"

"You have not tol- I don't know."

"I am Forredar, wizard to the King himself. Service in the capital. Have you ever heard of me before?"

"No"

"Good. Mr. Dorf, you either managed to lie your way through the interrogation or are possibly innocent. You may not leave town for the following week, for we have further business to discuss," Forredar said, his voice filled with malice.

"I did not take that crown! And why do you insist that I can use magic?" Nathaniel was furious. The questioning had been very unfair to him, and it was his turn for answers. Instead of giving an answer, Forredar twirled his finger, creating a yellow spark which shot at Nathaniel's chest. There was a loud crack, and Nathaniel felt his chest grow very heavy. He looked down to see many large lumps steadily growing in his shirt. Nathaniel's eyes opened wide, he gasped at Forredar. He felt something on his hands, and he saw that gray boils were sprouting all over them.

"I ask the questions around here! You will not continue this rebellious behavior! Good day, Mr. Dorf, because it may be one of your last!" With that, Forredar turned around, and Nathaniel felt himself fall out of his seat. The other two soldiers rose from their seats and walked briskly outside. Forredar clapped his hands, and the boils on Nathaniel's body seemed to disappear. There was a flash of bright, purple light. Nathaniel reached for his sword, but by the time he got to his feet, Forredar was gone. The door was closed, but there had been no sound of it ever opening.

Herbert flew down to Nathaniel and landed on the table in front of his seat. Nathaniel sat down and looked at the parrot.

"You want me to go to Ralf? Or are you okay?" asked Herbert. Nathaniel had only remembered Ralf's warning, but shook his head. Messing with a wizard could be tough business, and he didn't want the whole town turned into a pig pen. Still, the attack was rather disturbing. And Forredar seemed to dislike him, and his use of the word *dwarf* pretty much sealed it. What could a wizard have against dwarves? Or could he have offended him some other way? Whatever the reason was, Nathaniel hoped he wouldn't face that again.

"No, we shouldn't send for the militia yet. Let's just head over to the tavern and go back to work," said Nathaniel. Herbert flew over to his shoulder and stood, perched on it. Nathaniel rose to leave, but his door swung open and four people rushed in. Thinking of soldiers and wizards, he drew his sword and rolled to the right, sending Herbert flying into the air. He heard the door slam shut, and looked at the newcomers.

Colin, Renol, Gretchen, and the town gossip, Madeline, stood in front of the closed door. Madeline was a middle-aged woman with curly blond hair. She wore a black dress with a white apron over it. Though she was two feet taller than Nathan, she was short by human standards. Renol was holding his bow, and a quiver of arrows was slung across his back. Colin had his fists up in front of him, but put them down at the sight of Nathaniel. Gretchen held a flask with an orange liquid in it. At the sight of Nathaniel, she ran to him and leaned over him.

"Oh, no, no, no! Come here, sit, sit! Let's get you in order!" she exclaimed. She whisked him up and into his chair by the table. Gretchen then handed him the flask and told him to take a sip. "It'll help with the boils," she said.

"Thanks, but they're gone already. He flicked them away." He handed the flask back to Gretchen. "I take it you were interrogated also?"

"Why yes, yes we were!" yelled Madeline. "And he couldn't have been more pleasant!" Nathaniel noticed that she did not say this with sarcasm. "He was very complementary about my dish set!"

"Excuse me? He didn't say anything to me except the questions. Not even a 'hello', or 'good-bye'. Same for Colin and Gretchen here!" said Renol.

"Wait, why did all of you come down here?" asked Nathaniel.

"We didn't think Forredar would be too gentle with anyone, and you're, you know, smaller. We wanted to make sure you were all right. When did he leave?"

"He left just a few minutes ago. You would've ran into him, wouldn't you?" asked Nathaniel.

"No, I don't think so. Wizards don't just walk out the door like anybody else, they teleport. They wave their hands, there's a flash of purple light and -bang! No more wizard!" said Renol. "He's lucky he works for the King, or else I'd be one to teach him a lesson."

"I disagree," said Madeline, "he was a very charming man. I hope to see him again soon. And a wizard! That's the kind of person we need in this town!"

"Maddy, are you blind and deaf as well as dumb?" asked Gretchen." She looked very cross, and Nathaniel was starting to catch on. "That man was very improper. He wouldn't show any respect, and he told me not to ask any questions."

"Well, I think he was a very engaging person," said Madeline. The two women stared each other down, and it seemed neither one would ever blink. The impression Forredar had left on them was very different indeed. After some long seconds of silence, Nathaniel thought it was time to speak.

"Madeline, he did attack me. And he repeatedly hinted that I was in league with rebels. I also think he dislikes dwarves in general, although I'm probably the only one he has ever met in person. Either he believes that it is his right to get information at any cost, or the King is very desperate to get his crown back," said Nathaniel with more force than he had intended. Madeline turned to him and opened her mouth to say a very nasty remark, but Renol cut in.

"I don't think the King would authorize the torture of citizens to any of his men. In fact, he would probably forbid it; he is a very gentle and diplomatic man. Forredar may be working under the king's orders, but he doesn't need to worry about anybody reporting a slip-up, does he? The capital is two hundred miles north of here, so no one can get a message there quickly. Plus, he can teleport there right away and tell the King anything he wants, possibly do a little magic to persuade him. We certainly can't do anything about him or the soldiers, because the King would find out and send the army here, or even declare war. Now, -" he paused and looked at Madeline and Gretchen, "-I do not live here, but I would hate for the army to take this over or burn it. And who knows, with enough wizards, the whole army might be able to be teleported here in a few hours. But we must still be cautious and careful around Forredar. I don't want him to have an excuse to leave this place," finished Renol firmly. His voice carried through the cottage and sent a clear message into Nathaniel's head.

"You're right," he said. "If we drive the soldiers away, the King will think we're rebelling. By the way, what's happened with Ralf?" Nathaniel was very anxious to hear about the militia captain and bartender. Renol didn't look pleased about what he was about to say. His eyes fell, then rose very slowly to look in Nathaniel's.

"All five of them, they came to the tavern. That wizard clapped his hands and somehow closed every window and every door in the place. Then, he conjured some kind of a bear out of thin air and told us he wouldn't attack if we cooperated. Like we had any choice not to, anyway. One by one, he took us into the back room and asked us many questions about the positioning of town and the people living in it. And I don't know about the others, but he actually froze, yes *froze* my hands and feet to stop me from taking any action. But in the end, we were all okay, at least until Ralf went in. We could hear Forredar asking questions about the militia, and what happens when it is called into formation. We heard many loud bangs, and what sounded like broken glass. After about ten minutes, Forredar pushed the door open and dragged the bartender through by the back of his shirt and through him on the ground. He looked awful. There were cuts all over his apron, he had a bleeding gash over his eye, and he couldn't get up for a good bit of time. That wizard didn't give him any second looks. He just waved his hands like a madman and disappeared. The other soldiers simply left the tavern," said Renol, sadly. "Now, he's going to be okay, but I'm not sure he'll be around much longer. The wizard said somethings about purging the kingdom of traitors, and extra questionings." Nathaniel was shocked. Ralf was tough, probably the toughest man in Kumaiyan. If he was battered and bruised worse than anybody else, then nobody else would stand a chance against Forredar. Nathaniel hated to think of what would happen to anyone who showed open resistance.

"Anyway, we're glad you're okay," said Colin. "I'm going to write a piece on the thoroughness of the investigation. I'm sure that publishing my real opinion won't be welcome amongst the soldiers. They need to think I don't think anything is wrong with the whole situation. Nice to see you, Dorf." Colin strode to the door, then paused and looked back at him. "Oh, word to the wise? Stay inside. That wizard is patrolling the area with his men. They are interrogating anyone who is outside." With that, he grimaced, took a deep breath, and bolted out the door. Nathaniel looked at Madeline and Gretchen, who still looked stiff and strong.

"Sorry, but it seems I have to leave also," said Madeline in a way that didn't sound very sorry at all. "Dorf, be careful and most importantly, be nice. I don't want to see anyone else on the wrong side of those men."

"Good-bye, Madeline," said Nathaniel crisply. Though she looked thoroughly offended and hurt, Madeline curtsied in a girlish way and walked out the door, seeming to enjoy the prospect of another interrogation much more than Colin had. Nathaniel watched her go without blinking, then turned his attention back to Renol.

"Where are you off to, then?" Nathaniel hadn't known Renol for that long, but he thought him to be a good person to be around when things got dangerous.

"I've got no choice but to stay in town. I guess I'll be heading over to the bar, see how everything is going there. Remember to use that parrot over there in case you need to talk to any of us. He's a valuable asset, he is," said Renol, gesturing at Herbert. For the first time in minutes, Nathaniel realized that Herbert was in the house. The green parrot had nestled himself in Nathaniel's pillow, but his head poked up at once to hear the conversation. Nathaniel looked back at Herbert, seeking his approval to be "used", and looked back at Renol.

"All right then, but you'd better be quick getting around town. They might think a rebel gathering is taking place here or something, and I don't want him getting any close to us," said Nathaniel. It was obvious to everybody in the room who "him" was. Forredar was too dangerous and powerful to get into trouble with. Renol gave a quick nod, then moved even quicker on his way out the door. Now it was just Gretchen, Herbert, and Nathaniel.

"Gretchen, if you want to leave, feel free to do so. I'm okay now, thank you very much. I'll be sure not to cross him again." Even though they were close in age, Gretchen's height gave her a rather intimidating figure. She looked down at Nathaniel.

"We all have to look out for each other throughout the search, Dorf. Even those of us who haven't been so readily accused. You're not the only person I have visited today. I've been all over town myself, checking in on people after the wizard was through with them, rubbing herbs into their skin to help with spell scars, trying to keep everyone healthy. We can't afford to let the King put an iron fist on our town. If we show weakness, we might as well relinquish all of our power," finished Gretchen rather sadly.

"Power? What power?" asked Herbert.

"The power we have to stay strong, the power to never back away from a challenge. We are few, but each of us plays a large role in our own world, a powerful role that helps others and benefits many. So, Dorf, I will leave, but not because you told me to, or because you are feeling okay, which I still doubt, but because there are others who need help as well and I am able to give it. Good day Dorf, Herbert," said Gretchen, and she looked out one of Nathaniel's windows before going to the door. When no signs of danger revealed themselves, she ran out the door and closed it behind her in one fluid motion. Nathaniel watched her run down the path and vanish from sight heading to the west of town.

It was not easy to allow something of political importance to control the lives of the townspeople, particularly Nathaniel and Herbert. They had been used to working by their own schedule, going into town whenever they wanted to, even being able to just walk outside on a sunny day. Nathaniel walked from the window to his cabinet and grabbed a brown, thick, mostly blank book from inside it. If there was any time to finally start to use his journal, this was it.

# Journal Entry Number One

*Date:4254, 12, Half Day          Nathaniel Dorf*

*It has been two whole days, and I have not left my home since the soldiers arrived. I have been eating well, for I happen to have a large supply of vegetables and a parrot who can fetch plants from the outdoor world. What I would give to be able to go there.*

I have not heard anything except the usual creaking of the floorboards, the sound of my voice, Herbert's chatter, and the soft clinking of dishes before and after each meal. My thoughts have been concentrated on two things: food, and escape.

I never understood how men could fear prison. Sure, I knew of the constant boredom, the restricted freedoms, but I didn't understand what it does inside of a person. Being imprisoned in my own home for just two days has shown me a lot about what it must feel like to be an innocent man in prison.

I feel as if I have everything to do but no way of doing it. I cannot speak to anyone except Herbert, and we ended up repeating an entire hour of conversation over breakfast today. I would like to walk into town and see which people are entering the duel in two days, but I cannot. I would really love to visit Ralf and see how he's coming along after his encounter with that vile wizard Forredar, but I cannot. I promise, when I look back on this I will not be able to think of one activity, one method, one way that I could have used or done to keep myself busy.

The wizard in town is a most disgusting creature, though he looks like a very accomplished person with his short haircut and golden armor. During my meeting with him, he repeatedly used the word dwarf in a derogatory manner and forcefully pried information that is of no use to anyone from my lips. He even resorted to attacking me when I merely asked why he was *asking me the questions! Luckily, the boils he made grow on my body disappeared before Gretchen could give me her medicine. She's very skilled, really knows what she's doing, but the stuff she gives people stings wherever it is applied, or drank. The King could really provide her with a nice salary to work in his castle instead of letting her toil here for next to nothing. At least she's tougher than half of the men here, or else she might not be able to get by.*

*The King must feel very threatened by this whole crown business. I would too, if a valuable object of mine was stolen. I just wish he wouldn't put everybody else in a state of panic. There is no need to have a wizard running around torturing people to near-death and making people too scared to leave their homes just because he feels threatened. There is no need to send soldiers to a small village hundreds of miles south of the crime scene to investigate an occurrence from a day ago. I really don't want stuff like this to last for much longer, for I am breeding some rebellious thoughts.*

*Forredar thinks he's got us in the palm of his hand, which most people are inclined to thinking. Not me, though. I believe that we should play along and see if things get any worse. Once he starts attacking people again, or if I hear any spells coming from outside, I'm going straight to the tavern to rally the militia into action. Before and after the rebellion, we were not involved with the king, or any politics. But now, when he has invaded our home, I can see why people closer to the capital, or in cities closely connected to the king, decided that they would do better with a new center of power.*

# The Night Watch

Nathaniel woke up even before the chickens began making noise. He moved very slowly out of his bed, rubbing his eyes methodically to clear his vision. Herbert still snored from his perch above Nathaniel's bed, having no reason to wake up that particular day. In fact, nobody really needed to be awake at all.

Three days had gone by since the questionings had begun. The town was under siege now, but the invading force was laying siege to each and every home and building in the town. No one could go outside their homes, no one could go to work, no one could talk with neighbors, no one could even go to the market to buy food. Luckily, most people in town had enough food to last for at least five days. Unfortunately, three days had gone by.

Nathaniel and Herbert had spent the last three days confined in their cottage, often exchanging pointless, uninteresting conversation. Both of them ended up sleeping much longer than they would on any normal day. Their only perk was that Herbert could still fetch the newsletter by flying out the window, and Colin and the other writers managed to get it together. Although it was very short and tightly controlled, the newsletter was a connection to the outside world, where nothing was happening. Stories in the newsletter included recipes for making the most of your scant food supply, how to treat certain wounds and burns, how the King is definitely proving to be tough in such hard times, and why everyone should go to the duel the next day. What Nathaniel thought was strange was the fact that he was the only one who could still read the newsletter. No one else but Herbert could go outside, so only Herbert could get it from the town center, near where Colin lived.

Nathaniel felt that much of the information was being directed at himself and the soldiers in town. For one, there was a rather large article about the sword duel that was to happen tomorrow, and how it was town tradition for everyone to attend and place bets on their fellow villagers. Nathaniel thought that this was a clever way to get the soldiers to allow them back into their daily lives, and for him to know that such an event had not been canceled. Nathaniel and Herbert thoroughly enjoyed the duels, not so much because Nathaniel had a sword, but because it was a time to meet challengers from other villages and to win some money.

The End Day duel worked in a manner that was friendly to everybody there. Two challengers would cap their swords to prevent any real injury, and they would use them to duel in the town center. To win the duel, a person had to disarm their opponent and get in a killing position with their sword. Anybody who wanted to duel could, but they would have to wait until other matches were finished. A crowd of spectators, usually most of the town, would watch the duelists and could even place bets with one of the town's older, retired militia men, Oben. At the end of the night, people could win and lose money, and gain reputations as skilled swordsmen.

Nathaniel rarely dueled, mostly because of his height. It was too much to ask for someone who is three feet tall to block a heavy blow coming from a six foot high gladiator. Nathaniel had won one match in his life by knocking the sword from Colin's loose grip and threatening to stab him between the legs. Herbert had found the threat to be a little stale.

Nathaniel wondered if Forredar would allow the duel to be held tomorrow. He could imagine that it would be the last straw if he didn't. After all, though the soldiers know that they are under the king's protection, that doesn't stop them from being driven away or possibly killed. Even Forredar could be taken by surprise and used as a bargaining chip for their freedom. He doubted the King would want to lose a wizard, when there weren't even two-dozen in the world.

Just as he was filling a cup of tea for himself, Nathaniel noticed Herbert muttering in his sleep. As soon as he turned to listen in on it, there was a brilliant flash of purple light and the wizard Forredar stood right in front of Nathaniel's door.

The wizard was not dressed in his battle armor, but in a black shirt with black buttons down the middle of it. His sleeves were a little too long, and covered halfway down each palm. His pants were white, pure white, a complete contrast to his dark top. As usual, he was pointing his finger at Nathaniel. Or, where Nathaniel had been.

Upon seeing the wizard materialize in his home, Nathaniel had taken his sword from the table and rolled to his right, avoiding the spell that the wizard might decide to throw at him. When he rose, he held the sword in front of him as if blocking an attack.

"Not to worry, *dwarf*, if I was going to attack you would already be dead. I have arrived to personally inform you that you are no longer suspect in this case. From this moment forward, you are allowed to leave your dwelling, but you will not be allowed to leave the town just yet. Also, you may not hold large gatherings at any place at any time; I will not take the chance to allow rebellion to rise in this country again.

"The duel that is supposed to take place tomorrow will be held. However, though my soldiers will be competing as well, I will not be distracted by such tomfoolery. If there are any subtle attempts on the lives of any of my men, then you will have a very painful death.

"Since my soldiers are patrolling the area, I will allow yourself and four others to stand guard in town as well. Not to keep my soldiers in check, but so we can work together to put an end to these times of worry. Yourself, that large bartender, and three others whom you may send messages to yourself my keep watch. We wouldn't want the culprit to escape, would we?" Forredar's voice was cold as before, but he seemed to have gone through a small change since their last meeting. Nathaniel was about to ask about the other townspeople, but Forredar spoke first. "If you do not comply, I will turn you into a toad, maybe a bird, maybe even a pile of ashes. Ah, allow me to demonstrate," said Forredar, pointing at a glass on Nathaniel's table. A jet of sparks hit it with astonishing speed. The glass did not move as expected, but as Nathaniel watched it quickly sprouted green legs, grew a body, and was suddenly a large, green toad. Forredar gestured at Nathaniel warningly.

"Okay, I'll comply," said Nathaniel. Seeming satisfied with the answer, the wizard turned to the toad who was exploring his new 'home'.

"Undone!" said the wizard, and the toad turned back into a glass and floated back to its original position. "Now, I will leave you here. But listen carefully, dwarf. If I find out that you are using any .....powers behind my back, there's going to be hell to pay."

"I don't know how to do magic!" yelled Nathaniel. "And I certainly don't have any magical scrolls or staffs, you should know; you did search this place, after all."

"Well, you could have hid-never mind, then. I am off to rejoin the troops," said Forredar. There was a blinding flash of light, and he was gone. Nathaniel momentarily stared at the empty place where the wizard had stood, then turned to Herbert.

"I'm still not going out yet. It seems pretty odd, that I was ruled out. If he narrowed it down, he's closer, and can use more power to his advantage," said Nathaniel, with much effort.

"I agree, it's better if we play it safe. There's no sense in risking getting in the middle of a fight, now is there?" said Herbert. Nathaniel nodded, feeling Herbert and his relief spread through him.

"We should just take it easy here. Besides, tonight we are on watch duty, now that we're allowed. Let's get some rest."

Nathaniel and Herbert sat down at the table to have tea. Neither of them were excited to have been freed, but Nathaniel could feel anticipation at what was to come in the night.

Many hours later, when it became dark outside and the lights of other homes were lit, Nathaniel prepared his scouting gear. He slung his quiver over his shoulders, filled with arrows. He strapped his leather boots to his feet. He put his sword through his sheath at his waist, and put his bow over his right shoulder. Nathaniel Dorf was ready for patrolling the town.

As he and Herbert walked out the cottage door, the fresh air greeted them like a long lost relative. Though it was dark, the feeling of being out in the open again was very relaxing and oddly warming. When Nathaniel closed the door, Herbert promptly took off flying into the night sky. Though he had been able to fly beforehand, Herbert had not been allowed to be out for long. Now, Nathaniel reasoned, he could be free to fly the whole night.

Once Herbert disappeared from view, Nathaniel walked down the path away from his house and into the street. Many of the houses he passed had candles lit in the windows, illuminating the inside of their respective rooms and a small portion of the outside of the home. He was glad to know that he wasn't the only one staying up late in town. Nathaniel had the sneaking suspicion that other people in town were keeping watch from their windows to make sure the soldiers behaved. After all, many of the homes he passed belonged to militia members or regular Night Watch workers.

As he moved through the outskirts of town, Nathaniel saw a great, lumbering figure obscured by darkness. It was about twenty yards away, moving slowly around the town border and stopping every so often at a house or building. Nathaniel, thinking of wizards and soldiers, readied an arrow and aimed his bow at the moving mass.

"Stop! Identify yourself!" Nathaniel gave the commands with more courage and strength than he felt, nor he was pleased by the effect. The figure, taking notice of Nathaniel for the first time, started running towards him with growing speed. As he ran past a window with a candle in it, the light revealed that it was indeed Ralf the bartender, battered and bloody but moving with much enthusiasm.

"Dorf! Thank the Gods they let you out here!" exclaimed Ralf as he caught up to Nathaniel. As he drew closer, Nathaniel noticed he had a wooden shield bound to his left arm, and a long silver sword in his right. The light reflected with an impressive effect off of the blade.

"Ralf, are you all right? They told me you were roughed up, but...but..." Nathaniel trailed off, having not been prepared to address the bartender in his beaten state. But Ralf merely clapped him on the shoulder and gave a hearty laugh.

"What, this? Yea, it hurt, but it'll take more 'n that to finish me. That wizard didn't know who he was dealing with, but anybody else could've died from what he did," Ralf finished the sentence sadly and sighed. Nathaniel, feeling awkward in the ensuing silence, decided to speak again.

"Who else has he let out here tonight? He said there would be five of us."

"Let's see....there's you an' me right here, that fellow Soris from the tavern is supposed to be out, an' then there's Varon and Noah," counted Ralf off of his fingers. Nathaniel was pleased with the choice of the guard. Varon and Noah, young rogues from the south, were exceptionally skilled swordsmen each capable of fighting multiple enemies at a time. And even Soris had combat experience in the woods, fighting off the bears like he said. Of course, he had come to them running, but at least he hadn't been killed.

"What kind of a weapon is Soris using?" Nathaniel remembered the traveler being unarmed when he entered the town."

"I lent him an ax from the armory; he seemed pretty good with it. Nearly took my head off when he was practicing, but good enough. An' look," Ralf pointed at Nathaniel's sword, "you've got both your weapons here. Worst comes to worst, you might get a little practice in yourself before tomorrow."

"I hope not. I have Herbert watching what the wizard is doing, kind of acting as a spy for us. He's going to report to me every now and then, tell us where he's sending his men."

"Ah, that's good for him, good for him. Anyway, about tonight. The wizard's been letting people off the hook so far, right? Well, he might become even more forceful with the remaining suspects. If we see him go after anyone, or enter anyone's home, we've got to follow and take appropriate action. I'm not saying I can take on a wizard, but the five of us together can. I'm counting on us to be able to make short work of the soldiers if it should come to that. Ah, here comes the pair!" Ralf gestured behind Nathaniel. He turned to look at the newcomers.

Sure enough, Varon and Noah were striding towards them holding torches in their left hands and swords in their right. They were the same height, about a little shorter than Ralf which still allowed them to tower over Nathaniel. They wore black shirts and loose black pants. Both of them had dark brown hair. Also, both of them were laughing when they approached Ralf and Nathaniel.

"What's so funny?" asked Nathaniel, perplexed. Clearly something was funny, and Varon was glad to point it out.

"Well, you'd think with all the tight security and that reckless monster running around without a leash that you two would've thought to bring lights," said Varon, chuckling. Nathaniel cursed himself silently for forgetting, but Ralf let loose a string of swear words that lasted a full minute. This only resulted in more laughter from the two friends.

"Hmm, mouth like that and we're going to have to give you a light," said Noah, handing his torch to a red Ralf. "No sense in having us holding two anyway, gets in the way of our fighting style." The rogues were also known for fighting their way up the road to Kumaiyan back-to-back, holding off countless bandits and thieves. When asked for evidence, Varon and Noah showed the townspeople the bodies and the strangely empty looting sacks. Immediately following the incident, they promptly purchased a small house with bedrooms for each of them.

"Oh, now I'm holding a light for both of us? I'm docking you a day's wages, Noah," said Varon jokingly, referring to the swordsmanship lessons the pair taught. Even though they were Nathaniel's age, many older people came to their home to learn how to wield a sword. When they were fifteen and had just arrived in the town, the rebellion was starting, and they joined the militia and helped demonstrate which end of a sword to thrust at unfriendly soldiers to the townspeople. They only started making gold for it the year after that.

"How did you guys do when the wizard came to question you?" asked Nathaniel. The two rogues looked at each other, and broke out in fresh laughter.

"You see, that guy comes into our home pointing and shooting sparks all over the place!" said Varon, struggling to repress the laughter.

"Yeah, so Varon and I disarm his two goons and hold him at the tip of our swords. So, he says something and this light hits me in the face." said Noah, finding it humorous.

"It was all sparks and everything, looked like it was blinding him. But, while he was focused on Noah, I punched him in the face and he screams like a woman. What's more, I left a nice sized cut across his face," said Varon.

"So, the sparks disappear from my face, and I knock him in the chest with the back of my blade. The man staggers over and hits the floor in a mess. Then I tell him if he attacks us again, we'll slit his throat. Must've been pretty scary, because he gets up and apologizes to us. Then he asks us all these questions. By the time he was finished, he was sweating all over, and immediately disappeared. Then we gave the soldiers their swords back and threw them out the front door," said Noah, smiling. "It feels like it was only yesterday...."

Varon then looked at Nathaniel "Why do you ask, though? Something happen to you when he went to your home?" And so, Nathaniel recounted the events of a few days ago leading up to the present day. Their jaws dropped when Nathaniel described the apparent racism and anger displayed by Forredar. Eventually, they broke out in open discussion, describing what they heard from other people in town, what they thought would happen in the future, and soon Ralf joined in and told his story.

After about an hour, the four split up in two groups, the rogues in one and Nathaniel and Ralf in the other. Each group would patrol the east or west side of town.

Nathaniel and Ralf were going to patrol the west side of town. Nathaniel's cottage was near the middle of the west side, and it was where most of the family homes were in town. The east side was made up of a mix of businesses and taverns, and a few small homes fit for one person each. The east side was really louder at night than the west, but during the week it had been quiet. The  had decided to patrol that area because more people became drunk there and could start getting in trouble. When Nathaniel pointed out that everybody else was inside, Noah pointed out that bad things can often happen in the safest places.

Strangely enough, Soris had not shown up yet. At least the four scouts hadn't found him yet. Nathaniel thought that he would take the first opportunity to meet up with them. Hopefully, he would not waste the opportunity to be out and about the town he was visiting. Even though the siege had been nearly lifted during the morning, Nathaniel thought that being outside for one day after imprisonment for three wouldn't be enough.

Nathaniel and Ralf were walking through a row of small cottages that all had their lights extinguished. Everybody there was probably very tired and relieved to be able to get back to their normal lives the next day.

Though there was no light from the houses, the stars were brilliant and bright in the sky. Thousands of them glimmered around the half-moon up high. Nathaniel stopped walking to admire the beauty of the night sky.

"Look at it," he began, "It's really wonderful." Ralf, who had walked a few paces ahead of him, turned and looked up.

"Yeah, sure is better than a bunch of candles and torches, but I think I'm going to keep mine," said Ralf, waving his torch in the air. "Come on, if nothing happens, we could head over to an inn to have a drink."

The man and dwarf set off for the center of town. They decided that they would stop over at an inn, The Inn of the Full Moon, to have a quick drink. As they neared the center of town, they noticed that more candles and torches were lit, making the area brighter. When they passed one cottage, Nathaniel heard a loud scream. But, when he peered in the windows and all around the house, no one was even awake, and no lights were lit. In fact, Ralf hadn't even heard it.

"Darn, I'm getting delirious," said Nathaniel with a sigh. "Let's hurry up." Deciding that the dwarf would be back to himself with a glass of water, Ralf quickened his pace and they soon approached a two-story building with two windows facing the street on each level. The inside was brilliantly lit, and

Nathaniel and Ralf walked inside, the door swinging shut behind them.

The inside of the inn was very bright, but empty. The circular counter towards the back of the room had many stools set out, but no one sat in them. The walls were brown and drab, the same shade as the chairs at the small table beside the counter. A nice layer of dust seemed to have built up on every surface in the inn. The stools and chairs looked as if they hadn't been used for some time.

"Can I help you?" said a voice from above. Nathaniel turned to look at a staircase in the far right corner, and the innkeeper Mit walking down it. He was dressed in loose night clothing. His hair, which was the talk of the town on several occasions, was brown and curly, but stuck up oddly like a giant ball. One of Mit's distinguishing features, along with the hair, was a sizable black mole which clashed with his tan skin on the left of his chin.

Mit was about thirty years old, but marched to his own beat. The inn used to only be his house, but when he learned that he needed a way of making money to live he turned it into an inn and kept a small bedroom in the upstairs section of the inn. All he figured he had to do was let people sleep in his house and pour drinks, and sometimes serve food to them.

"Oh, hey Mit, you were asleep," said Nathaniel apologetically. He immediately knew why: Mit hadn't been expecting customers to come tonight, and they hadn't been able to for the past few days. "You mind if we sit down, at least?"

Mit eyed them skeptically, then motioned for them to sit at the counter. Nathaniel and Ralf walked over and each sat at a stool while Mit poured water into three glasses.

"So, are you guys out here on patrol duty?" asked Mit. Mit was not an active member of the militia. He liked to keep to himself as much as he could, even though his business depended on other people coming into his home.

"Yep. The wizard let five of us go out tonight. You know, to keep a balance with both groups of soldiers," said Nathaniel. "Of course, Forredar could probably turn us all into toads or something, but I'm glad I could go out tonight." He took a sip of water, then put his glass down. The water was very cold.

"Oh, is that his name?" asked Mit. "I've never actually met him, but he sounds like the devil." Nathaniel found this to be very odd, and wondered how Forredar had never met the innkeeper.

"But, Mit, didn't he come here? Didn't he question you?" asked Nathaniel. Mit looked away, not meeting anyone's eye.

"I hid. I simply ran upstairs as fast as I could, and hid under the bed. I saw some small lights go into my room after the door was blasted open, but no one came after me. I guess when they found no crown, they decided it didn't matter if I was there or not," said Mit sadly. "I know I shouldn't have hid, but I heard about him attacking people," he turned and pointed at Nathaniel, "and about what could happen to anyone who didn't do exactly as he said, so I had no other choice. Heck, even then he could've burned the inn down and left me to die, but I wasn't willing to face him." Ralf looked positively sympathetic for Mit, and although he did not show it, Nathaniel felt the same. It was too much to ask for anybody, let alone a non-militia member, to be in the same room as someone with a history of anger and violent outbursts. "But, what has happened with you two? I heard you got it pretty bad from the wizard, and I'm surprised to see you here."

"Oh, it hasn't been much," said Ralf, "just got roughed up a little by Forredar, was told I was allowed to have some men posted out here tonight, and met up with Dorf and the rogues a short while ago. Not really much going on now, though."

"Well, you don't look like it's been a little rough," said Mit, indicating Ralf's many cuts and bruises. "What'd he do, take an ax to you or something?" Before Ralf could respond, the inn's door opened, and Nathaniel turned around to see Varon and Noah striding towards them, with their swords tucked into their belts.

"I don't know, Mit. It looks more like he was used as a sword sharpener," said Varon. The rogues sat down at stools next to Ralf.

"Nah, little friend, looks more like a bear got him," said Noah.

"Probably some kid with a knife got him, right Dorf?"

"All right!" boomed Ralf. I know my face is cut up, all right? And it actually was a bear, Noah," he said to the astonishment of everybody. "Well, that wizard conjured one out of thin air, and had it hit me when I gave a 'bad' answer to a question. So, I believe that's a coin for Noah." Varon reluctantly placed a coin on the counter and slid it over to Noah, who pocketed it with a quick swipe of the hand. Mit filled two more glasses with water and handed them to the very disappointed rogues.

"Mit, what's with the water? Why no mead?" asked Noah as he spilled water down his shirt front.

"I'll tell you why no mead – you didn't pay me anything! Cough up, and I'll give you some," said Mit bitterly. Noah banged his glass on the table.

"Over my dead body!" he exclaimed. Mit shrugged and turned to pour some water for himself.

"Fine then, more for everybody else who comes in here…," he muttered under his breath.

"Have you seen anyone else outside yet?" asked Nathaniel, thinking of the other soldiers and Soris. Varon took a sip of water and put his glass down.

"Yeah, we saw two of the soldiers walking around a few shops. They seemed to be guarding the front entrance, as if keeping someone out," said Varon, "or in. We haven't run into the wizard or the other two yet, so we think they're back at their camp."

"Camp?" asked Nathaniel.

"Yes, camp," said Noah. "That's where the soldiers have been staying, you didn't think they actually stayed in town? They don't sleep anywhere in town, anyway, so that's the only logical conclusion." Noah shrugged and went back to his water. Nathaniel remembered the wizard's two visits, then thought of where the soldiers really could be staying.

"The soldiers may be at a camp," he began, "but I don't think the wizard sleeps here. He probably teleports at night back to the capital. That also allows him to relay messages to the King without our knowing." The rogues obviously thought that through, but Noah didn't quite believe it.

"Then why didn't he just teleport here?" he asked.

"Well, I've heard that a wizard can only teleport to places that he or she has been. So, I guess Forredar hasn't been to Kumaiyan before, so he had to ride on a horse here. Now, since he's been here, I'm sure he can teleport back and forth as he wishes," finished Nathaniel. Noah looked dumbfounded along with his best friend, but Ralf rubbed his eyes and yawned sleepily.

"Look, nothing is happening tonight, and if it's all the same to you, I'm really tired. I'm going home, and if you guys want to stay out here a little longer that's fine," said Ralf as he stood up and walked to the door. The rogues and Nathaniel turned to wave to him, but he stumbled out of the door and into the night.

"Okay, good, he's gone," said Varon.

"Yeah," said his rogue, "now we can begin planning." Nathaniel found this comment rather odd, so he decided to speak.

"Planning what?" he asked as innocently as he could.

"Look, Dorf, we can't have that wizard around here much longer, even if we're allowed to live again," said Varon. "The way I see it, he's taken over the town, and we've got to get him out of here."

"Oh, that's great, but haven't you noticed his magic and four bodyguards? We'd be no match for them if we decided to rebel!" said Nathaniel warningly. The rogues grinned slyly.

"Dorf. It wouldn't be rebellion," said Noah, "I'm not sure the King really wants this anyway. He probably doesn't know what is really going on. And we're not suggesting that the three of us do it. We've got to have the whole militia out to chase them away. Maybe those travelers who came by a few days ago would help;

they seem to hate him also." Nathaniel couldn't believe what he was hearing, but did not dislike it.

"Maybe we shouldn't do anything until after tomorrow, after the duel. I think the town would be pretty demoralized if something disrupted it, and then we don't have an army," said Nathaniel evenly. "And why didn't you want Ralf to hear about it?"

"Well, we don't think he would take to kindly to the idea, might not want to face the wizard again," said Varon.

"After all, he already has been through a lot," said Noah optimistically. "Hopefully, he won't have to do a thing."

"Fine, then I'll think about it," said Nathaniel, "but let's finish our shift."

# The Surprise

The next morning, Nathaniel was out and about helping some of the local men get the town center ready for the duels. Chairs and benches were placed in a square leaving a considerable amount of space for the actual fights. Outdoor tables were set up with cloths draped over them for people to place drinks and food platters on. And of course, a wooden booth was dragged out of an old shed for the betting to take place at.

Oben, a retired militia man, would sit behind the booth with a sack of gold and many sheets of parchment. If the townspeople wanted to place bets, they would walk to the booth, deposit what they would risk, and Oben would record it on his ledger. At the end of the matches that were bet on, the gamblers would be paid appropriately and allowed to continue betting or stopping while they had enough gold. Nathaniel found that the whole betting process was rather fun and exciting, especially if he bet on a match involving one of the rogues or, on the rare occasion, both of them. He would often flip a gold coin in his hand to choose which rogue to bet on; if it landed on the knight on horseback, he would bet on Varon, but if it landed on the moon and sun symbol, he would bet on Noah. He often prided himself for the true genius he was.

That fifth and final day of the week, End Day, was an absolutely beautiful day to hold an outdoor event. Without a cloud in the sky, the sun shone brilliantly all across the land. Its heat permeated every inch of the outside world, but a gentle breeze would come from the west to cool the town, creating a positive atmosphere for everyone.

Birds of all colors and sizes flew in every direction in an around the town. Nathaniel wondered if they had been acting like this since the wizard and his men showed up, or if this was a response to the bright spring weather. The latter was confirmed when he saw Herbert shoot out of the cottage window and join his fellow birds in the frolic.

Once the ring was drawn up and the benches were in place, Nathaniel and the other workers began placing bets of their own, for Oben had already arrived and was sitting comfortably in his booth.

"Yes miss, you have sixteen on Gillens, and seven on Morcim," said Oben to a tall woman at the booth. Oben was a fairly old man with gray hair and a bad posture. He was very slow-moving due to his age, but didn't miss a trick with his mind. He always dispensed the correct amount of gold to the winners of a match, no matter how little time he had.

Nathaniel reached the booth, and with some difficulty managed to place five gold coins on the edge with his outstretched hand. He couldn't see Oben, but knew he must've smiled at the sight.

"Okay, Dorf, who will you be placing your gold on?" he asked.

"Who is going to be fighting today?" asked Nathaniel, wanting to see what options he had. Oben began to rattle off a list of names.

"There's Gillens, Morcim, Destrell, Emerett, McKringle, Noah, Varon, and a few of the soldiers who rode in here. Of course, Noah and Varon are each taking on one, but the other hasn't been challenged yet, even though he isn't the wizard," said Oben. "So, who do you think your gold is worth?"

It really wasn't a difficult decision. Noah and Varon could each take down five soldiers if they had to, Gillens was a baker who barely knew how to swing a sword, Morcim was a large man who had a lot of strength but little coordination, Destrell was very small and spent time reading books rather than practicing with a sword, and McKringle was an average swordsman, but probably not capable of holding up to a well-trained soldier for any long amount of time.

"I'll say that both rogues win their fights," said Nathaniel confidently. He heard Oben brush the coins off of the counter.

"Are you going to duel anyone today, Dorf?" asked Oben.

"No, I don't think so," said Nathaniel, "I would be stuck against a soldier, wouldn't I? There's no way I could win."

"Oh, sorry to hear it, very sorry indeed," said Oben, "but if you would reconsider, the offer is open until the duels start. The soldier is the odd man out, after all."

"Thanks, Oben, but I'd rather go to the tavern and put a few hours of work in before I need to take that gold back," said Nathaniel, and he walked away from the booth and headed into The Golden Tavern.

The tavern was the same as Nathaniel had left it the last time he was there. The only difference was that a few tables and chairs were missing, having been provided for the duel. A crowd of people was inside, some standing, some sitting, around Herbert who was perched on the back of Ralf's chair.

"And I thought to myself, 'This isn't right, he's got to be at least a foot shorter than that....'" Herbert trailed off as he saw Nathaniel stride behind the counter. "Oh, hello, Dorf, I was just, er, entertaining.....right, people...."

"It's okay," said Nathaniel, though he was a little tired of all of the height jokes. "Anyone want anything?" he was answered by a massive movement of outstretched hands holding coins. After surveying the hands and counting the gold, Nathaniel began poring drinks and handing glasses to the patrons. "Hey, I might need some help, I've got to serve twenty people!"

"Fine, fine, but I was just getting' comfy," said Ralf as he slowly rose out of his seat, knocking Herbert to the floor. A rush of laughter ensued. "Oh, sorry Herb, I'm a little big, you see!" As Herbert picked himself up, Ralf walked behind the counter and helped Nathaniel fill their massive order. "So, Dorf, you fighting today?"

"Nah, I'd rather not. The only other applicants were soldiers, and I don't think I want to get beat in front of the town. I placed a few coins on it, though. Maybe I'll get lucky," said Nathaniel hopefully, but remembering that he rarely was lucky.

"Oh, there are slots open?" asked Ralf somewhat eagerly. "I'd love to have a crack at those imbeciles!"

"Yeah, Oben said that there were a few soldiers left. I'm sure you'd take them all on, but that's not allowed. If you want to go over and register with him, you should do it now. I'll hold the fort down." Ralf considered this for a moment, mulling it over in his head. He then put down the glass he was filling and spread his arms out in a stretching position.

"I guess I'm in good shape and all," he said, and for the first time Nathaniel realized that most of his cuts and bruises had gone, except for a thin one across his left cheek, "I think I'll do it. Oh, Dorf, we're going to go out again tonight. I think it'll be good to keep doing it until they leave. I'd hate it if they managed to attack anyone right after the duel. We're all in such good spirits anyway!" With that, Ralf quickly walked out from behind the counter and out the bar door. Nathaniel

sighed and started polishing the used glasses when Herbert flew over and stood on the counter.

"Dorf, nice to see you, nice to see you again," he said, holding his wing out as if to shake Nathaniel's hand.

"I saw you this morning," said Nathaniel, but cracked a smile. "What have you been doing so far? Comedy, tragedy, what sort of drama?"

"Eh, a little of each, actually. Oh! Oh! How many wizards does it take to light a candle?" Herbert jumped up and down excitedly.

"Er, one?" guessed Nathaniel, though he understood Herbert's sense of humor. Herbert looked simply delighted to reveal the answer.

"No! None!"

"None?" asked Nathaniel, confused.

"Yep, they use magic to do it for them!" said Herbert, then he started laughing. Nathaniel eyed him quizzically.

"So, that's good, isn't it?" asked Nathaniel. "I mean, not having to light a candle by hand would be pretty convenient, actually."

"And that, Dorf, is why you're smarter than everyone else here," said Herbert, suddenly serious. "Though I never thought about it that way..." Herbert trailed off into whatever thoughts were kept in his parrot-head. Nathaniel shrugged and went back to his glasses. Herbert moved closer, accidentally knocking a glass over. Surprisingly, it didn't so much as crack. Nathaniel picked it up and placed it far away from his friend's reach.

"So, what are we going to do today?" asked Herbert.

"I expect to work for a few more hours, then we can watch the dueling," said Nathaniel. "Looks like we're back to our lives again." Though he would rather not be couped up inside his home all day, Nathaniel couldn't help but feel as if he should do something different once in a while. His life wasn't necessarily boring, but for some odd reason he thought that it could be more, more......, well, just *more.*

"Oh, we'll be here all day?" said Herbert. "Dorf, what do you think has been going on lately? You know, with the crown and all?"

"I have no idea," said Nathaniel, "there hasn't been any real news for a few days. But we don't have to worry about that, as long as everyone in town is okay, we're okay. Besides, we know that no one here has the crown, don't we?"

"Yep, but what I'm interested in isn't who has the crown, but why. I don't think anyone would go through all that trouble just to prance around at home with it," said Herbert. Nathaniel suddenly had a rather vivid image of a man wearing the crown, walking around a group of admirers. He shook the thought from his head.

"Herb, I think it was just some thief who can do a little magic and who wanted a valuable object," said Nathaniel in what he hoped was a reassuring voice. Apparently it wasn't.

"Aha, then explain this!" said Herbert. "Only sorcerers can use magic, and all of them are trained in the capital, so that means a wizard would have to be working for the King to do magic!"

"So?"

"So, I think it was an inside job. Maybe some wizard saw something in that crown that no one else did. Or, he could try to enchant it into killing the king. I've heard they can do that," said Herbert knowledgeably. "Wouldn't it be something if I could do magic?"

"Oh, it definitely would be something," said Nathaniel. "I'm not sure you can even hold a twig properly, let alone shoot sparks from your claws."

"Hey, I have held plenty of things in my life!" replied Herbert.

"Oh, my mistake, anyone can point at people and start turning them into frogs," said Nathaniel. "Heck, I couldn't do it, and I'm not sure animals can do magic."

"Until a few years ago, you were pretty sure animals couldn't talk," retorted Herbert. "Anyway, I think I could do some good in the world! Imagine, being able to conjure food for the poor, create light in the darkest areas, and all of that stuff that only the gods can do!"

"Yeah, but I'm not sure you'd want to leave this place," said Nathaniel, "you would need to go to the King for permission, for starters. Then you would have to be instructed by a wizard, at the capital most likely." Herbert gave a snort.

"Instruction...not with a brain like mine! I can imagine it, standing on your shoulder, the wind whipping wildly, and suddenly poof!" He jumped up and flapped his wings. "A nice new scarf appears out of thin air. Oh, I bet I could even make a statue of myself!" Nathaniel gave an awkward chuckle.

"Sure, I get it. Hey, how about you magic up some more glasses for me to fill?" Herbert looked dumbfounded, then took flight to the back room to fetch more glasses.

The day continued on smoothly. Customers regularly flowed in and out of the tavern and Nathaniel was kept very busy. Herbert had been working the whole day as well, keeping the patrons entertained with his antics and dramatic sequences.

As the light from the windows faded, the last of the tavern's customers had exited the building and Nathaniel, Herbert, and Ralf were left to clean up the mess and close up the bar. Well, Herbert really wasn't much of a help. He often dropped things, and eventually gave up the whole process and flew onto a chandelier to crack some jokes at Nathaniel.

"Dorf, we're done for the day," said Ralf as one of the three chairs he was carrying landed on his foot. "I'm ready to leave." Nathaniel thought that "ready" was a bit of an understatement, considering the excessive swearing and jumping done by Ralf, but he followed him out of the tavern.

A large crowd of people filled the town center. At least one hundred and fifty people from around town had gathered to watch the fights. Men, women, and some of the older children sat on benches or at chairs around tables. Nathaniel spotted Oben sitting in his booth poring over a long roll of parchment, presumably the record of the gold bet on each fighter.

Herbert had fluttered back onto Nathaniel's shoulder, angry that they hadn't alerted him to their exiting the tavern. Nathaniel lost sight of Ralf as he made his way through the throng to cross town and reach his home.

"What are we stopping here for?" demanded Herbert as Nathaniel unlocked his cottage door. "I thought the duels were taking place where the crowd is!"

"I've just got to grab something," said Nathaniel as he quickly snatched his sword from his favorite chair. When Herbert looked at him hopefully, he shook his head. "I'm only taking it in case something happens, not to duel." The parrot chuckled and together they left the house.

By the time they had gotten back to the town center, the first duel had already started. Nathaniel could hear the cheering and clashing of swords, but could not see the fight until he had climbed onto a bench. Being three feet tall really had its disadvantages.

In the center of the ring, Varon was dueling a man that Nathaniel had never seen before. He was tall with short blond hair and plain clothing. Remembering what Oben had said about who was fighting, Nathaniel reasoned that he must be one of the soldiers.

Even though he was up against a highly trained soldier, Varon was certainly making short work of his opponent. Nathaniel saw the two exchange blows at the same rate, but

Varon wore an expression of boredom whereas the soldier seemed to be putting all of his energy into the encounter.

The soldier was strong though. As Varon made to attack his left flank, he pulverized his sword down with a quick strike. Varon quickly recovered with another attempt to disarm his opponent, but clearly kept a more vigilant watch on the soldier's movements.

Not two minutes afterwards, Varon caught a particularly heavy blow from the soldier on his sword and flipped it out of his grasp. The soldier stood before him, defeated. The crowd roared, and the two opponents bowed to each other and left the ring for their seats.

The next two fighters were two townspeople, Gillens and McKringle. Gillens was about at the average height of an adult male, with long brown hair covering his ears and shoulders. McKringle had a relatively comical appearance, his stout figure draped in a doublet and brilliant pink pants.

Gillens bowed deeply to his opponent, who stiffly tilted his head downwards. On a count of three, both men drew short swords from their waist and went at each other.

This duel, however, proved to be a hilarious scene instead of a contest of dexterity and skill. McKringle, who was short by most standards, was actually parrying most of Gillens' blows with ease, but wasn't able to follow up with any attacks of his own. After ten long minutes of frustrated fighting, Gillens had resorted to simply swinging his weapon wildly, hoping to catch his opponent's blade in the process. But McKringle, who wasn't agile or quick, somehow avoided these strikes rather then put his sword up to block them. Giddy with laughter, he ran circles around the frenzied Gillens until his opponent grew tired of the random chopping and swinging. Fortunately for McKringle, Gillens dropped his sword. Before he could pick it up, McKringle had jumped on it and held it down with all his might. Many spectators laughed, and the fight was over. McKringle gave the sword back to his opponent, and fled the scene without pausing for a bow.

Two people entered the ring for the next fight. Nathaniel saw that one of them was Oben, and the other one was a soldier dressed in full battle armor. Oddly enough, Oben did not have a sword in his hand, but a piece of parchment.

"Attention! Attention! Everybody, we have a new challenge!" cried Oben. "This soldier would like to challenge one member of the town to a duel! Sir, would you be as kind as to point him out?" This resulted in much whispering and muttering within the crowd. Usually, all of the challenges were finished before the duels began.

The soldier turned around, surveying the crowd through his mask. No one could tell who he was looking at, but everybody in a certain section of the crowd seemed to whimper if he turned towards them. As the soldier turned towards where Nathaniel was sitting, he abruptly stopped. He stood perfectly still, and Nathaniel knew that he was looking right at him. The soldier raised a gloved hand and pointed at Nathaniel.

"Him," he said in a deep voice, "the dwarf. I challenge the dwarf." Nathaniel felt the eyes of everyone on him. The crowd had gone quiet. Everybody was looking at him, waiting for his response. Should he decline? Or would that make him seem cowardly, or afraid of the soldier? What if he accepted, would he be beat like never before? His face burned, sweat rolling down his cheek. Herbert nudged him by digging his claws into his shoulder, and Nathaniel stood up. He was ready.

"I accept your challenge!" said Nathaniel. Though he was not exactly a crowd favorite during the duels, he received much cheering and clapping from the spectators. Oben clapped his hands wildly, calling the crowd into silence.

"Great! Good! Now, if anyone would like to place some gold on the outcome of this match, we will conduct a ten minute intermission. Please go to my booth, yes it's right over there, if you would like to win some coin from the efforts of these fighters!" With that, Oben walked off to his booth where a few people had already lined up to place bets.

Nathaniel had not been expecting to fight anyone. He also didn't expect to win. Could he possibly, by some stroke of luck manage to be victorious in battle? As he slowly made his way towards the center ring, he grew less and less confident with each step. Nathaniel remembered that he was a dwarf, and of all the disadvantages he was burdened with because of it. He was not tall enough to match a grown human in battle. He was someone who had trouble mounting horses, opening doors, or reaching counters. He even experienced difficulty purchasing things in the market. No, Nathaniel Dorf could not win a fight.

When he reached the ring, the soldier was waiting with his sword in his hand. The crowd clapped and cheered when Nathaniel walked towards the center of the ring and took a bow. He did not know why the crowd was cheering him on, why he was suddenly so popular, why he was being supported even though everyone knew the soldier would win.

Nathaniel now stood fifteen feet away from the soldier. Once again, he was not sure of the soldier's reaction to his presence, but he had a pretty good idea what he was thinking. The soldier had probably challenged him because of his size, and was now chuckling to himself at seeing his opponent before him. Nathaniel instead looked at the crowd. He saw many familiar faces, mostly townspeople, he even saw Herbert exchanging gold with Oben. Then, Nathaniel saw Forredar sitting behind his opponent, wearing all black clothing and looking with...with interest at Nathaniel. Their eyes slowly met, and Nathaniel felt very afraid for a few seconds. Why could the wizard be there? Perhaps he had placed a large sum of gold on the soldier, and wanted to see how long it took for him to succeed. Or he could try to attack Nathaniel during the fight. After all, he had acted towards him with a lot of hostility, and Nathaniel was sure that he wouldn't waste an opportunity like this.

Nathaniel pulled his eyes away, forcing himself to look back at his opponent. He was bowing. Remembering the proper etiquette, Nathaniel bowed also, making himself even smaller than he was, and felt.

"One!" said a voice, and Nathaniel turned to see Herbert perched on a table. "Two!" This was it, he must be prepared. He faced the soldier again. "Three!"

The soldier rushed at Nathaniel, and swung his sword at an alarmingly high speed. Nathaniel brought his sword up just in time to block the blow, and the soldier drew his sword back. Making another attempt to behead him, the soldier swung high again, but Nathaniel simply ducked, something you really don't do that often when you're three feet tall. Missing wildly, the soldier's arm crossed his body. Seizing the opportunity, Nathaniel thrust at the soldier's arm, going for the sword, but his opponent beat it down with a backhand strike. He kicked at Nathaniel, but he had rolled to the left just in time, hitting the soldier's armored legs along the way. The soldier spun around to Nathaniel and lunged at him with his sword. Nathaniel parried the attack and leapt into the air, aiming a blow at the soldier's arm. He missed, and fell to the ground. The crowd gasped.

The soldier was standing over him now, holding his sword high above his head in both hands. Nathaniel managed to pull himself up to his knees when the soldier brought his sword down. Then things became strange.

It was as if the world was moving slowly around him. Nathaniel brought his sword up to meet the attack, and a blur of green light covered his own hand. He heard the clash of steel, saw the sparks fly, but they were moving very slowly. In fact, the soldier seemed to be moving very slowly also, drawing his sword back at a snail's pace. Acting instinctively, Nathaniel swung his sword at his opponent. It did not move slowly like everything else, but very quickly. He saw an intense flash of green, his sword hitting the soldier's, and his opponent's weapon flying behind him.

Then the world was brought back up to speed. The soldier staggered back, looking at his hand with disbelief. His sword had fallen not a foot away from the spectators behind him.

The crowd cheered and clapped. Nathaniel saw many people looking positively shocked and surprised. Herbert was flapping his wings wildly and jumping up and down, showing his enthusiasm to a much larger degree than anybody else. In fact, after the spectators had finished their applause, he was still celebrating.

Nathaniel looked back towards his opponent, but he saw Forredar first. He did not look shocked as the others did, but his expression was one of pure loathing. He was also sitting perfectly still, and his eyes seemed to absorb everything that was going on around him in addition to focusing their hatred on Nathaniel.

Nathaniel exited the ring but did not go back to his seat. He would have to sleep on this.

## The Statue

As it turned out, Herbert had been the only one to bet on Nathaniel. Apparently, the townspeople would rather see Nathaniel upset the soldier and lose a few coins than see him lose. That is why Herbert was carrying a small sack that was jingling with coins as they made their way home.

Once Nathaniel was inside his cottage, he placed his sword in his cabinet and sat down on his bed. He looked down at his hands, wondering whether or not he could make them glow again. His performance during the match had been unexpected; he wasn't supposed to beat a trained soldier in combat, and from his point of view, make everything glow green and slow down in front of him.

It had happened without warning; he had had no control over it. All he had done was move as quickly as he could and swing his swords as fast as he could. Somehow, he had moved so fast that everything seemed to slow down for him. Or had he slowed down time itself so that it would seem as if he was moving really fast?

Of course, there was another possibility, a very rare possibility. A quality so rare that only thirteen people in the world currently had it. It was almost impossible to imagine.

*Magic* thought Nathaniel. Could he, no matter how many years of training were required, no matter how many people had failed, become a sorcerer or a wizard? No, it was not possible. How could he have accidentally used magic? It was known that a person needed to train their body and mind for many years to use magic. Nathaniel had been holding a sword, not a magical staff, during the match.

If he had used magic, then he should learn how to use it again. If properly trained, if properly harnessed, he might be able to become a decent magic-user. But the only way to be trained was to be taught by an older wizard, and all of them were in major cities and at the capital.

It really was unlikely, but a spark had lit in his head at the notion of it. How could he be a wizard? No one else in his family was, and that was how everyone thought that magic was passed down.

There had never been a story about a wizard who lived in Kumaiyan. The wealthy nobles were packed into the cities, and they were the ones who had their children taught to become wizards. Wizards were recruited by the King or the counts of cities to perform tasks for them that a menial servant could not. Many of these wizards had played an important role in protecting various cities and villages during the rebellion by using sorcery and magic to keep enemies away from the protected areas. It was even rumored that the king's true personal bodyguard was the most experienced and most magically gifted wizard at the capital.

Then again, wizards were not always well behaved within Arcoiris. The wizard who led the rebellion forces, Talitenkus, had gone against the laws of the land and made many attempts to take the throne with a series of failed assassination attempts and minor skirmishes. That had been the first time in centuries that a wizard had broken the law. They were a large part of the law enforcement of the capital, taking orders only from the King himself. They never needed to steal because they could conjure food and water. They certainly wouldn't kill people; a quarrel could be settled with a non-lethal spell or a meeting with the King. What Talitenkus had done was revolutionary, but he had never succeeded.

Nathaniel sighed deeply and looked at his watch. It was almost ten o'clock. He had worked late, after all. He was pretty tired, so he decided to turn in. Herbert had already fallen asleep, clutching his bag of gold like a mother holding a child.

As he fell into darkness, Nathaniel remembered that he was supposed to be on duty that night. Oh, well. Soris hadn't shown up the other night, anyway. He closed his eyes and quickly fell asleep.

After what seemed like only seconds to him, he was awakened by a loud bang at the door. Rubbing his eyes and slowly making his way out of bed, Nathaniel walked to his cabinet and took his sword from its hanging place. The door banged loudly again.

"I'm coming, I'm coming!" he shouted as he pulled the door open.

Forredar stood in the doorway dressed in all black clothing. He looked down at Nathaniel with a menacing glare. His four soldiers were behind him also, all dressed in full armor with their masks on. Their swords were sheathed.

"Nathaniel Dorf, you have been found guilty of royal theft. You will be taken to Vikelad to stand trial," said Forredar, sneering at him. "If you will not come quietly, we will use force to apprehend you." But Nathaniel hadn't stolen anything! He had never even been to the capital!

"Excuse me? I haven't taken anything! What have I taken?" he yelled, incensed.

"You should know, dwarf," said Forredar, "that crown is worth more than your weight in gold. Then again, so is my left boot."

"This is outrageous! I have done nothing of the sort! Where is your proof, wizard?"

"We had found the crown at your....residence approximately two hours ago. We have taken it in safekeeping for now, and will return it to its rightful owner once we reach the capital."

"Liar!" he bellowed at the top of his voice. He saw several windows light up behind the soldiers. "You damn well know I didn't take anything, you searched my place with that bit of magic you did!"

"Ah yes, that little spell you used was rather effective," said Forredar smoothly. "Such tricks will not work for you in the future, I'm afraid."

"I-DON'T-KNOW-HOW-TO-USE-MAGIC!" screamed Nathaniel, brandishing his sword. He heard many doors open, but that was nothing compared to the pounding between his ears. This was insane, it was preposterous!

"Are you threatening me, dwarf?" asked Forredar. "My, my, that won't hold up well in court. And please do not befoul the air with your hideous lies. They will only extend your sentence. Now, will you comply or do we have to hurt you?" His finger was now pointed right at Nathaniel's chest.

"Maybe you should listen to me instead," said Nathaniel. He lowered his voice to a whisper. "I am not going anywhere. I have not done anything wrong. And I'd rather fight you instead of tell you I am guilty of anything." He stood up on the tips of his toes and tried to stick his face right up in Forredar's, but he wasn't quite tall enough. He was three feet tall, after all.

"Fine," said Forredar. "We'll do it-" he was cut off by a loud scream.

"Incoming!" yelled what must have been one of the soldiers. Something rocketed through the air and struck a soldier in the chest. Everyone at the door turned to look for the source of the missile.

Varon and Noah were standing to the right of Nathaniel's cottage, holding rocks and swords in their hands, shouting and jeering at the soldiers. Neither of them wore shields, but their sword tips shone brightly in the torchlight from the many lit houses.

The soldiers drew their weapons, and Nathaniel took his chance. As Forredar turned his gaze back to him, undoubtedly to make a toad of him or something, he sprinted around him and into the street. Looking back, he saw Forredar stagger, a rock rolling away from him.

"Nice one!" he yelled to the rogues. As well as giving them encouragement, the shout directed two of the soldiers to Nathaniel instead. Lovely. He decided to run for it, and ran towards the rogues, who were bracing themselves for the charging soldiers. He also heard a loud scream.

"No!" It was Forredar's voice. Suddenly, something shook the earth and Nathaniel was lifted off his feet and thrown forward. The air grew hot, and he was twisted and turned and tossed as easily as a small bird in a gust of wind. He heard air rushing past him, saw flames jump up before his eyes, and held onto his sword for reasons unknown to even him at the time. Then, with a final push, he was thrown up, or what he thought was up, and fell to the ground none too lightly. Dirt was swept up into his face, and he pushed himself off of the ground coughing.

He saw a thick cloud of smoke covering the area around his house. Nathaniel heard shouts and bangs and saw jets of flame leap up from the thick of the smoke. He made a move forward to investigate, but a soldier materialized out of the cloud in front of him.

The soldier drew his sword slowly, as if unsure what to do, then rushed at Nathaniel holding it high above his head. Being ready for the strike, Nathaniel parried the first blow without even flinching and aimed an attack at the soldier's face. It was blocked, but his opponent lost his balance momentarily and staggered backwards.

Pressing to his momentary advantage, Nathaniel stepped forward and hacked at the enemy's legs. The flat of his blade clashed with the heavy armor, and he felt a stinging sensation in his palm. The soldier managed to regain his balance and bring his sword coming down, and it would've split Nathaniel's head in two had he not put his blade up to guard it.

This was a situation he did not like to be in. Here he had a tall man pressing a sword down on top of him. He had the disadvantage of being a dwarf again. He was straining every muscle in his body to hold off the soldier. His face was contorted strangely, and he cursed the soldier for wearing a mask. He could not see how much effort his opponent was putting into the struggle, but he felt that he was giving off a pretty pathetic expression.

Nathaniel felt beads of sweat fall like raindrops down his brow. How long had he been at it? A minute? Two? He still heard shouting but now heard the clashing of metal on metal. He didn't hear any spells, though. He was sure that the wizard was trying to find him through the smoke, probably blowing up anything in his path. But he didn't hear it.

Nathaniel felt the strength leave his arm, and he dropped his weapon with a howl. He was surely dead. The soldier would bring his sword down any second now. Any second....what was going on? Then it happened again.

Time seemed to slow down for him. He saw his enemy moving at an incredibly slow pace, his sword moving less than an inch every five seconds. Seeing that he had a chance to live, Nathaniel dove to the left. That lifted the slow effects.

The soldier's blade cut through the air and slammed into the dirt beneath him with a hard thud. He screamed and let go of his sword, clutching his right arm with his left. He ran in circles, howling in pain, and tripped over Nathaniel's sword.

Wasting no time, Nathaniel grabbed his sword from where the soldier had fallen over it and stamped on his opponent's head. Hard. It was driven to the ground and bounced up. The soldier stopped moving. He was unconscious.

Nathaniel stood, wondering what to do next. Should he hide? Surely Forredar had not been stopped, and he would likely hunt him down with whichever men he had left. But how could he hide from him? Every home would be searched, every building would be raided. He couldn't hide....but he could run.

As he made to sprint off towards the end of town, a bright silver light expanded through the cloud. It temporarily blinded him, and when he could see again the smoke was gone.

A battle was revealed to Nathaniel. Back to back, Varon and Noah were battling two soldiers, their blades moving faster than the eye. About twenty feet to their right, Ralf was dueling a soldier, a shield bound to his arm and a long sword in his hand. Unlike the rogues, who looked as though the fight was amusing, he looked utterly frenzied, hacking and slashing with a madman's drive. Then in between them, in front of Nathaniel's home, Forredar was spinning on the spot, moving incredibly quickly and pointing his fingers at the crowd of townspeople around him. Nathaniel saw that he was directing the flights of several jets of flame, which chased the townspeople and held them away from him.

Sighing with relief, Nathaniel saw that no bodies were on the ground. No one was dead. Deciding that he couldn't let the town hold them off, he dove into the fray. He ran towards Ralf, who seemed to have been knocked down a peg some time into the fight. He was moving slower, his attacks were weakened. Nathaniel hoped that he got there in time.

He did, though. Right when Ralf's opponent drew his sword back to deliver a powerful blow, he dove at his waist. His face hit the soldier's armor, which happened to hurt a lot, but by hitting the waist he had attached himself to the soldier. He stuck his fingers in the belt of the soldier, who was frantically trying to shake him off.

"Whee!" cried Nathaniel as he spun in the air, his legs suspended by the force of the soldier's movement. He wondered what Ralf was doing at the moment. The soldier stopped trying to shake him off. Nathaniel heard him bring his sword up. *Come on, where are you? he thought.*

Suddenly, he fell forward and felt the soldier fall over too. The soldier made a loud grunting noise then stopped shaking and writhing all together. Disentangling himself from the belt, Nathaniel rose to see Ralf holding his fist out at about the place that the soldier's head must have been. He smiled broadly.

"Sorry about that," he said, "I lost my sword after you tackled him." He helped Nathaniel to his feet. Nathaniel brushed the dirt off his face and looked back towards the main fight.

Varon was holding a soldier in front of him while Noah was whacking him with a sword and kicking it. Another soldier's body was on the ground, but all of its body parts were intact. Forredar was in the center, but was not chasing anybody. A globe or purple light surrounded him, and ten men with bows were pointing arrows at him. Several arrows lay around the globe, revealing that it was indeed a magical barrier designed to defend the wizard. Looking back towards the rogues, Nathaniel saw that the second soldier was on the ground, stirring feebly as Varon and Noah took turns stamping on him. It looked as though they had won.

He walked towards Forredar, using all of the anger he could muster. His fists were tightly clenched. He addressed the wizard, who looked neither scared nor angry.

"You piece of ragged filth. You know I haven't done anything wrong, you just attacked me! Now, I will give you this chance," he felt as if he was suddenly in a position of power, "to tell me why you attacked, or we will kill you." He liked the idea of the last part, but killing in general was a nasty business to get into. Forredar smirked evilly.

"The King will know who the culprit is, dwarf, before anyone else can get to him. I am after all a wizard. I am giving you a last chance to surrender. You have fought bravely and well, but that won't help you where you're going," he said, with an odd air of confidence considering his position.

"Absolutely not!" yelled Noah. "He hasn't done anything wrong! I bet you're just mad because he bested your fighters twice!"

"Yeah! There's no place for cheats and grudges in this town," said Varon. "We're not letting you take any of us to your capital. Just deal with your loss and leave this place. Hell, you can take your henchmen with you." He gestured towards the two fallen soldiers at his feet.

"I am not jealous or defeated. You see, I can do things that none of you can even dream of, things that I am employed to do for only the highest honors in the land. I can do things such as this-" he pointed his finger right at where Ralf was standing. "Gargoyle!" A beam of sparks flashed in between the two men, and Ralf went rigid. A gray substance began to spread quickly across his body. He didn't make any movements. The gray moved up and down, covering every inch of his body that it could cover. When his whole body was encased, he looked just like a statue. Correction: he was a statue. Nathaniel gave a start. The rogues' mouths opened wide, gaping at Ralf's statue.

"Never, ever, dare to underestimate me!" said Forredar. "Your resistance will not be tolerated!" Nathaniel charged through the barrier to kill him. He felt a shock go through his body. He pushed against what felt like stone and finally broke the magical wall and thrust his sword at the wizard. A split second before it made contact, the wizard disappeared with a flash of light, and the barrier fell from around him. Sparks flew in every direction and flickered into nothingness.

Nathaniel looked around wildly, but the wizard was truly gone. His eyes then found Ralf. The statue was pointing right where Forredar had been standing, and its mouth was open in a scream that was never heard. Ralf's eyes looked maddening, as if cursing his attacker.

Several people were beginning to crowd around the statue and gasping when they noticed who it was. The men with bows lowered them and formed a small group behind Nathaniel. The rogues had rushed forward the moment Ralf was hit, and they were now examining the statue and tapping it in several places.

He really wished he knew how the magic worked. He suddenly realized that about a hundred people had formed a crowded circle around him, the rogues, and the statue. Many people where whispering furiously and pointing at the statue with outstretched arms. Nathaniel caught a glimpse of the traveler April holding a hand cupped over her mouth, a look of horror etched on her face.

He turned back to the statue of Ralf. More people were beside it know, touching it and rubbing it. Mit had even emerged from the darkness of his inn, and was currently muttering s string of curses under his breath.

Madeline, dressed in a horrible blue striped nightgown, was pacing around the statue and shaking her head. Her behavior would have been acceptable, but she didn't look upset, but instead looked as if she was merely disappointed. Beginning to feel angry towards her again, Nathaniel strode forward and stopped her as she was pacing. Though they were close in height, she was still taller than him.

"What's the matter with you?" he asked. "Someone has been turned to stone, and you don't even seem to care!" Madeline looked offended at the question.

"Of course I care!" she retorted.

"Yeah, you care enough to go gossiping about it to everyone tomorrow," said Nathaniel, ignoring the cruelty in his own voice.

"No, I care that we have driven a very powerful man away from our town! Now what do we do? The king's army will come for us, you know that? That Forredar is a smart one. Oh, yes," she said, somewhat delightedly, "he'll get the troops here quick enough all right. He'll also be able to tell who is loyal," she pointed at her chest, "from who is a traitor!" She gestured towards where Nathaniel stood. "When they come, you had better be quick, Dorf! You'll be next!" Varon stepped between them and held a hand out to both sides.

"As much as I disagree with this old witch's idea of who is loyal and who is not, she has a point, Dorf. The army will come, and they are going to raid the village or possibly destroy it," he said. "I think that we'll have to prepare the militia for battle."

"No, my little friend, our militia cannot keep the army out for any long stretch of time," said Noah. That seemed to give Noah an idea.

"How long until the army can get here?" he asked. Noah and Varon looked at each other blankly for a few seconds, as if to decide who would answer, then Noah did.

"Well, they've got to travel about two hundred miles....I would say a few days, but that teleport magic messes everything up," he said. "I don't know how many of these the wizard can transport with magic, or how many have to walk." Noah pointed at a soldier at his feet. This gave Nathaniel an idea.

"You may not, I may not, but I think I know someone who might," he said. "In fact, I would say that thanks to their wizard leader abandoning them, they have to know."

## The Pathway Forward

It was very, very late when Nathaniel returned to his cottage. To his profound surprise, Herbert had slept through the whole battle. The green parrot was snoring away on Nathaniel's pillow. Ignoring Herbert, Nathaniel threw his sword into a corner and sat down at his favorite chair.

"Huh? What time is it?" asked Herbert, who had suddenly woken up at the sound. "Dorf, it's still dark out! What's going on?"

"It's about one, Herb," said Nathaniel, "and I've been out for a while." Herbert looked confused.

"What have you been doing there? Has something been going on?" he stood up on both feet, suddenly alert.

"No! Of course nothing has been happening! Well, unless you count, I don't know, the EXPLOSION! The fighting? All of the loud banging noises that should've woken you up?" he asked. Nathaniel was not angry at Herbert, after all, his being awake or asleep wouldn't have changed anything that had happened. Herbert looked rather taken aback.

"Fighting? An explosion? Goodness no, I haven't heard anything! Who's been fighting?" said Herbert. And so, Nathaniel recounted the battle scene from his point of view, explaining how Forredar had attacked him without solid evidence and what happened when he tried to destroy him. Herbert looked awed when he said that he had helped defeat two soldiers, but then looked saddened when he told about Ralf's statue.

"Is he...is...he.....dead?" asked Herbert nervously.

"I don't know," said Nathaniel, "but we're going to find out. We captured all of the soldiers, thanks to yours truly and the rogues, so we'll be interrogating them tomorrow. We're going to get every piece of information from them that we can- how Forredar's spell works, what's really going on with the king, what kind of pow-, well, you get the idea." Nathaniel wanted to keep his personal question to himself for as long as possible. Thankfully, Herbert didn't pick up on his pause.

"Yeah, and we'll kill them if they don't want to talk!" he said, flapping his wings together. Nathaniel smiled and shook his head.

"Sorry, but we aren't going to resort to killing just yet. I don't see why they wouldn't talk, it's not as if we're at war with them.....or are we? Anyway, we can't beat up the representatives of the King during an investigation, or he'll think we're up to something. Things are already tight enough with the wizard escaping," he said.

The thing Nathaniel had turned over in his head countless times on his way home that night was that they had failed to stop Forredar from escaping. This now meant that he would be able to give the King any information, true or false, before they would, and the King could act upon it. Had their village been doomed to the might of the Royal Army simply because one man escaped capture?

The next morning at about eight o'clock, Nathaniel was already at the tavern polishing glasses and getting ready to work. Because Ralf was currently situated out in the street, he was the only bartender working that day. True, Herbert had followed him to the bar bright and early, but all he did was make jokes and practice his daily drama for the patrons.

---

Even though Forredar had fled and the soldiers were safely locked up in holding cells, few people wanted to leave their homes that morning. The usually busy streets had been empty when Nathaniel had walked through them.

After no more than half of an hour, the tavern doors opened and a group of townspeople entered. Nathaniel saw Noah, Varon, Gillens, Gretchen, and Madeline walking into the tavern. Well, Madeline wasn't exactly walking, but was being dragged by the arms by Gretchen and Noah. They threw her into an open chair, then took seats around a table. Nathaniel noticed that her feet were tied together.

"Hello, Dorf," said Noah as he brushed dust off his hands. "We decided to stop by and show you what else has been salvaged from the incident last night."

"What do you mean?" asked Nathaniel.

"What he means," said Gillens, stepping forward, "is that we've caught ourselves an old hag, that's what."

"How dare you!" exclaimed Madeline. Gretchen clasped her mouth shut with her hand.

"I found her last night while she was attempting to apprehend Nathaniel over here," said Noah. "She tried tackling him while he was engaged in a duel with one of our prisoners. Luckily I managed to take her down. Then I was attacked by one of them, and I left her behind. Amidst all the confusion, we didn't find her until she made that ridiculous threat." Madeline looked outraged behind Gretchen's hand.

"She tried to capture me? Why?" asked Nathaniel. He was beginning to feel confused. "You might want to let her talk, Gretchen." Looking with unflinching hatred at Madeline, Gretchen withdrew her hand and placed it at her hip. Nathaniel knew that she carried a knife under her dress.

"Oh, you know damn well why, you little dwarf!" yelled Madeline. "We can't have thieves running free with something that belongs to the king! I'm outraged that you all helped him escape!" She pointed at Varon, who swatted her hand down with a flick of his wrist.

"Escape? Look, you old witch, he's right there! I don't think he escaped, but your knight in shining armor certainly turned tail, didn't he?" replied Gillens scathingly.

"Why you!" cried Madeline, and as she forced herself out of her chair she collapsed to the ground with a loud thud. As she kicked and thrashed with frustration to free herself, Herbert flew past and left a nice scratch across her cheek.

"When you attempted to take Mr. Dorf into custody, you didn't take many key points into consideration," said Herbert from his perch on Nathaniel's shoulder.

"What sort of points?" asked Madeline, still struggling with her feet.

"Well, for starters, you're an old bat. Seriously, what are you, four hundred? No, most witches only live to around two hundred or so, but how could you possibly conceive the absurd idea that you were able to take down Dorf? Secondly, you're an old bat. Nobody takes pleasure in your company. No one is going to help you capture him. And lastly, Dorf's innocent. He doesn't have the crown, that's been proven already. And if he did, he would have most likely skipped town also, but innocent men don't run." Madeline snorted.

"Men, not dwarves," she muttered. "They don't think like we do, you realize? It's probably some sort of plot..."

"Listen here, witch," said Noah, "Dorf's innocent, just drop it. And he was out there fighting last night, just like the other men." He looked at Nathaniel. "You know we believe you, right?"

"Of course I do!" said Nathaniel. "You all stood up for me last night."

"And we still will," said Gretchen. She looked very strong and intense. "I propose jailing this old hag or banishing her from town."

"Preposterous!" exclaimed Madeline. "I have the King and his law on my side! You can't do that, he won't stand for it- Ow!" Gretchen had kicked her sharply in the chest. She rolled on the ground in pain, gasping for breath. Gretchen knelt down and leaned in close to her.

"In case you haven't noticed, the King's not here," she said. "And if his army does show up, you'll be in the front lines of the battle, whether it be as a soldier or shield." Madeline coughed loudly and stared up at Gretchen in horror.

"Oh, if he comes I will be freed," said Madeline. "in fact, I will be rewarded beyond that of any loyal servant! I will be showered in gold, my name will be set in stone, my home will become larger than all of Kumaiyan, and I will be seated at the king's right at each and every event of the century!" She shook her fingers wildly up at Nathaniel. "And you, yes, you will be punished for the rest of your sorry little days! He'll jail you for a lifetime and feed your corpse to the rats in an uncovered grave! Oh, yes, and your bones will be-" she was cut off as Herbert once again attacked her. Showing no signs of restraint, he hacked at the flailing woman and scratched every inch of skin he could find.

"You will never, never, never say anything like that to Nathaniel Dorf again!" he yelled, just as he put a particularly deep scratch on Madeline's neck. Nathaniel grabbed him and placed him on the counter before he could kill the woman. Herbert looked at him reproachfully.

"Can't I please just get a few more kicks in, Dorf?" he asked, doing his best to make the impression of a child asking his mother to stay out for a few more minutes. Nathaniel chuckled to himself.

"No, sorry Herbert, but there has to be enough left of her to at least deliver to the cells. Maybe you can have another go while she's incarcerated," he said. Nathaniel turned to the others. "By the way, why didn't you jail her in the first place? Isn't that what's going to happen anyway?"

"Sure, but we just wanted to let you have a chance to hand out any other necessary punishment first. Herbert seemed to catch on to the idea fast enough. She did try to give you to the wizard after all," said Varon. "Just give the order and we'll lock her up." Nathaniel looked from the flailing woman, the despicable traitor to his own hands. What should he do? Why was he suddenly in a position to hold such power? Then he thought of Madeline, how he had never really liked her much in the past, and that this incident could not be counted as a simple mistake.

"Yeah, lock her up," he said. Madeline gasped as Noah and Varon lifted her off the ground.

"You can't, you can't!" she screamed. "They'll come for me, yes, they'll send the whole army here and burn every building to the ground!" Gretchen laughed at her.

"Well you'll be in one," she said, and the rogues dragged Madeline out of the tavern. The woman's rantings and threats could be heard for about another minute, then a dull thud sounded through the air and there was silence. Nathaniel looked at the still seated Gillens, who seemed to be thoroughly enjoying the reprieve from Madeline's screaming.

"So, what happens now?" asked Gretchen. Nathaniel looked around, as if expecting someone else to answer. Then he looked back to Gretchen, who was staring right at him.

"Me?" he asked, pointing at himself.

"Yes, you Dorf," said Gretchen. "You are Ralf's assistant after all. I think he'd want you to take over in his place while he's....he's..well, you know." Nathaniel was stunned. What was he expected to do?

"I didn't think I was second in command of the militia," he said nervously. "Wouldn't the rogues be better suited to take charge?"

"I have no doubt that they would take care and responsibility while working, but you....well, I think you're stronger than them. I saw you fight, I saw you take down those men," she began. "Yes, I saw what happened, you've really improved as a fighter. And right now, no one else seems to be in any state to take over. Ralf wasn't the only one who was injured; both of the traveling men were wounded during the explosion. They're staying in my home, actually, recovering from their painful ordeal. The burns look pretty bad, by the way."

"But, isn't there anyone else?" asked Nathaniel, in desperation. "What about Gillens over there? He can definitely organize our defenses!"

"Dorf, we will not give that burden to one person. In fact, we will have a meeting here shortly to discuss it. And before we can decide anything else, we have to interrogate those prisoners and get whatever bits and pieces of information that we can. Ah, yes, here they are!" She pointed to the door, which was not blocked by another group of men. The rogues were back, along with Colin. The captured soldiers, stripped of their masks but left in their armor, were kneeling in a row on the floor behind them. All of them had ropes tying their hands together.

The townspeople grabbed chairs and organized seats around the table Gillens was at. Gretchen too took a seat and beckoned for Nathaniel to sit at her right.

"This is it?" asked Nathaniel as he made his way onto a chair. "Only six –seven, sorry Herbert – people?"

"Well of course there's seven of us," said Noah. "Most other people are worrying about another attack, but we decided to actually do something about it." Nathaniel looked in disbelief at the group in front of him. How could they organize the defense against the largest army in the known world?

"Okay, the first order of business: bashing these guys from head to toe until we get some answers," said Varon as he punched his fist into his hand. "That okay with you, Dorf?" Once again, Nathaniel was being put in a position of leadership. Before he could force out a response, Gretchen took over.

"Dorf isn't quite our captain yet," she said. "He hasn't had any time to *prepare*." Varon nodded, then rose from his seat and walked to the soldiers. They were all trembling violently.

"So, you there," he pointed to a pale, young soldier, "what the hell were you people thinking when you attacked him? I'll bet you knew he was innocent, didn't you?" The soldier lost the remaining color in his face, then spoke.

"Please, don't hurt us....we was just doing as told, sir. Master Forredar," Noah coughed loudly as if to cover up the title, "told us he had found the culprit, see? I mean, the whole week he was using his spells and powers to unravel this here mystery, see? And three, maybe four days after he searched his house," he nodded towards Nathaniel, "he comes to us and explains, see? Said the dwarf was hiding the crown with sorcery, said he weren't able to detect it that day. I'm telling you, we hadn't any idea he was innocent!"

Varon observed the trembling man, then turned to the group at the table.

"Well, do you think he's telling the truth so far?" he asked. "It's okay if he's not, we can smash it out of him." Nathaniel didn't look at Varon, but at the soldier. He was clearly afraid, and may not have been any older than he himself was. Sweat was now steadily dripping down his brow and forehead. Nathaniel did consider Forredar's personality. He liked to have other people do what he ordered. He was indeed the head of the operation.

"I think he's speaking true, but that isn't enough information for us," said Nathaniel, as kindly as possible. "Tell me, soldier, what perpetuated this investigation? What has been going on in Vikelad?" The soldier flinched again when Nathaniel looked his way, but cleared his throat to speak again.

"About a week or so ago, the King goes into his secret room, where he keeps the crown, see? It's got all sorts of guarding and spells put on it. Anyway, it's not there anymore, simply vanished by the looks of it. The King summons all sorts of stewards and wizards to get inside, and they block the palace off to anyone else, even the guards. I was inside at this time, I saw it with my own eyes. He has these wizards put all sorts of things around the room, walls and barriers and guard animals. You know, bears, trolls, and the like, see? Then he has some of them hunt around the city, pushing through streets and all, entering homes and taverns and shaking up people. Of course, Master Forredar told us not to let anyone off easy. Said anyone within a hundred miles was a suspect, he did. Had us question people, even the children, and put them in detentions if they're stories didn't check out, see? Some of us tried to slip the little ones bits of sweet if they were nice enough, but Master Forredar didn't approve of that at all, and had us turn in our sweets to keep away from the children. By that very afternoon, the whole army had been out getting reports, and the streets were swarming with us troops. Master Forredar soon told everyone to stay in their homes, because anyone in the streets who isn't in one of these here uniforms could be mistaken for the crook, see? A few people were arrested by night. Then, that very night, Master Forredar has four of us mount our horsemen and follow him down south, through this forest. Strange, though, it was right in the dead of night. None of the others were out, it were almost as if they'd been held back.

"We had passed many villages, but we didn't make any stops, see? Master Forredar told us to come straight here, even though we needed to talk with the peoples in the surrounded area. Once we got here, we settled down for a while and began our inspection. And now," he said, "here we are, at your mercy."

It was unlikely that he was lying. The man seemed to be terrified! Nathaniel stared at him and they locked eyes. The story seemed to fit in with what they'd experienced; it had all happened out of the blue, and the one person who had known about it was miles away.

"That is all you know?" he asked. "You don't have any idea why he really wanted to capture me?" The soldier shook his head.

"No, no sir." Nathaniel looked hard into his eyes, and the soldier flinched. "No, please sir, I was just doing my job! I hadn't any way of knowing you was innocent, I swear!"

"It's all right, I understand," said Nathaniel kindly. "I just wanted to make sure that was all, okay? No one's going to hurt you, I promise." He looked up at Varon who incidentally looked like he wanted to hurt the soldier very much. "You hear that? We're not hurting them, we've got no reason." Varon shook his head.

"I'm surprised that you of all people would say that," he began, "I'd have thought you would want revenge."

"I *do* want revenge," said Nathaniel, "and I'll have it in time. But now, we have to shift our discussion to our actions. We have gained all that we could from these men. I am deeply sorry to say that we must hold them here, at least until the army comes." The already nervous soldier seemed to yelp a little. Gretchen stood and clapped her hands once loudly.

"Fine. Dorf, are you ready to give us a plan yet? I'm sure you must have something," she said. Nathaniel stared at her blankly. After rolling her eyes, she said, "Fine, I'll start us off. Based on his information," she pointed to the interrogated soldier, "Forredar cannot transport the army here by teleportation, which means we have about five days before they come. Nathaniel, how do you suggest we defend ourselves?" Nathaniel had been thinking of a plan in the few seconds that it had taken her to speak. It wasn't very good, and luckily Gillens interjected with his own idea.

"I say we forget the defense. Be real, Gretchen, we can't hold off the army, especially not while Ralf's a statue. We have to get a message to the King first, before his army even reaches this place," he said. Gretchen looked rather impressed.

"Interesting, very interesting. Do you think you would go to deliver this message, or plead our case to the king?" To Nathaniel's surprise, Gillens shook his head.

"No, I'm not fast enough, even on a horse. I suggest that he does it," he said, and while his stomach lurched, Nathaniel found Gillens's finger pointing at him. Everyone, even the helpless soldiers, looked in his direction. His face burned, he felt the same nervous feelings that he did when he was challenged in the duel. Sensing that he was expected to speak, Nathaniel cleared his throat and made eye contact with Gillens.

"Me?" he said, rather stupidly. So much for speaking.

"Yes, you Dorf," said Gillens. "Think about it, you're light, easy for a horse to carry, you're the best scout that we have, that's good for traveling through the maze, and you've got to clear your name in the capital. There's probably a bounty for your arrest by now. You have more of a reason to go than any of us."

"And he's got me to help him out," said Herbert proudly, flapping a wing against his chest.

"Wait a moment, just a moment," said Nathaniel. He was still trying to absorb the shock of things. "Aren't I supposed to be taking charge of the militia here?"

"Dorf, if you succeed, we may never need the militia," said Gretchen. "You will be doing the militia, the whole town, and yourself a favor if you tell the King what has happened. Oh no," she said, seeing the look on his face, "you can't opt out of this. You're just right for the job. You actually fought him, you were the one who was threatened. It, well, it just wouldn't make sense for anyone else to say it, would it?" Nathaniel thought that it would perfectly well make sense for anyone else to make the journey, but kept his mouth shut. He didn't seem to be able to open it at the moment.

"Dorf, you're not going to argue," said Noah. "You had the guts to come here in the first place, while most of the town stayed inside. You stood up to that wizard, and you even managed to take down a few warriors. So, how hard could a two hundred  mile journey on horseback be for you?" Nathaniel still thought that it would be pretty hard, and managed to find his voice just in time to defend himself.

"Aren't you concerned about us having every available fighter here? What happens if I meet up with the king's army while they're traveling down here? I'll be caught alone, and they'll take care of me before coming here. Shouldn't we have as many men here as possible?" he asked, praying that he was breaking through to his friends.

"We are concerned, Dorf," said Varon, "but not about our defenses. Like Gillens said, we really don't stand a chance. I think everyone else agrees with me when I say that I'd rather take the chance of having one less person and possibly staving off any invasion rather than accumulating troops for a futile resistance." His words were reflected on the faces of Gillens, Noah, Herbert, and Gretchen. Colin was furiously scribbling words down on a piece of parchment. "Colin, what are you doing?"

"I'm keeping the minutes," he said, without pausing to look up or elaborate. Varon unlaced his shoe and tossed it at him. The leather smacked into Colin's face and Noah roared with laughter. Colin shook his head wildly and readied to throw the shoe back, but he found his quill first and hastily wrote something that could not have possibly had anything to do with the category of "projectiles in politics". When he was done, he found that the shoe was not still in his hand, but in Herbert's claws. Herbert flew above their table, flapping his wings to keep himself suspended. Varon laughed.

"Good boy, Herbert. Now, give it here," he said, gesturing with an open palm. Herbert simply looked at him, and flew even higher. "Come on, Herb, give me my shoe back." Now it was Colin's turn to laugh.

"Looks like he's turned on you, eh?" he asked.

"I wear two shoes to work each day, did you know that?" asked Varon. Colin seemed to shrink a little. "And we don't want this meeting recorded, either. What are you going to do, write an essay for the newsletter about us? No, if the King has any chance to find out what we're up to, we're even worse off." With that, he strode to Colin and tore his notes into pieces. Colin shrank further into his seat as he watched the parchment scraps fall to the floor.

"I propose that Dorf delivers our message and clears his name with the king," said Gretchen. "Is everyone in favor?" Varon's, Gillens's, Noah's, Colin's, and Gretchen's hands rose into the air. Herbert made an effort to raise a claw and dropped Varon's shoe in the process. Nathaniel sighed.

"Looks like you're outvoted," said Gillens. "Then it is decided. We will send Dorf up north to the capital. In the meantime, we will work to fortify the village against any possible attacks." He stood, and the others followed suit. Only Nathaniel stayed in his seat.

"Wait, when, exactly, will I be leaving?" he asked.

"You mean we, don't you?" said Herbert. "Do you think I'm going to let my best friend take a trip to Vikelad and miss out on the fun? I'm coming with you."

"Fine," said Nathaniel, "when will *we* be leaving?" His question was directed to the group in general. Gretchen decided to answer.

"The journey could take about a week. I'd say you will be leaving in about, say, two hours?" Two hours? That wasn't enough time!

"But, I don't have anything ready...."

"Well then," said Noah with a grin on his face, "you'd best start packing up. I know we will." Then he grabbed a soldier by the neck and led him outside. The other townspeople gathered the hostages and left Nathaniel and Herbert in the tavern.

# The Departure

Nathaniel and Herbert hurried back to their cottage to gather any supplies they would need for their journey. Nathaniel unearthed a small pack that he could store food in and carry over his shoulder. Herbert decided that it could be a nice bed.

Nathaniel laid out his supplies on the bed. He had his pack filled with food, his quiver with a large number of arrows, his bow, his sword and its sheath, and his canteen filled with fresh water. Herbert had also laid out a small food supply, comprised of mostly nuts and small fruits.

Checking his watch, Nathaniel realized that he had spent nearly an hour rummaging around his house and looking at a map to learn his route. It seemed to be pretty straight forward; all he had to do was go straight up north until he reached the large city of Vikelad. He decided to keep the map with him, just in case he would need to refer to it later. He packed it in his bag and made to leave the house.

"Ready, Herbert?" he asked. The parrot flew over from his perch and rested on Nathaniel's shoulder. "Good, let me just put my stuff on." He put his sword at his waist, slung his quiver and pack over his shoulders, put his bow in his hand and went to the cottage door. As he was about to leave, he looked back into his home. He would miss it, there was no denying it. He had never been away from home for a long stretch of time.

Nathaniel had also accepted the fact that he may never see it again. If he was too late getting to the King and the army burned the village down, he would not be able to come back. If he was killed by the soldiers or locked up by the king, then he would definitely never see home again.

"We'll be back, Dorf," said Herbert as if he knew what he was thinking. "We'll be here again." Nathaniel nodded and left his cottage. He locked the door behind him and pocketed the key. *I wonder when I'm going to use that again*, he thought. He walked down the path leading into the street and made for the border of town, where he knew that someone would be waiting to lend him a horse.

As he walked through town, Nathaniel noticed that people were beginning to step outside. He saw children simply opening doors and walking into the streets to play. He saw men and women stick their heads out of windows or go outside with the children. But that wasn't all. The more people that came outside, the more Nathaniel was convinced of why they were suddenly showing themselves.

Nathaniel had assumed that word would get around of his departure, and it had. He noticed that while children in the street wrestled or talked with one another, the adults were looking at him. They knew, then, that he was leaving. They knew that he was their messenger, that he was the one who was supposed to save them. Though it made him feel very pressured and nervous, Nathaniel liked feeling taller than other people for a change. He felt as if he was boldly going into danger, towering above the other men and women as if they were dwarves.          Someone shouted, "Good luck!" from a window. That broke the silence; people on all sides began saying things such as, "please come back," or, "take care." No one else followed him, though. He, along with Herbert on his shoulder, made their way to the edge of town where they saw a man and a tall brown horse.

When they drew nearer, Nathaniel recognized the man as Oben. He was steadily stroking the horse along its neck with his left hand as he adjusted its saddle with his right. He looked towards Nathaniel and smiled.

"Dorf, glad you're here, nice to see you," he said. "I was just getting Kiel ready for you. She's a fast one, no doubt about it. I picked her out myself once I heard about your little mission." Oben looked down at Nathaniel and pointed to the horse. "You might have a little trouble mounting her, though, but what are you going to do with a guy who's three feet tall? We can't overwork the small horses, and the others aren't as fast as she is." Nathaniel glanced at Kiel. She was a large, muscular horse with a smooth, black mane, who definitely looked as if she could carry several fully grown men. A leather saddle and reins were already equipped on her body.

"She's great," said Nathaniel. Kiel tapped a hoof appreciatively. "And intelligent."

"Yep, she'll be just fine on your journey north," said Oben, "but will you?"

"What are you talking about?" asked Nathaniel. "Sure, I'll be fine." Though he tried to say it with confidence, his voice wavered and Oben seemed to pick up on it instantly.

"Listen, Dorf," he said. "I know that you need to go, we don't stand a chance otherwise. But remember those travelers? The hardship they faced? That one man spoke of the bears increasing attacks on travelers. You will undoubtedly be a little faster on your horse, but you will have to be very careful. The Maze used to be a safe place."

"Yeah," said Nathaniel, "but Kumaiyan used to be safe also." Oben accepted the retort with a grin.

"Odd, how things change, isn't it? Only a few days ago, people here were concerned about their jobs. Now they're preparing for a battle. And you, you work behind a counter all day! What a shock this must be for you, eh? You've gone from polishing glasses to speaking with the King of Arcoiris!"

"Yeah, pretty amazing isn't it?" asked Nathaniel dryly. "I mean, why send me? Sure, I'm the one who needs to be cleared, but I wouldn't mind if someone else did it for me." Oben stared at him for a few long seconds. Just when he thought he wouldn't receive an answer, Oben spoke.

"Don't think I didn't see what happened yesterday," he said. "How you won?" Nathaniel shuddered. "I'm surprised that I am the only one who saw that movement. You moved faster than anyone else could, and your hands were glowing green. Dorf, was that magic?" Nathaniel had not been expecting this. He had believed that no one else had witnessed his outbursts of speed.

"No, Oben, I'm not even sure how it happened," he said, truthfully. "I remember being in the fight, then everything was a bluish blur, and my opponent's sword flew out of his hand. How come you saw it and no one else didn't?" Oben smiled broadly.

"Dorf, how many people do you think wanted to see you lose? Most people didn't watch. I was the only one who saw it through, because people had gold on it and everything. But when you disarmed him, the noise was nearly deafening. Everyone heard it and turned to see what had happened. So they saw you, standing there, victorious against all odds and your enemy at your feet. What else would they do? They applauded you and you left. I remember your expression, you looked as if you'd just seen a ghost."

"So you mean, no one else saw me fight like that?"

"Well, not during your duel, no. But I heard you took down two of the soldiers last night. Good work, by the way."

"Thanks. Do you have any idea how I did that?" Oben's eyes widened and he pointed at himself.

"Me? No, of course not! But if I had to guess, I'd say it was some kind of sorcery or magic. You don't see many people, let alone a dwarf, move like that by themselves. And here I didn't think you knew how to do that....." he finished, looking off into the distance.

"Yeah, and I don't. But I hope to find out; maybe someone at the capital can tell me. Anyway, what are you going to do once I'm gone?" Oben shrugged.

"Not sure. I bet I'll have to end up helping out with our defense. I had been the best fighter here under other circumstances." Nathaniel had an idea of what those were, but wanted to hear him say them.

"And those circumstances are?"

"Well, for one, I was younger. I had all of my strength and my vision was magnificent. Also, those darn kids weren't around to make a fool out of me during practice. Damn rogues ruin everything. Now I'm just an old man who takes people's gold and gives it to other people," he looked away from Nathaniel as if he was looking into the sun. "Aww, now go away before I get all emotional, will you? Besides, I think your bird is getting antsy." Nathaniel turned to see Herbert standing on Kiel's back and rapidly flapping his wings. The horse didn't seem to mind, but Nathaniel felt that it would not work for her to have any reason to be upset with them during their travels.

"Okay, I guess I'll be off then," he said. He extended his hand for Oben to shake. They shook hands for a brief second. "I hope I'll see you again. Be careful. I hope that I get all of this settled before any more harm is done." Nathaniel waited for a response, but Oben simply stared at him. Deciding that he really needed to be going, Nathaniel walked to Kiel and began to climb onto her. He struggled for a few seconds, but managed to pull himself on top of the horse and into the saddle. Oben had not equipped him with a dwarf-sized saddle. "Herbert, on my shoulder."

Herbert, who had flown off of the horse when Nathaniel had clambered onto her, came back to his shoulder and planted his claws there. Just as he pulled on the reins and started to kick into Kiel's side, he looked back at the town he was leaving behind. He first saw what was far away; the shops and houses, people in the street looking in his direction, the statue of Ralf pointing in front of him, and his tavern which would now be closed indefinitely. Then he saw Oben looking up at him from the ground. Nathaniel was not higher up than anybody all that often.

"Good luck, Dorf," said Oben. "We're going to need all of your help." Nathaniel nodded and pulled on Kiel's reins. The horse responded to the command and took off with incredible speed away from the town. Nathaniel held on tightly, fearing that he would be thrown off at any moment, but Kiel was not reckless and kept moving straight and smoothly. As they neared the Maze, he gently tugged the reins. The horse stopped moving and grunted. Nathaniel slowly turned his head to look at the edge of Kumaiyan.

He knew that he might never come back. He knew that his home may not be standing if he was to return safely. The many small cottages and shops may not exist for any longer than a week. The town, which looked peaceful and silent, could be turned into nothing but rubble and smoke. Feeling a tear fall from the corner of his eye, Nathaniel realized that he could stop it. He could plead their case before the king, he would be the one to stave off the army. He tried to feel brave, he tried to feel confident, but he still felt uneasy about his mission.

He was a dwarf. The smallest race of humanoids on the planet. Suddenly, his thoughts were filled with visions of bears and other enormous creatures that not even a grown human stood a chance against. But he battled the thoughts, and mustering his courage, he kicked into Kiel's side. The horse jumped and sprinted into the Maze, taking Herbert and Nathaniel Dorf away from their home.

# Journal Entry Number Two

*Date:4254, 16, First Day                    Nathaniel Dorf*

*We have been traveling north for almost four hours now. Herbert, Kiel, and I have made camp in a small clearing. The Maze is easy to navigate through, but we have been careful to watch out for any bears or other beasts in between the trees. I am not sure how far we have gone, but we don't see any end to the massive forest.*

*Herbert has been behaving very well considering that he's been riding on my shoulder for the duration of our trip. He hasn't been arguing with Kiel much, but how they communicate in the first place is what amazes me. How does a horse talk with a parrot, especially one who speaks our language? I wonder if it has something to do with magic.*

*Kiel is a magnificent horse. Though our precautions have forced us to move slowly, she has kept a steady pace and hasn't shown any signs of tiring. She is able to feed off of the grass and other plants around us, while Herbert and I eat off of our packed rations.*

*I admit, I have another motive for traveling to Vikelad. Yes, our current situation is important, and we cannot afford to lose any time in bringing a message to the king, but I would also like to consult a wizard about my....well, powers. Oben remarked to me that he had witnessed my power also, and I would like to know what exactly it is. Have I become some sort of a wizard or sorcerer? Could it have anything to do with my encounter with Forredar? Answering these questions is my second priority once I enter the capital city.*

*The town seems to be determined to stand their ground if the invasion does indeed take place. We do have some skilled fighters, but "some" is the problem. Our militia, when fully formed, has about eighty members in it. The king's royal army is rumored to have over ten thousand troops enlisted in its ranks. If the King finds the he is desperate to retrieve his crown, or just feels it is right to punish Kumaiyan for our resistance, then we won't stand a chance. I admire the bravery of each and every man and woman who decide to fight when the time comes.*

*True, a lot has happened over the course of a week, but the image that is most prominent in my mind is the statue of Ralf.  Ralf, our militia leader, turned to stone by the wizard Forredar. He was the one who kept things together, he was the one who could rally the militia into formation in mere minutes. His strength and courage in the face of adversary impress me the most, and my third priority once I have reached Vikelad is to* try and find out if there is a way to cure him. I truly hope that he is not dead.

Varon and Noah will make excellent substitutes as leaders of our militia. Their ingenious use of skill and strategy will be very helpful in aiding the town through any battles. I am sure that they are formulating a plan as I write this, or that they are training and preparing Kumaiyan for battle.

Though I am sure that Kumaiyan is in good hands, I cannot bear the thought of an actual battle occurring there. The largest violent encounter that the town has ever seen was that of last night, in which a few men were injured and we captured Forredar's henchmen. No large-scale battle has ever taken place in our streets, no invading army has ever tried to raid the town with attacks. The devastation that the royal army could cause is horrifying. The entire town could be leveled or burned to the ground in an hour. The streets could be swarming with soldiers of the king, each one bearing bloodied weapons and merciless expressions. After all, what would the King have to lose if Kumaiyan fell? In his eyes, we could be nothing more than a handful of gold coins retrieved from tax collectors. What difference would it make if we no longer existed?

If I am intercepted by the army before I reach Vikelad, then were are indeed doomed. It is hard to accept that I am the one who is supposed to save us, that I'm the one people are praying for, who holds the fate of our small town in the palm of *my hand. I have never been in a position to make a difference before, both because of my upbringing and my size. Dwarves, though very rare, seemed to be cursed. We are short. Many things in our lives are dictated by our height.*

*For example, at the tavern I work at, I have to use a barstool just to serve drinks. Now, climbing up on that stool can be a little tricky, and I cannot do it very quickly. When I am talking with someone, I am very intimidated because I always have to look up at them. It makes me feel as if I were a child being scolded by a parent. Until yesterday, I was no good at duels because my opponents are always bigger and stronger than myself. But now there is hope.*

*If I have inherited some magical powers, I can be different. I can be a significant person, I could even be a powerful person. No longer would my height slow me from reaching my goals. No longer would I be forced to simply watch the End Day duels. No longer would my mountain of a barstool be a bother. I could have a new life, possibly a better life. A life with adventure, knowledge, and importance.*

*As I watch the fire in front of me begin to die, I see my own hopes flare. This is it, this is possible. I will be great, I will become powerful. It's too bad, though. I'll have to get to Vikelad first.*

## Through the Maze

Nathaniel woke up as the sun blazed overhead. The rays warmed him and he felt drowsy. He was lying on the grass in the makeshift camp under a small blanket he had brought with him. Herbert was curled next to him, snoring as usual with his eyes closed tightly shut. Kiel was already awake, dipping her neck to feed off of the grass.

As he stood up and rolled his blanket into a small bundle, Nathaniel realized that they had already lost a day to get to Vikelad. How far had they gone? It was very hard to calculate, considering that his map showed no units of measure and they had to slow down during their travels to look out for potential attackers. His watch showed that the time was eight o'clock. They had not even been traveling for a whole day.

"Herbert, wake up," said Nathaniel. The parrot did not respond. "FIRE!" Herbert abruptly leapt into the air and flapped his wings wildly.

"Fire? Where's the fire? Dorf, you're on fire!" he shouted. Nathaniel shook his head and laughed.

"Do I look like I'm on fire?" he asked. Herbert was stunned into silence. "No, we actually need to get going. We haven't covered that much ground yet, and Forredar has had a whole day to talk with the king. C'mon, let's go." Herbert gaped at Nathaniel.

"Did you...did you trick me? Dorf, I trust you to alert me when there really is an emergency! We can't have false alarms like this!"

"I distinctly remember the last time there was a fire, and you slept through it," said Nathaniel. Herbert looked at him quizzically.

"Evidently I was out of town for such an event," he said.

"Herbert, it happened nearly two days ago. Forredar nearly blew up the house? Anything ring a bell?" Apparently it didn't ring a bell, for Herbert continued to survey Nathaniel as if he had just announced the beginning of some foreign holiday.

"No, Dorf, I really don't think that happened. As you said, we should go. We can talk about what fires happened where and which sorcerer blew up what, but right now we have a job to do."

Herbert flew over to Kiel and landed on her shoulder. Nathaniel chuckled as the parrot flapped and jumped on the horse's back, thoroughly entertaining himself and irritating Kiel. Deciding that it would be better if the two animals weren't at odds with each other, he grabbed his pack and ran to the horse.

"Herb, stop tormenting Kiel. She is a lot bigger than you, after all." Herbert pointed his wing at Kiel defensively.

"She started it," he said. "She said that horses aren't made for nonsense." Kiel grunted angrily.

"You were jumping on her," said Nathaniel. "Anyway, move. I've got to get on." Herbert flew off of the horse's back and Nathaniel clambered on with much difficulty. Herbert returned to his perch on his shoulder, and they set off through the Maze.

As Kiel carried them through the massive forest, Nathaniel began to observe the wildlife around them. Small creatures such as squirrels ran in circles to avoid the horse's hooves. Birds flew high above them and over the tall trees. Many deer froze whenever the trio passed them and stared at them until they had gone.

Nathaniel had not spotted any bears during the day. In fact, he hadn't seen any creature that looked one bit dangerous. If Talitenkus was using training bears like Renol said, then he wasn't using them in this part of the woods. Once Herbert had kindly observed that their current speed was similar to that of a baby snail, Kiel sped up considerably, nearly throwing Nathaniel and Herbert off of her back. After much swearing, the little parrot decided to keep quiet for about an hour, a feat he had never accomplished, even in his sleep.

They continued to gallop through the Maze until it grew dark. Nathaniel felt that they had made a significant dent in the distance they needed to travel, and suggested that they find a place to sleep for the night.

Even though they had found a clearing the previous night, the middle of the Maze was densely populated with thousands of trees. They dedicated at least an hour and a half to their search, but made up for it by continuing to move north while looking. They found many things that they were not looking for. Herbert managed to locate an arrow with an interesting head. Instead of a point, it had what looked like a hand with all five fingers, sharpened of course, spread out and pointing forward. Nathaniel made to toss it away, but Herbert insisted that he keep it and he finally placed it in his quiver along with his other arrows.

Nathaniel found a small leather glove that fit his right hand perfectly. Once he tried it on, he flexed his fingers and wrist. The smooth leather bent with his movements and he decided to keep it. It was surprisingly clean for having been nestled deep into the forest.

Eventually, they began to feel very tired and settled on camping out a few feet next to the path. Besides, the trees would provide cover for them if it were to rain or storm.

Nathaniel laid out his blanket and stared up at the sky. Though the trees obscured most of his view of it, Nathaniel caught a small glimpse of the moon shining brightly overhead. It shone through the small gap in the trees and illuminated their campsite. Nathaniel could see Herbert lying next to him, shielding his face from the light with his wings. He may have already been asleep, but he acted strangely even when he wasn't conscious.

Kiel was fast asleep, having worked like a horse for the length of the day. Unlike the small parrot, she was very quiet while asleep. That may or may not have had to do with the fact that she was possibly too tired to make any noise.

Nathaniel was proud of their day's journey. They had covered at least three times the ground they had covered in the previous day. He felt as if the world had suddenly grown a lot smaller. Traveling a long distance just didn't seem to be much of a challenge for him. As he fell asleep, he thought that the road ahead had become a little easier.

Nathaniel woke up to a gentle prod in his side. He turned over and tried to shut his eyes again.

"Herb, it's too early, the sun's barely out," he mumbled. He heard laughter in response.

"You hear that? My name's Herb now, it is!" said a cracked voice from above. "Turn him over." Nathaniel felt something push him over rather roughly. He hit his head on the ground and looked up for the source of the blow.

Two men were crouched over him, one looking very shocked and another with an expression of delight on his face. The shocked one looked to be about Nathaniel's age, dressed in a dirty, ruffled shirt and sporting hair that was tangled and knotted in many places. Nathaniel noticed that he had a small club in his right hand.

The other, larger man appeared to be much older than the first. His skin was dark brown, and he had a think black beard around his mouth and chin. The top of his head was covered by a thin layer of dark hair. This man carried a large ax in his hand, and Nathaniel guessed that it wasn't used for the sole purpose of chopping wood.

"Look at this one," said the younger man, "he's a dwarf!" The older man laughed.

"A dwarf? We've found a dwarf? Weird, I thought they had all gone. Maybe he's got some coins on him," said the older man gleefully. He reached down, and Nathaniel raised his arms out in front of him.

"What do you think you're doing?" he asked. The older man stopped and pulled his hand back.

"Well, we're robbing you blind, that's what we're doing!" he said proudly. "What do you think you get for camping out here all alone? No horse or nothing." Despite the fact that he was being robbed by two potentially dangerous bandits, Nathaniel jumped up to look over the older man's shoulder. Sure enough, Kiel and Herbert were not with him.

"So, dwarf," began the younger man, "how shall we be doing this? The easy way or the hard way?" Nathaniel knew he would have to stall the two brigands long enough to at least come to his full senses.

"Easy way?" he said rather stupidly. "No, I'm not sure what you mean by that. Easy for you, or easy for me?" The younger bandit stared at him for a few moments, then looked back to the older man. The old man opened his palms and thrust them towards the young bandit. He turned his attention back to Nathaniel.

"If we are to do this the easy way, you will need to do exactly as I say. First, you'll get up and fetch your belongings from wherever you've stashed them. Next, you'll hand over your belongings to us and we'll sort through them and decide what you can keep and what's ours. Finally, we'll take what we want and we'll be off. Any questions?" Nathaniel looked back at him, trying to feign an expression of misunderstanding and confusion. The bandit turned back to the older man, who seemed to be in charge of the duo. The older man rolled his eyes and the younger bandit looked back at Nathaniel. "If you have any questions, please express them now." Nathaniel began to feel himself becoming more awake and aware of things, but he wasn't done yet.

"Where did I put my pack?" he asked. "I could've sworn I'd kept it right next to me for the whole night, maybe someone else took it. Do you folks know where it is?" The young bandit peered at Nathaniel curiously.

"What's the matter with this one, Blake?" he asked. "He seemed fine enough when he was asleep." The older bandit, Blake, didn't look amused.

"I think he's a terrible actor, that's what," said Blake. "I think we're going to have to roughen him up a little." Blake made to grab Nathaniel's collar, but the young bandit stopped him with a wave of his arm.

"No! If we kill him, we won't find out where this pack is! We would lose everything!" said the young bandit. "Dwarf, do you want to tell us where your stuff is? Please, do tell us where your valuables are!" Nathaniel now thought it was time to change the course of the conversation.

"No, I don't think that's going to work," he said. "You see, I've worked very hard for my things over the years, and I just don't think it's right that you simply take them from me." Blake did grab his collar after he said that.

"Think it's fair if we slit your throat, dwarf?" he asked menacingly. "Or if we decide to break a bone in your body for every minute you refuse to give us our loot? You won't think it's fair, dwarf, but we'll do it anyway. Now, tell Marko what he wants to know." He released his grip on Nathaniel, but kept his glaring eyes fixed on him.

"Please be calm, Blake," said Marko, "he's just a dwarf."

"With a nice watch on him!" exclaimed Blake as he reached for Nathaniel's wrist. His eye had caught the gleam of the golden wristwatch Nathaniel wore. Blake wasn't ready for Nathaniel to move, however.

Nathaniel jumped to his left, propelling him several feet away from the bandits. His sword, still in the sheath at his waist, was quickly drawn as he turned back to the bandits.

Marko was still crouched on the ground, looking in disbelief at the place where Nathaniel now stood. His mouth was opened as if to shout a warning to his partner, but no sound came out of it. Blake had been faster to act; he held his ax high above his head and rushed at Nathaniel. Nathaniel reasoned that now would probably be a nice time for everything to slow down for him again.

But it did not. The world continued moving at the same speed it always did. Blake swung his weapon just as he came within an arm's length of Nathaniel. However, the bandit had swung to high, the ax cleaved the air above Nathaniel's head. Nathaniel quickly aimed a blow at his opponent's leg, and Blake had to back away to avoid being cut. The bandit, apparently deciding that Nathaniel's height would impede him into the fight, stepped closer to him and brought a heavy strike down towards Nathaniel's head.

Nathaniel whipped his sword up to block the ax. As the two weapons made contact, he felt his entire body vibrate from the shock of the blow. He brought his sword away and dove to his right just as Blake brought his ax down again. Nathaniel hit the ground hard, smacking his knee on a particularly hard patch of earth, and recovered to face his opponent. Blake was holding his ax high in the air, and slowly advancing on him. Nathaniel tried to stand, but his knee flared and he was forced to kneel. Then, before the bandit could get in range, Nathaniel did something that he did not think about: he flicked his sword.

It spun through the air like a disc and caught Blake on his right shoulder. Howling in pain, the bandit dropped his ax and grabbed the sword as if to pull it out. The sword did come out, but Blake fled, clutching his bleeding shoulder. Nathaniel remembered Marko, and was lucky to have done so. Just as he faced the younger bandit, he had to duck to avoid a crushing blow from his club. He looked up into Marko's face, then a split second later it was replaced by a green blur.

Herbert had seemingly appeared out of nowhere and attacked the bandit. Nathaniel saw the parrot attacking Marko, clawing him and flapping his wings.

"Take that, you slimy worm. Not so tough with a guy on your face, now are you?" The bandit was so surprised by Herbert (his attack and his voice) that he dropped his club and tried to swat him away. Nathaniel then struck out with his fist and hit the bandit in the stomach with a pretty hard punch. Marko doubled over and tripped over his fallen club. Herbert took the opportunity to rip the bandit's shirt down the back, then flew to Nathaniel's shoulder. Marko looked up at them from the ground.

"Please....wasn't my idea....need to make a living.....went along with Blake for gold....don't kill me!" he screamed.

Nathaniel shook his head.

"No, we're not going to kill you," he said. Marko's face seemed to lighten a little. "In fact, I'm going to let you go, but I will not return your weapon. You may leave now." Looking thoroughly stunned, the bandit picked himself up and made to leave. A moment later, he faced Nathaniel.

"Thank you. Thank you very much. But I would like to know: What is your name?" he asked. Before Nathaniel could open his mouth to speak, Herbert cut in.

"Dorf," he said. "His name's Dorf. And you won't be so lucky next time. Now get on, shoo!" To Nathaniel's slight irritation, Marko appeared to be more intimidated by Herbert than by himself, but was glad to see him leave all the same.

"Thanks, Herbert," he said. "You really helped me out. But where were you and Kiel? I woke up and you were gone."

"Well, you didn't expect us to just stick around, did you? No, we heard them coming from a distance, but we couldn't pick you up and we didn't want to make too much noise. So, we hid out behind a large bush until you started fighting. Then I stepped in and saved you before he beat you over the head," he summed up proudly. "Kiel! Come out!"

The horse trotted towards them from behind many thick bushes and trees, and Nathaniel's pack was tied to her saddle.

Nathaniel strode over to his blanket and rolled it up and stuffed it in his bag. Then he walked over to the edge of their camp, where his sword was lying in the grass. The shiny metal was tinged red at the tip, but Nathaniel ignored the stain and stowed the weapon at his side. His knee ached from the fall, further impairing his efforts to mount Kiel.

"Are we leaving?" asked Herbert. "Don't you want to take a rest?" He shook his head.

"No," said Nathaniel, "I'll rest while we ride. But we might as well be moving anyway. No point in waiting around, especially where bandits have been."

"Dorf, I don't think you need to worry about any bandits," said Herbert. "In case you haven't noticed, we just took down two of them."

"Yeah, but I'm not sure I could do it again, and there could be more next time. We can't defeat more than a couple of bandits on sheer luck." Herbert settled on his shoulder and clinched it tightly with his claws.

"Luck? I don't think there was much luck there, Dorf. You impaled that big one with a sword, and I saved your neck when the little one went at you. How did we get lucky? Well, I know *you* were lucky when I intervened," he added brightly.

"It was a lucky throw," said Nathaniel. "I wasn't looking or aiming at anything in particular. I just flicked my wrist and let it.....let it fly out of my hand. I was fortunate that it hit him." Herbert snorted.

"Well, I think we could do it again. As long as you've got me to cover your back, we're invincible. Heck, I'd wait here for more bandits to come just for the fun of it." Nathaniel pulled on Kiel's reins.

"Sorry, maybe if we're not so lucky it'll happen again. But for now, we've got to keep traveling north. We don't have much time." He kicked into the horse's side, and they sped off through the trees.

Nathaniel was worried about how much time they had left. His watch showed him that it was eight o'clock. It was the third day that they had been venturing north, and Nathaniel had hoped that they would be in Vikelad by the next day. Now, at least, that didn't seem very likely.

The Maze revealed itself as the truly massive forest that Nathaniel had only read about. There was no end in sight, and the thousands of trees seemed to block most of the sun. There was, however, a change as they made their way further towards the capital.

Part of the forest looked as if it was being destroyed. There were no major clearings, but many trees were on their sides or jaggedly cut in half or hacked off at the trunk. The air smelled of burnt wood, but there were no burnt trees in sight.

The Maze was the central road for many merchants and travelers, but apart from the two bandits they had encountered earlier, Herbert and Nathaniel found it to be strangely empty. There were lingering footprints in the dirt path, but when Nathaniel stopped to look at them they looked as if they were very old. They did not pass any camps on the side of the path. It was as if they were the only ones in the Maze.

The bleak, desolate atmosphere continued through the thick of the forest. It wasn't very light where they were, and the lack of noise save for Kiel's galloping added to the dark mood. Even Herbert was keeping quiet, either too scared to speak or too tired to comment on anything.

True, it was frightening to travel through the soulless Maze, but Nathaniel assumed that they were at least halfway to the capital, if not more. The thought of victory burned through the fearful chill, and they pushed on, not daring to stop and waste any time.

Around four o'clock, according to Nathaniel's watch, they arrived at a fork in the road. The way forward was clear, however, as the path straight ahead was long and the path to their left was only a few yards long and led to a small, gated hut. A sign next to the gate read: Inn the Maze. Kiel stopped at Herbert's command, which made Nathaniel feel a little diminutive.

"You want to check it out?" asked Nathaniel. "I'm sure we could use some hot food and some wine." Oddly enough, though he was a parrot, Herbert did enjoy the taste of wine.

"Absolutely! I really need to stretch!" exclaimed Herbert, and he promptly took off of Nathaniel's shoulder. Nathaniel hopped off of Kiel and led her to the fence surrounding the inn. He tied her to a fence post and opened the gate. Then he strode to the inn's door and entered Inn the Maze.

The interior was similar to that of Mit's inn, except it was rather dusty and dark. A small counter was in the far right corner of the inn, and a few chairs were situated around it. Two small, round tables with chairs were in the center of the inn, both with lit candles on their tops.

Nathaniel heard a knock behind him, and opened the door to reveal Herbert hovering in the air several feet above him.

"Gee, how do you think I could get in there? I'm a damn parrot!" he yelled and flew into the inn. "Hey, I wonder where the innkeeper is?"

For the first time, Nathaniel noticed that there wasn't anyone behind the counter. The whole first floor was empty. The only signs of any inhabitants were the burning candles on the tabletops.

"Anybody home? Hello!" There was no answer. "Maybe he's upstairs," he suggested. "I think we should look there." Herbert let out a loud groan.

"Nah, let's just forget it. I really don't need anything to drink anyway. Let's go. Dorf?" But Nathaniel had already walked to the staircase behind the counter. He slowly climbed up the wooden steps to the attic floor.

The attic was dark and dreary. The floorboards were covered in a solid inch-thick layer of dust. Cobwebs hung in every corner of the room, some of them with live spiders dangling from them. No torches were mounted in the attic, so Nathaniel could only clearly see the first few feet of space in front of him.

"Wonder if he's out?" asked Herbert from behind.

"I don't think so," said Nathaniel, "where could he go? And there would probably be some sort of a sign outside if he was." He proceeded to move further into the small attic, feeling his way along the wall with his hands.

"Maybe he's moved away," suggested Herbert, "or he doesn't keep very good care of his home."

"Yeah, but how else would those candles be lit? Someone has to have been here in the past day, at least." Without knowing why, Nathaniel found that he was whispering as he spoke. He continued to walk through the attic until he touched the far wall. Once he began to feel his way towards the middle of the room, he stumbled upon a small bed, barely visible in the darkness of the room. Upon further examination, he found that a blanket was strewn across the bed instead of neatly folded under. "I think he's been sleeping here, Herb." He moved away from the wall, tripped, and grabbed onto the side of the bed to break his fall.

"What was that?" asked Herbert.

"Nothing," said Nathaniel. He stood up straight and pulled his hand away from the bed. Then he felt it. The inside of his hand was covered in a thick layer of dust. He brushed it off on his pants and turned towards the doorway.

"Herb, I don't think he's here, but I'm not sure he went away either. This place is a mess."

"What do you mean?" asked Herbert.

"I mean, that I think he went for a walk and never came back," said Nathaniel gravely.

"You mean he could have been killed on the road?"

"Yeah, probably this morning, by the look of it. He might have lit those candles earlier, and then left."

"Good theory, Dorf," said Herbert, "but I think I see a problem with it."

"What?" asked Nathaniel. "I think it all makes sense."

"The door was unlocked, remember? You'd think if he went for a walk, he would lock the door until he got back. Probably to stop people stealing from the inn, most likely."

"Unlocked.....?" What? Surely, the innkeeper would only leave his door unlocked if he was around to greet the customers. Could he have possibly forgotten this one time? Could it be purely coincidental that the very day he disappeared he forgot to lock up his inn?

"Come on, Dorf. Let's just get on the road and forget about all of this," said Herbert. "We really need to be moving, just like you said." Nathaniel sighed, resigned.

"Fine. Let's go." He heard Herbert flap his wings and fly down the staircase. He walked across the middle of the room, and just before he reached the doorway, he heard a loud cracking noise. He turned around, expecting to see splintered wood or broken floorboards, but didn't see anything except the darkness of the room. "Herbert, are you okay?"

"Yeah, except I can't get out of here! Get down here, now!" Nathaniel started to head down the stairs when the room was suddenly illuminated with bright, purple light.

"What the....?" began Nathaniel as he turned back towards the attic room. It was now dark again, the light having lasted for only a second. Then he heard an awfully familiar voice split the silence.

"Gargoyle!" A jet of bright sparks soared over Nathaniel's head and struck the wall behind him. The silver light lasted for a short time, but allowed Nathaniel to glimpse the intruder.

Forredar was standing in front of the dusty bed, dressed in all black and pointing at Nathaniel. "Gargoyle!" The spell was aimed at Nathaniel's chest this time, and he dove down the steps to avoid it. He briefly saw the wall behind him, now transformed from wood into stone, before he fell painfully down the small flight of steps. He felt his knee smash into a step and skidded to a halt at the foot of the stairs.

"Herbert, fly away!" he yelled hoarsely. Herbert, who was hovering at the door, shot towards a corner of the inn just as Nathaniel heard Forredar scream again.

Nathaniel heard a loud roar and his heart sank. He hurriedly got to his feet as he heard something very large thunder down the staircase. He ran into the center of the first floor and turned to face his opponent.

A large, seven-feet high black bear stood before him, bearing his teeth and opening his claws, ready to fight. The beast roared and rushed at Nathaniel. He rolled to the left and drew his sword, the bear missing by inches. He heard a loud crash, and saw the bear bounce off of the far wall.

"Kill him!" Forredar's spell, a long jet of fire, missed Nathaniel by several feet and hit the wall behind him. "Dance, little dwarf!" He struggled to dodge the spells, and then the bear came back at him.

It swiped its paw at him, but it merely whipped through the air above his head. Believing the beast to have overshot him, Nathaniel turned to face Forredar, but felt something hit him very hard in the back. He was thrown forward, towards the door, and crashed into the wizard who was shouting and waving his hands over his head. Both of them fell to the floor, and Nathaniel heard the wood beneath them break. Nathaniel swung in his enemy's direction and missed badly.

Forredar, though fallen, pointed his finger quickly at Nathaniel and opened his mouth to speak. Reacting instinctively and faster than ever before, Nathaniel grabbed his wrist with his free hand and directed the spell towards the ceiling.

"You pay now!" yelled Forredar before he realized that he was no longer facing Nathaniel. The ceiling exploded. With a loud bang, hundreds of chunks of wood fell to the floor and caught fire. Flames burned through the wood and spread through the rest of the building. Blinking through the smoke and falling splinters, Nathaniel saw the attic's bed fall from above and smack the roaring bear. It crumpled and was covered by the smoke. He felt his wrist burn, and he let go of Forredar's arm and was pushed backwards. He hit a remaining section of the ceiling and crashed to the floor.

"I'll flood you in, then!" screamed Forredar. Nathaniel suddenly felt very wet and saw that the inn was steadily filling up with water, which was flowing from Forredar's finger. The wizard didn't seem to see where he was, and Nathaniel remained on his back until the water rose higher. "Gargoyle!" A falling section of ceiling and flame collided with the spell and was immediately turned into stone. Nathaniel saw Herbert fly up through the destroyed attic and out of sight.

Once the water rose above Nathaniel's lying body, he decided that he needed to escape. He jumped to his feet and made for the door, but tripped on a broken floorboard. Forredar whirled around and clenched his fist tightly. Nathaniel felt the heat of the spell before everything fell to pieces.

The already destroyed inn was incinerated in the blast. Nathaniel was pushed backwards and through the door, landing outside. Miraculously, he landed on his feet, and without looking back he sprinted towards where Kiel was tied up. Suddenly, the bear sprang up in front of him and made to grab him. Nathaniel ducked and swung at it with his sword. He made contact with the bear's middle, and it fell, howling. He stepped around the body and hurriedly untied Kiel.

"Herbert! Get out here! Come on!" he yelled, and he scrambled up to mount the massive horse. He felt the reassuring thud of Herbert landing on his shoulder, and he kicked into Kiel's sides with both feet.

The horse jumped higher than any of them expected and sped forward. She found the central path easily and took off to the north.

"What the hell was he doing there?" asked Herbert. "I'll bet he's trying to kill us!"

"Yeah, he probably is. But how did he know where we were? It was a pretty good trap, if you ask me, but I know he teleported to the inn. He wasn't hiding there," said Nathaniel as they rode on. "I'm just glad we got out okay, though my knee is still killing me."

"Oh, I wouldn't say we got out just yet," said Herbert. "Look behind you." Nathaniel turned around and saw what looked like an enormous lizard with wings flying towards them. It had black scales covering its body, and a long tail.

"It's a dragon!" yelled Herbert. "But I think it's killed the wizard!" Nathaniel felt his stomach lurch as they jumped over a large pile of rocks and fallen branches. He drew his sword and held it in front of him, not knowing how much good it would do against a dragon. When the dragon was within three yards of them, it opened its wings wide and screeched. The noise was loud and deafening. Nathaniel could hear it pierce his eardrums and clapped his left hand over his ear to protect it. He closed his eyes too, scared to face the beast. The shrill cry disturbed Kiel, who jumped and ran in a berserk circle, galloping to escape yet disoriented. Then it was over.

Once the dragon stopped screaming, Nathaniel looked back at it. Without warning, a jet of fire burst to life and missed him by inches, singing the edge of his hair. Then he noticed that the dragon was not there anymore. Instead, at the ground behind him, stood Forredar.

"Run!" yelled Nathaniel. He jumped off of Kiel just as another jet of fire exploded from the wizard's finger. Herbert flew off of his shoulder, and Kiel, thoroughly scared, took off through the trees to the side of the path. As he hit the ground, Nathaniel felt his sword fly out of his hand. He looked up t Forredar, who was now clapping his hands and muttering under his breath. Then he directed his gaze at Nathaniel and yelled.

"Catch him!" A wolf, a large, white wolf, burst from the tips of his fingers and dove at Nathaniel. He dodged it and grabbed his sword from the ground. The wolf recovered from the missed attack and began to circle around Nathaniel. He held his sword in front of him and watched the creature, as if daring it to strike. The wolf charged, and he felt the world slow down around him.

Nathaniel saw a bright green light cover his hands, saw the wolf slow down dramatically in midair. He jumped forward and swung his sword, beheading the wolf at the neck. Because he was the only entity moving at full speed, Nathaniel saw the wolf head slowly begin to float away from its body, then the whole creature turned to smoke and disappeared. He turned to Forredar, who was attempting to cast a spell on Nathaniel. But he too was moving slowly, and Nathaniel rushed at him and stabbed at his middle.

The wizard then moved impossibly fast. A jet of fire shot from his palm and met the tip of Nathaniel's sword. Both combatants were blown backwards with the force of a storm. Forredar hit the ground on his back, and Nathaniel was thrown backwards into a tree. He felt his leg smash into the trunk and he fell down just as Forredar yelled, "Clear!". The spell ripped past him and burned through the tree behind him. The tree made a splintering noise, and Nathaniel dove out of its path as it fell over with a loud thud. Recovering, he saw that it had fallen right where Forredar *had* been standing, but the wizard had avoided the falling tree. Forredar was standing with his back to him, pointing towards the inn. Nathaniel scrambled to his feet just as he heard what sounded like a horse gallop into the path.

"What in the hell have you done to me home?" bellowed a man's voice. Nathaniel saw a man on top of a large horse accompanied by three other men on foot. The horseman was holding a bow in his right hand, and two of the other men held axes in theirs. The third man held a long sword. "You there! Sorcerer!" The horseman loosed an arrow that surely would have hit a normal person, but Forredar knocked it out of the air with a bolt of lightning. The wizard yelled incoherently, and the man's horse jumped and threw its rider off. The horseman crashed to the ground with a sickening crunch.

"Get him! Take him down!" yelled the man with the sword. One man with an ax moved to Forredar's right, the other to his left. The three men formed a circle around the wizard, and he pointed his finger at the ground in front of him. "Charge!"

The men with axes both rushed at Forredar. In one motion, the wizard knelt and spun on the spot, silver parks spewing from his hands and hitting the charging men. Both men froze immediately, then Nathaniel knew what would happen next. The gray substance that had covered Ralf now covered them, and in seconds two statues stood with their axes held high. Their faces were stuck contorted in looks of shock.

Forredar then turned to the man with the sword. Seizing the chance, Nathaniel charged at his back and tackled him just as he cast his spell. The jet of fire shot into the ground and burned a small hole in the dirt. They both fell, Forredar collapsing under the unexpected force of Nathaniel's attack. Then Nathaniel saw it happen. Forredar's right hand hit the ground hard, and Nathaniel heard a loud crack.

Wasting no time, he struck at Forredar with his sword. The flat end of his blade smacked into the wizard, who screamed in agony. Then Nathaniel felt it stronger than ever, as if he had prompted its return. The world began to slow down.

He had time, he knew it. He raised his sword slowly, not quite as slowly as the wizard was moving at the moment. He grabbed its hilt with both hands and pointed the blade down at his enemy's chest. This was it, this was the end of the evil one who had terrorized his town and turned others to stone. He felt strangely nervous, as if he was afraid to make a mistake. He shut his eyes and plunged the sword down......and was knocked over by an unseen force.

The world came back into motion, and Nathaniel felt himself rolling along the path, having been pushed away roughly from Forredar. He was clutching his sword very tightly, and his knuckles were white to prove it. He slammed into a tree and stopped rolling. Feeling very dizzy, he glanced up to see a very large, black mass standing beside Forredar. As his vision came back into focus, he realized that it was a bear. The wizard must have summoned one.

He saw Forredar stand up and point to the horse and its fallen rider, who did not appear to be conscious. He was lying down on his back, his right arm oddly bent over his chest. Then Nathaniel nearly jumped with excitement. He had another chance.

Meanwhile, the man with the sword had backed away towards the ruins of the inn, holding his sword in front of him as if to ward off any attacks. He was cowering in front of the gate, not daring to look at the wizard. Nathaniel gestured to him with his sword, waving it towards the bear, but the man shook his head and put his arms over his face. Nathaniel thought this to be very cowardly, and looked away bitterly.

Forredar's bear gave a small growl and began to walk towards the horse, who ran in the opposite direction, leaving its owner behind. Now, Nathaniel knew he was no match for a bear, but he decided that someone else needed his help, and that took precedence. He held his sword above his head, which really wasn't that great of a height (but hopefully intimidating nonetheless) and ran past Forredar at an astonishing speed. The wizard made no attempt to stop him. He ran up to the bear, who turned around at his appearance. Without hesitation, he swung his sword and cut through the center of the beast. It fell, howling, and vanished in a puff of smoke as Nathaniel drove the blade through.

"Hey! You!" On instinct, Nathaniel spun and turned to the source of the shout. Forredar was standing up with his right hand stretched out. "Gargoyle!" The nearly-lethal jet of silver sparks flew over his head. Then Nathaniel heard the twang of a bow string and saw an arrow speed towards Forredar from behind him. The wizard clapped his hands once and disappeared in a flash of purple light. The arrow continued its flight and stuck in a tree twenty feet behind its target.

"You all right there, dwarf?" Nathaniel turned to see the man who had seconds earlier been lying on the ground now standing up with a bow held in his right hand. He appeared to be about fifty years old, with a thin beard and a wrinkled face. The man wasn't exactly tall, but he dwarfed Nathaniel in height. He wore a thin fur vest over a plain white shirt. Judging by his appearance, Nathaniel deduced that he must be a hunter or an outdoors man. "Gave you a nasty fight, didn't he?"

"Yeah, that's the second time he's tried to kill me," he replied wearily. "Thanks, by the way. I don't think I would've lasted much longer against him." The supposed hunter chuckled and shrugged.

"I figured if I shot before he recovered, that I might be able to at least scare him off. Shame, though," he said, looking down, "had I had a second more, he may have been finished. My name's Jason, by the way."

"My name's Nathaniel, but most people call me Dorf," said Nathaniel. "And to be fair, I'd like to see you try putting yourself in front of that guy. Not to be rude or anything," he added as he saw the smile fade from Jason's face.

"No, of course not. I know, especially for someone in your....your condition, fighting a wizard isn't any simple task. I didn't mean to insult you, I was just hoping I had gotten him. In case you haven't noticed, he destroyed my home." Jason pointed to the ruins of the inn. The swordsman was not there anymore, and Jason's horse had trotted back to it and stood near the fence post. Smoke rose from the ruins and formed thick clouds in the sky. Wooden boards stuck out at odd angles, charred and splintered.

"I noticed," said Nathaniel with a shudder, "in fact, I was in there while it was happening. He blew the place up trying to kill me." He remembered that he had almost been part of those ruins if he had not pushed Forredar's spell out of the way. "Wait a minute....where were you while this was happening?" Jason coughed loudly.

"I haven't been home in over a week. I was out on a hunting expedition with some other men who live in the forest. Those damn bears have been giving us all trouble, so we decided to hunt them down. They were scaring people, killing people. It was all bad for business, and it wouldn't take long for them to start coming after us. Anyway, we've been killing what we thought were many different bears, but now it seems that the wizard created them. What happened to them?" Nathaniel pointed to the statues of the two other hunters. Jason looked hurt.

"Damn. Those were some good men, good warriors. I'm really going to miss them. Got me out of a few tight ones, they did. I assume it wouldn't be right to hold a funeral service. They aren't dead, after all," he said. Nathaniel felt a smile spread across his face.

"So, you're saying when someone is turned to stone, they aren't killed?"

"Yes, why?" Jason looked confused, as if he had not been expecting to discuss the topic.

"Back in my town, the same thing happened to our militia captain," he said, relieved. "Is it possible to put them right again?"

"It is, but only a certain spell can do it, and I'm very sorry to inform you of this, but I'm no magician. I'm sure any wizard in Vikelad could do it. Are you by chance heading there?"

"Yeah, that's where we're off to. We have to forestall the king's wrath on our town."

"What do you mean?" Jason eyed him suspiciously.

"A few days ago, that wizard and a few other soldiers showed up in Kumaiyan. They claimed that they were searching for the king's crown, but never found it. Then, before I left, he came to my home and attacked me. We outnumbered him greatly, and we forced him to flee. We hadn't done anything, we still don't know why he really attacked."

"And he has been following you and trying to kill you this whole time?" Nathaniel shook his head.

"No. This is the first we've seen of him in the Maze. Your inn, it was rigged. He set up a trap and nearly got me. He teleported into it, probably from the capital. I suppose he may have been following us, but he would have had to have been very stealthy about it," said Nathaniel. "Of course, couldn't he simply make himself undetectable with magic?"

"Like I said," began Jason, "I'm no magician. I only know a little bit about how sorcery works from reading books and listening to the traffic coming through my inn. But after seeing the things he can do, such as destroying my damn home and turning men to stone, I have no doubt that it is possible he hid himself from you during your journey. Where is your horse, by the way?" For the first time since the fight, Nathaniel realized that Kiel and Herbert weren't in sight. He shrugged lightly.

"Oh, she'll be with my parrot. I'm sure they haven't gotten too lost, they can talk these things through," he said, amused at the puzzled expression on Jason's face. "You know, how animals communicate and such."

"Oh, I see. But they can't talk, can they?" asked Jason.

"You know how birds are," said Nathaniel. "They can understand the basics." He spun, took a deep breath and called for Herbert. "HERBERT! GET BACK HERE! IT'S SAFE TO COME OUT NOW!" He turned back to Jason. "They'll be back in seconds." True to his word, Kiel came running out of the thick of the forest with Herbert perched on her head. The parrot held one wing stretched forward, pointing directly at Nathaniel.

"Ya! Ya! Forward, forward!" cried Herbert. Kiel galloped to Nathaniel's side and stopped inches before colliding with him. "What happened here, Dorf?" Jason looked very bewildered, as if it was all too much for him to bear.

"But, but, he can t-talk...b-bird," he sputtered, as if he was a child learning how to speak. Herbert looked him over curiously and turned back to Nathaniel.

"Like I said, what happened?" he asked.

"Forredar fled, again," he said. He gestured towards Jason. "He saved me, matter of fact. Nearly killed the wizard also. That was his inn that was blasted apart, by the way." Herbert's expression immediately softened.

"That's terrible. These other men, were they friends of his?" he asked, pointing at the statues with his wings.

"Briefly," said Jason, who seemed to have found his voice. "Didn't know them for more than a week. Still hurts, of course, but there's nothing we can do about it yet. I'm more shocked that I'm talking to a bird, to be honest with you. No offense or anything," he hastily added, picking up on the angry stare that immediately came to life on Herbert's face. "It's just a little odd, that's all. I've never done it before." Nathaniel seriously doubted that a "little" odd was what Jason really felt, but he knew how Herbert dealt with people who "didn't respect" him and supported Jason's choice of words.

"Well, I would say that we need to be going," he said, eager to change the subject. "We still have a lot of ground to cover, and now that they know where we are, we have even less time. Thank you, I suppose. I hope things start turning in your favor soon." He untied his quiver from Kiel's side and swung it over his back. Just as he was ready to begin the climb on top of the horse, Jason interrupted.

"Excuse me, but you don't mind if I come along, do you?" he asked. "I'm sure I could be of some assistance, after all. In case you want someone to watch your back." Herbert scowled, but Nathaniel knew what Jason meant.

"Are you sure? It could be dangerous up ahead, and I don't want anyone else to get hurt." Jason nodded.

"Of course I'm sure. I'm used to these parts, I nearly killed that wizard, and I have a bone to pick with him once we get there. Someone is going to pay for me home," he said, grinning. "Even if it's the King himself." Nathaniel had no doubt; the man was definitely determined. The way he saw it, Jason was being forced to travel north also, and there was no point in denying his aid.

"Very well, you may join us," he said. Herbert coughed loudly. "Oh, Herb, please try to get along with him. No one else in the capital is going to believe that you can talk either." Herbert fluttered over to his shoulder and perched himself on it.

"I'd be careful, though," he said, "I don't trust many of these 'humans'." Ignoring the comment, Nathaniel hopped up to mount Kiel when he felt a stinging pain shoot through his left knee. He fell and broke his fall with his hands.

"Are you all right, Dorf?" asked Jason. "Do you need any help getting on your horse?" Nathaniel picked himself up and shook his head.

"No, I can do it. I just need a little more time," he replied. Clenching his teeth, he slowly and painfully brought himself up and onto Kiel's back. The injury would slow him on foot, so he resolved to spend as much time as possible on horseback. He grabbed his bow from Kiel's side and gripped it tightly in his right hand. Looking towards Jason, he saw that their new companion was walking towards his ruined home.

"Jason, what are you doing?" he called. Jason turned around and called back to Nathaniel.

"I'm going to see what I can salvage from me home," he said. "I kept a fair bit of gold stashed away in there." Then he continued on towards what used to be the inn. As soon as he had disappeared within the depths of the ruins, Herbert flew off of Nathaniel's shoulder and landed on Kiel's neck, facing him,

"Okay, I'll allow him to come with us," he said. "I'll tolerate him. But I just want to lay down a few ground rules."

"All right," said Nathaniel, rolling his eyes. "And what might those be?" Herbert cleared his throat, as if he was making an important speech.

"Number one: He must not draw his weapon in your presence unless you allow him to do so. I don't trust him, especially with all the valuables we have."

"Herbert, he's already saved-"

"Was I finished?" demanded Herbert. "No, I don't think so. Number two: the human may not, under any circumstances, come within ten feet of you. To be allowed to do so would give him endless opportunities to sneakily attack you."

"Herbert, this is insane-" Herbert glared at Nathaniel.

"Do I need to remind you of the sharpness of my claws?" Nathaniel shook his head vigorously. "Good, then. Number three: If the human acts in any way that could endanger our lives, we kill him. I won't tolerate recklessness on this vessel."

"Herbert, we're not on a shi- wait, kill him? Don't you think that's a little- no, you don't think anything is extreme, but I'm sure as hell not going to kill him." Herbert snorted.

"Fine, then we will, right horsey?" He tapped Kiel's neck and she grunted angrily. Herbert's smile flickered for a moment.

"I take it that means no," said Nathaniel. "But Herbert, if he does anything like make too much noise, which I'm sure he won't do because of his experience out here, then we'll deal with him *with out killing anybody!*" He saw a scowl flicker across Herbert's face, but it vanished in an instant.

"Good. Oh, look, here he comes," said Herbert. Sure enough, Jason was walking out of the ruined inn, holding a small sack at his side. As he came closer, Nathaniel heard it jingling with what must have been coins.

"I managed to find most of me gold," said Jason. The rest of the home...well, you've been in there. Everything else perished." Jason pocketed the sack of gold and easily mounted his horse. His bow was now slung over his back with his quiver. "Sorry for delaying us, but shall we get going now?"

"Yes, of course," said Nathaniel. Herbert flew back to his left shoulder and they sped down the dirt path, heading north.

# Brutus

Fortunately for Jason, none of Herbert's rules came up in their discussions as they made their way to the capital city. Then again, their discussions weren't particularly thorough. In fact, they were traveling so quickly through the Maze that by the time they decided to make camp (about one o'clock in the morning), they were too tired to speak. Nathaniel, though he felt very stupid and foolish, elected to spend the night on his horse so that he would not have to face the pain of mounting the next morning. Jason made no comment on the strange behavior, and Herbert was too drowsy to care.

The next morning, after a mere five hours of sleep, they promptly set off to cover the final distance to Vikelad. Nathaniel knew they were close, he could almost feel it. Their journey was coming to a close. They had left behind the thickest part of the Maze the previous night. Now, the trees weren't sparse, but they weren't very dense and more sunlight broke through the thin covering. This part of the Maze was significantly brighter because of this, resulting in Nathaniel's cheerier mood despite his injured knee. Herbert, however, was still suspicious of Jason, flying off of his perch on Nathaniel every once in a while to check on their companion. Jason either ignored the parrot's antics or did not notice them, for he did not comment on the strange behavior at all during their travels.

Indeed, their ride was uninterrupted until they arrived at a small, worn bridge that crossed over a thin rivulet. They stopped their horses before the bridge.

"Should we cross?" asked Jason. "It looks all right to me."

"I don't know," said Nathaniel. "It looks a little old. But the water isn't deep at all. Let's just walk through that." He nudged Kiel forward, and when she was a few yards away from the water she grunted loudly and stopped. "What's the matter? Come on, go! Herbert, what is it? Can't you make her keep moving?"

"No, I'm afraid not. She's scared of something, probably around the bridge," replied Herbert from Nathaniel's shoulder. "Or maybe it's a certain *human*..."

"I say we find another way around," suggested Jason from a little ways behind them. "Hopefully, she won't be scared of whatever is over there." Jason turned his horse to leave, but then a roar split the air.

"Oh no, you don't!" yelled a deep voice. "No one can just pass through here!" Nathaniel looked to the bridge, where a very large, slightly green-skinned humanoid creature was standing. It was very muscular and about eight feet tall. Its head was a little larger than Nathaniel supposed it should be, and sharp, curled teeth stuck out of its bottom jaw, in front of its lips. It had black hair which was overgrown and apparently braided several times falling at its shoulders. It wore a ripped, gray shirt that exposed its enormous muscles and a tarnished loincloth. The monster held a wooden, spiked club as long as Nathaniel was tall in his right arm. "You don't pass unless you answer riddle!" Jason was off of his horse now, his bow drawn.

"What are you?" he asked, ignoring the monster's statement. "And why won't you let us pass?" The monster grunted.

"You do not pass unless you answer riddle!" it yelled. Herbert leaned a little closer to Nathaniel.

"He's a troll," he whispered. "We have to answer his riddles to get through."

"And if we don't answer them?" asked Nathaniel.

"It depends. If he's a nice troll, he'll just tell us to go around and not to disturb him again."

"What if he isn't a nice troll?" Nathaniel asked nervously.

"Oh, well, I'm not quite sure what *he* would do. But I think we'd only have a few seconds to run." Nathaniel shuddered.

"You answer riddle!" yelled the troll, pointing a finger at them. "Or I use your bones to clean teeth!"

"I take it he's not a nice troll," whispered Nathaniel.

"Don't worry, my vertically-challenged friend," said Herbert. "Just let me do the talking." Herbert flew onto Kiel's head and addressed the troll. "Hello! I'd like to answer your riddle!" The troll lost interest in Jason and turned towards Herbert. Nathaniel felt Kiel tremble under his gaze.

"You will answer riddle, little bird?" he asked. "If you do not answer right, you all belong to me."

"Yeah, but I'm feeling pretty confident," said Herbert. The troll looked a bit confused. "So you know, that means I think I'll answer 'right'." The troll's wide nostrils flared angrily, but he restrained himself from crushing the parrot.

"If you so con-fy-dent, then answer this: A man want to cross a bridge, just like you. The bridge can only hold weight of three-hundred pound. The man has three balls: one that weigh five pound, one that weigh ten, and one that weigh fifteen. Man weigh two-hundred eighty pound. How does man cross bridge with balls?" Though he could not see his face, Nathaniel knew that he must be thinking hard. After half of a minute, Herbert raised his head to look at the troll.

"I'm sorry, but when you say 'pound', do you mean 'pound*s*?" he asked. The troll, rather than explode at the flip remark, looked up at the sky as if searching for the answer.

"Yes, yes pound means pound. Proceed with answer, little parrot." While Herbert rapidly muttered to himself, Nathaniel tried to solve the problem for himself. How could a man carry three balls that added to his weight so much that he could not cross the bridge without breaking it? It seemed impossible at first. Could he throw the balls? No, that wouldn't work, some of them might not make it across, or someone might steal them at the other end of the bridge. Nathaniel wasn't particularly skilled in numbers, but he knew riddles pretty well. He knew that people used very literal terms on several occasions while telling riddles, just to throw them off track. He tried to juggle all of the variables through his head, the possible conditions when it struck him: juggling. The man would only be weighing a maximum of two-hundred and ninety five pounds seeing as only one ball was added to his weight at a time, which allowed him to cross the bridge.

"May I answer?" asked Nathaniel, trying to be as polite as possible. The troll grunted a reply and nodded. "Good, thank you. I would like to suggest that the man juggles the balls, like a court jester, across the bridge." Nathaniel heard audible gasps from both Herbert and Jason. The troll kept a stony expression.

"Yes, tiny man. You answer right. But is one riddle for one person. You need to answer two more before you can all pass." Herbert started to argue, but a look from the troll silenced him. Nathaniel looked at the troll and nodded.

"All right, then. What is your second riddle?"

"What weigh more: a pound of parrot's feathers, or a pound of dead parrots? Is simple question." Herbert swore loudly, but the troll merely laughed. Obviously, a dead parrot would weigh more, no matter how morbid the riddle was. Before Nathaniel could answer, Herbert cleared his throat to speak.

"They weigh the same," said Herbert. "A pound is always equal to the weight of a pound, no matter what it is made of." The troll nodded reluctantly.

"Yes, but 'same' would have been just right. Now two of you can pass. But third riddle, third riddle never been answered correctly. You ready for third riddle?" he asked. Nathaniel nodded and Herbert squeaked. "Good, very good. Another question: what came first, chicken or egg?" Now, Nathaniel had often heard this question used in an analogy to something that could not be figured out. Could the troll possibly know the answer to it? Could he be the only one to have found the answer to the question? Nathaniel exchanged glances with Herbert and Jason, neither of whom seemed to know the answer. But did the troll really know the answer? And then it came to him.

The riddle was the perfect trap for a troll. All he would have to do was say the answer was the opposite of whatever the traveler said it was. If the traveler said, "chicken," the troll could simply say, "no. Is egg." A plan formulated in his head. He knew how to beat the troll.

"Herbert!" he yelled. Herbert looked at him, and he mouthed, "chicken," to the parrot. Herbert nodded. Nathaniel then caught Jason's attention and mouthed, "both." Jason nodded. The troll did not seem to pick up on what was going on.

"Well, tiny man? Are you ready to say answer?" he asked eagerly.

"Yes, I think we're ready," said Nathaniel. "Egg!" At the same time, however, Herbert and Jason both spoke.

"Chicken!" yelled Herbert.

"Both!" yelled Jason. The troll's face fell instantly. His eyes grew sad and wide as he looked from traveler to traveler, trying to decide which one was correct.

"Well, what is the correct answer?" asked Herbert. The troll stuttered and stammered for a few seconds, then threw his hands in the air.

"Oh, I don't know!" he wailed. "I bad troll, bad troll! Just use riddle to keep people away, see? No one ever know how to answer correctly, even me!" The troll broke down, sobbing, and Nathaniel felt a strange pang for the creature. "I only wanted to be big, strong troll who protect territory, like mommy, but I can't do it, see? I never learned. My mommy I-left me whe-when I was just a baby and I had to take care of myself. Never learned h-how t-to eat like b-big troll, but feed like deer, on p-plants. Oh, mommy I failed!"

"Gee, that's a tough break," said Herbert, "but can we get moving, please?" Nathaniel said nothing, but continued to observe the crying troll. Could such a thing feel human emotions?

"Uh, excuse me, do you have a name?" asked Nathaniel. The troll's sobbing slowed as he spoke.

"B-Brutus," he said.

"Brutus, how old are you?" asked Nathaniel. Brutus seemed to think about this very hard, for his eyes looked up to the sky again and he started whispering very quickly to himself.

"N-nine years old," he said, evidently proud of himself. Seeing the surprised look on Nathaniel's face he added, "We trolls grow very big very fast." Nathaniel nodded understandingly.

"And why do you live here?"

"This w-was m-mommy's bridge, she guard it for long time. S-She say i-it almost like c-child to her, she b-been with it ever since h-human built it. I w-want to guard mommy's bridge, i-it what mommy wants for me. But no, Brutus fail badly as troll!"

"How so?" asked Herbert sarcastically. Brutus didn't seem to pick up on it.

"W-when people no answer riddle c-correctly, me no eat them! I j-just scare them off or t-tell them to l-leave! I d-don't know how to h-hunt, but I play with deer, make friends! I-it's not h-how troll should b-be, but I never learn how to be!"

"Well, Brutus, maybe you don't have to be like your mother," began Jason. "Maybe you are a bet-different kind of troll."

"How?" asked Brutus. There was longing in his voice, as if he was eager to hear more.

"Well, you don't eat people, or meat," said Jason. "In fact, you haven't harmed a living thing. That's something very noble, Brutus. Instead of killing deer, you have made friends with them. You have a truly compassionate personality. That's not a bad thing!" he desperately added as Brutus lowered his head. "I'm sure your mother would be proud of you." Brutus slowly lifted his head.

"S-she would?"

"Absolutely," said Jason. "You're obviously smarter than any other troll, probably smarter than some humans. Those first two riddles were pretty tough to answer. How did you learn them?" Nathaniel silently applauded Jason's performance; Brutus was looking, and probably feeling, much happier now.

"Three, no four, year ago, man come to bridge, not much different than you. I very small at time, and just tell man to go around bridge and not bother me. Man, who was riding horse, dropped large bag of parchment and ran other way. So, I picked up large bag and look through parchment. I didn't read back then, but I look at letters for long time. Later, old woman come passing through with a man, and they talking. Instead of yelling, I hide under bridge and listen to them. Then, like magic, the symbols on parchment make sense to me. One of the letters was report on contest in small village. Contest use many riddles, and I read them and understand. Letter said only a few men answer right, so I decide that no one passing through bridge could answer right, either. And until now, I right." Jason looked mildly impressed.

"What a feat," he said. "I did not learn my letters until I was twelve years old. You definitely have been blessed with talent, Brutus. But now, do you really need to scare anyone else away from your bridge? Couldn't you let people through, as long as they agree to not hurt you?" Nathaniel now understood Jason's motive behind the conversation. The troll was so

inundated in his own pride and self-satisfaction that he was in a
state of high vulnerability.

"Yeah, I no need to scare anymore....probably smarter
anyway!" said Brutus. Jason looked pleased.

"Excellent, excellent. Now, as your first...customers,
could we pass over your bridge? We really need to be getting to
the capital city, and quickly too." Brutus took one gigantic step to
the side, clearing their pathway forward.

"I let you through. But capital no very far from here, only
few miles. Me ran there six times!" he added, thumping his
chest.

"Thank you very much," said Jason. "I hope we'll see
each other again." Then he pulled on his horse's reins and it
carried him across the bridge.

"Bye, friend!" called Brutus. "Bye, bye, little man!"
Nathaniel kicked into Kiel's side, not entirely trusting of the troll
just yet. "I'll see you again!"

"Yeah, hopefully," Nathaniel added reluctantly. He
followed Jason over the bridge and down the dirt path. He
imagined Brutus standing there, waving frantically, until they
were out of sight. Nathaniel caught up to Jason, who was
looking very proud.

"That was incredible," he said, for lack of a better word. "What made you think he wouldn't kill you?" Jason laughed and replied without taking his eyes off of the path.

"It was simple, really. I could tell from the moment we met him that he wasn't really vicious. See, even though he is big and strong, he was over-compensating for his emotional weakness. Maybe you didn't pick up on it because you were many times smaller than he is, but I knew that he wasn't really a monster."

"But you knew how to talk with him? How did you know he wouldn't take offense?"

"I have met trolls before. Each and every one of them share the same flaw: an bottomless appetite for accomplishment. It goes back all the way to when the first troll guarded the first bridge. See, trolls are very territorial creatures. She guarded it to hold her territory. In doing so, she felt as if her purpose in life was being fulfilled. These days, trolls count how many people they scare away, how many they kill, or how many years they have guarded their bridges. No other troll has ever learned how to read, but it is the principle of accomplishment that matters to them. So, as we exit the Maze, I believe that Brutus will be much better off now than he was before, and so will we," he said, grinning.

Nathaniel looked around at the mention of the Maze. Just like Jason said, they were out of the massive forest. The trees lining the road were thinner and fewer. They now saw the sunlight in its entirety. For the first time in days, Nathaniel looked up at the sky and saw the blue and white above. They had left the Maze behind, and their long journey would soon be complete.

"Dorf, what time is it?" asked Jason. Nathaniel turned over his wrist and glanced at the golden watch.

"It is about noon," he replied. "If what the troll said is true, we should be in Vikelad by this afternoon."

"Oh, that reminds me," said Jason. "I'm not so sure that we can just walk in there." Nathaniel nodded. He had thought about the potential danger there would be once they arrived in the city. Forredar could have the city's guards on patrol for him, or he could be there himself, supported by many warriors. They definitely needed a plan for getting into the city undetected.

"We need a plan," said Nathaniel. "By now, there are probably wanted posters hanging up all over the place with my face on it."

"Come now," said Jason. "Do you really think they would need your face?" Nathaniel looked at him quizzically.

"What do you mean?"

"Well, all they would really need is your height," he said. "Seriously!" he added when Nathaniel glared at him. "It would be so easy to have everyone in the city keeping their eyes peeled for a dwarf! They wouldn't even need to look twice. They're

probably rounding up any adults your height as we speak."
Though a little angry, Nathaniel knew Jason was right. It would
be illogical to deny that his height was a distinguishing feature of
his, one that would immediately lead to his capture.

"All right, but that doesn't lead us any closer to a
solution," he said. "Unless you can make me grow three feet in
the next hour or so."

"I can't do that, but I have a better, more realistic idea."

"Well, do tell." They slowed their horses to a trot and
discussed their plan.

The Culprit Revealed

At two o'clock, the stone walls of Vikelad came into sight. The walls were tall, with battlements set apart about every thirty feet. The dirt path led Nathaniel, Herbert, and Jason directly to the southern gate of the city, which was guarded by five armed men in battle armor. The guards did not see their approach from a distance, the first part of their plan working perfectly.

When they came into sight of the guards, Nathaniel hopped off Kiel, landing hard on his injured knee. The pain still bothered him, but its intensity had weakened since the previous day. Half-walking and half-limping, he hurried behind the west wall of the city, taking care to go unnoticed by the guards. Once he reached the wall, he knelt and caught his breath. Now it was Jason's turn to act. Glancing around the wall's corner, Nathaniel saw Jason dismount his horse and take both horses' reins in his hand. He led both horses to the gate, and the guards blocked his path with their halberds.

"Not so fast there, mate," said one of the guards. "We're going to need some information before you enter this city now." Jason shrugged.

"What information?" he asked. Another guard held up a small roll of parchment and handed it to the first guard.

"Let's see....name," he read.

"Jason."

"Do you have a last name?" Jason shook his head.

"Not that I know of, sir."

"I see, very good, very good. Next....what goods are you carrying with you, and what is the purpose of your weapon?" he asked, indicating Jason's bow, which was slung over his shoulder.

"I have a small bag of food, a map, a bow, a quiver full of arrows, and some gold. I had to use this bow in the Maze, to defend myself."

"From what?" the guard asked, evidently suspicious.

"Bears," said Jason, trembling a little. "Killed one of my friends as we were passing through. I brought his horse here, to take care of it." The guard nodded.

"Yeah, we've been hearing many reports about these bears giving people trouble and what not. Anyway...why have you come to the city?"

"I would like to walk through some of the shops," said Jason. "I would like to buy my wife a birthday gift, and I was told that Vikelad deals in the best goods in the country."

"Married, eh? Where's your ring?" the guard asked. Jason lifted up his ring finger, apparently showing the guard something that Nathaniel could not see. The guard gasped.

"Yep, cut clean off by the monster," said Jason. "I'd also like to replace it, but I'll have to wait til the skin grows back."

That was Nathaniel's cue. The guards had moved closer to look at Jason's finger, and he now had their full, undivided attention. Slowly, Nathaniel tiptoed around the corner, towards the city gate. "Even though there were two of us, doesn't matter when it's right in front of you."

"How did you escape?" asked one of the guards, all official manner forgotten. Nathaniel continued towards the wall, and Jason put a hand to his forehead and shook it dramatically.

"We managed to kill one of them, but by the time the other two were upon us, we knew we had to run. I jumped on my horse here, but my companion wasn't quick enough. The beast knocked him over and the last thing I saw was him being dragged away and clawing at the dirt." The guards gasped.

"How horrible!" exclaimed the guard closest to Jason. Nathaniel reached the gate and was directly behind the formation of guards. He didn't dare make eye contact with Jason, for fear of being detected. He pulled the gate open, inch by inch, just as Jason's grip on the reins slipped and he screamed.

"No!" he cried. Though the guards did not know it, Herbert (who was hidden in Nathaniel's pack) had told both horses to run when Jason screamed. Both horses took off towards the south. "My horses!" The guards sprinted off after the horses, some of them yelling to grab the reins or block their path. Jason winked at Nathaniel, and ran after the horses. Nathaniel slipped through the gate and was in the capital city.

The city was enormous. Stretched out before him were large stone buildings and streets turning in every direction. Hundreds of people walked through the paved streets. Beautifully carved pillars supported several buildings, vendors on the street sold jewels, amulets, and all other kinds of shiny trinkets, and never before had Nathaniel seen so many people bustling about through shops and markets. It was as if Kumaiyan had been multiplied a thousand times over and decorated extensively. As he walked through a street picked at random, Nathaniel realized that he could hide very easily. No one paid him any attention, and as long as he was careful not to bump into anyone, his short height allowed him to go unnoticed.

Everywhere he looked, he saw squares of parchment posted to building doors, but whenever he tried to read what was on it, he would have to duck or move out of someone's way. At last, through several minutes of walking blindly, he came close to a shop door and hopped up to see the sign. Posted on the sign was a sketch of two figures, with no details on them whatsoever. One figure was half of the size of the other, and Nathaniel understood the sign before he read the description.

*Wanted*

*Nathaniel Dorf, suspect for taking part in theft and assaulting officers of the Kingdom. Is three feet tall, accomplices include one green parrot and a middle-aged man with a bow and arrows. Both man and dwarf are dangerous, so alert an officer instead of trying to apprehend them yourself. Any sightings should be reported to a watchman or Palace Wizard. In addition, we have set spells around the city preventing any teleportation in or out. Don't hesitate to run if attacked by either fugitive, but any wizards should take care to not attempt to break the spells, as Master Guera has set them up himself.*

So he was being hunted. If sighted, he was doomed. Watchmen were patrolling every street, armed with bows and swords. The wanted posters were placed on almost every door. There was no chance of him going unnoticed entirely for the next five minutes or more. As he ducked behind a group of large workers, Nathaniel wondered who Master Guera was. Then he realized that there was a serious flaw in his plan.

He didn't know how to get to the palace. If he tried to ask for directions, he would be turned over to the watchmen immediately. If he wandered around the city much longer without a clear idea of where he was going, he would be spotted and turned over to the watchmen. His mind racing, Nathaniel pushed open a shop door just as a watchman materialized around a corner.

The shop was very small and consisted of a counter and a staircase in the back. Behind the counter was a young woman dressed in a very expensive-looking dress. Her long hair was jet black, clashing with her pale skin. Though he was only three feet tall, Nathaniel deduced that she was shorter than the average human.

"Oh!" she shrieked when she saw him. "D-Dorf!" She was pointing at him now, and backing away. Nathaniel held his hands up over his head.

"No! No, it's okay, it's okay!" he yelled. "I'm not going to hurt anyone, honest!" The woman backed right into a shelf full of clothing and abruptly stopped.

"Please, I'll do anything! Just don't hurt me!" she yelled. Nathaniel resolved to end the scene before anyone else heard her screams. That would cause some trouble.

"Listen, please. I do not want to hurt anybody, I'm not a criminal," he said, in what he hoped was a soothing voice. "I haven't stolen anything, and I'm sure as hell not dangerous. I need some directions, and quickly!" The woman nodded, still worried.

"Where you you need to go?" she whispered.

"I need to go to the palace," he said.

"The palace? Why would you want to go there? If you are innocent, you should flee!"

"I need to clear my name," said Nathaniel. "I've been set up. I never took the crown, I can prove that I don't have it." The woman smiled a little.

"Well, of course you don't have it. It was recovered yesterday and returned to its rightful owner."

"It was?" asked Nathaniel. "Where did they find it?" The woman shook her head.

"They didn't say. But I suppose if they found it on you, you would be in prison. I guess you really are innocent, after all." She looked rather thoughtful and shrugged absently.

"Good, I'm glad we got that straightened out," muttered Nathaniel. "Now, how do I get to the palace?"

"I could give you the directions, but I think it would be best if I led you there," said the woman. "If you need to stop and think about any directions, you have a chance at being spotted. If you follow me, however, then you only need to concentrate on walking where I walk. Sound good to you?" Nathaniel nodded.

"If I follow you, how will I go unnoticed?" he asked. "Are you going to hide me somehow?" The woman shook her head.

"No, that is a chance we'll have to take. The wizard Forredar is adamant to the notion that you are guilty. I'm sure he'll have people looking all over for you, but if we are quick we might get around them." Nathaniel's jaw dropped.

"Forredar is here?" he asked.

"Yes, he is. He got back here yesterday with the crown, said he had retrieved it. Why do you ask?"

"Because he's been hunting me for the past week all the way from Kumaiyan. He's tried to kill me a few times, and has turned some of my allies into stone. He even destroyed a man's home to try and get at me," he said as the woman's eyes widened with horror. "Has he done anything since his return?"

"Oh, yes he has. He's been placing those posters all over the city and placing spells all over the place. I overheard one of the watchmen saying something about a trap, but as far as I saw, Forredar hasn't laid out anything of the sort."

"Aha, I'll bet he has. He sprung a trap on me in the Maze and the next thing I knew, he was blasting an inn apart trying to get at me. Those spells are probably designed to alert him when I walk into the city," he reasoned. The woman behind the counter merely shrugged. "But why hasn't he attacked me yet? Unless...unless the spells will alert him when I am in the palace! Yes, that's probably it. He'll leave the rest of the population to keep on their toes for me, and he'll immediately know if I get past them. So, I'm stuck between a rock and a hard place." Surprisingly, the woman behind the counter didn't look very troubled. In fact, she looked very calm and controlled.

"Well, your way ahead is simple, then. Just hand yourself over, and plead your case before the King. I'm sure he'll want to speak with you anyway. And let's face it, as soon as you walk out of my shop's door, you will be seen. You might as well be seen surrendering to the watchmen. It couldn't hurt your case."

"But....but," he said stupidly. She was right. He had ran out of ideas and was trapped. After all of the narrow escapes he had made, this was how it was going to end. He would have one last chance to tell the truth to the King, and he'd better not waste it. "If I surrender, will the guards still roughen me up? Or will they let me walk in chains to the palace?"

"Normally, they allow people who turn themselves in to walk alongside them, generally unharmed. But in this case....I'm not sure what they'd do. The King is pretty trusting of his wizards, and with all of the stuff Forredar has put out there, he probably won't take too kindly to your appearance. But what are you, afraid of them?" she asked, almost mockingly. "You've said that a fully-trained wizard has been chasing you for a week, and you are afraid of the watchmen?"

"I'm not afraid," replied Nathaniel, more forcefully than he intended. "I'm already injured, and I wouldn't like to be beaten at all if I can help it."

"Oh, I see. Right, an injury, of course. Were you hit by a spell?" she asked, suddenly very interested.

"No, I was thrown down a flight of stairs and beaten down by a large bear. But it hurts just the same as if I had been."

"So, he never actually hit you with his magic?"

"Well, when he first started interrogating me, he placed some sort of boils all over my skin, but they went away quickly. That was painful, but my knee is still a little hard to walk on."

"Ah, the non-magical injury is worse than the magical? That's odd. He placed a curse on someone a week ago, and that person has a terrible fate."

"What does the curse do?"

"Well, this man, he wakes up every morning with a full head of hair, like it was before he was cursed. Over the course of the day, his hair steadily falls out until he is completely bald by sunset. The man says that it feels as if the hair is being ripped out of his skull, piece by peace, until he is bald. Then it happens all over again the next day."

"That's disgusting! Why did he curse the man? Did he do anything wrong?"

"As far as he said, Forredar asked him if he had any part in the theft of the King's crown. When the man told him that he had not, Forredar pressed on, asking more and more questions until the man grew fed up and kicked him out of his home. Though it wasn't legally correct for Forredar to intrude on the man after the interrogation was over, Forredar threatened the man with his magic. But the man continued to insist that the wizard needed to leave, so Forredar recited the incantation and cursed him. Mind you, that was at night, so the man took the brunt of the pain in seconds. I'm surprised he didn't go crazy from it."

"If it wasn't legal, but it happened in the capital city, then why hasn't anything been done about it?" The woman sighed.

"Well, do you think Forredar would tell the truth about that sort of thing? Of course not! And the poor cursed man is scared to death that if he comes forward, Forredar will finish him off! And he's probably right!"

"Wait....do you think the King even knows what Forredar is really doing? I'm not sure he would really approve of it. He turned a few people to stone, blew up a man's home, and attacked innocent people for no good reason. Would the King allow any of this?"

"No, come to think of it, I don't think he would. King Krellin has always been generous and kind to our people. I don't believe that any crime would cause him to inflict unnecessary pain upon the people of the country. Well, at least you can be a little confident when you appear before him." The woman walked out from behind the counter and closer to him.

"What do you mean?" But the woman didn't say anything. She strode forward and grasped the door handle behind him.

"Good luck," she said, and with that she pushed the door open with one arm and Nathaniel backwards with the other. He fell back and collided with a person walking towards the shop. He hurriedly stood up and looked at whom he had bumped into.

He had ran straight into a watchman. The watchman, three feet taller than he was, held a halberd and was outfitted with a silver helm revealing his hardened, weathered, face. The watchman looked apologetic at first, then his expression turned to surprise as he registered who Nathaniel was.

"Dorf..." he whispered. "Dorf! I've got you now, I have!" The watchman lunged at him, and fear spread through Nathaniel. He quickly stepped to the side and the watchman crashed to the ground. He stood up and pointed the halberd down at Nathaniel, looking very angry. "Ah, he said you'd be slippery!" Nathaniel raised his hands in front of him.

"I give up! I surrender!" he yelled, much to the surprise of the guard. "But I can explain everything, I really can! Just take me to the King! I need to speak with him!" The guard seemed to contemplate what he had said, and cocked his head to the side as if finding Nathaniel for the second time.

"Yeah, I was going to be takin' you to the King, anyways. Pretty odd that you'd want to go there, but all right. Come, I'll let you walk next to me, but try anything an' I'll attack you, all right?" Nathaniel nodded, and the guard brought his halberd back into a position across his chest. "Okay, you'll be wantin' to follow me, then." The guard motioned with his halberd and another watchman appeared in front of them out of the crowded street. "Get behind him, make sure we aren't stopped." The other guard obeyed, and Nathaniel found himself being escorted through the winding, packed streets by the men.

He was glad that the guards had him covered. Amidst the crowd, very few people could see him, those who could being small children. He did not want to cause a large scene with his appearance, but could not help feeling a little uneasy at the prospect of going to the King. Though it had been his plan from the start, the circumstances had changed drastically and he felt as if he was a fugitive rather than a messenger.

As it turned out, the palace was located in the very center of the city, all of the housing and market districts sitting around it in a circular pattern. Nathaniel swore aloud when he realized just how close he had been to the palace after all, and how easy it would have been to get to it. Still, he hadn't known the way, but he felt a little cheated that he needed to surrender in order to do so.

After at least fifteen minutes of walking, the guard in front of him stopped moving. In order to see what was up ahead, Nathaniel stepped to the side and peered around the guard.

Laid out in front of them was a magnificent palace that could have been the size of his hometown. It was painted pure white with tall towers protruding from the corners of the building.

Directly in front of them was a gate twice the size of the average human. The iron gate blocked a straight, paved pathway that trailed for about twenty yards and led to what must have been the palace's front door. He noticed that the gate was guarded on either side by two soldiers wearing the same masks as the soldiers in Kumaiyan had worn. The soldiers had shields fastened to their left arms and swords sheathed at their sides, and their golden armor glittered brilliantly in the sunlight.

"This one would needs to speak with the King, and soon," said the guard in front of Nathaniel. The soldiers flanking the gate turned to each other.

"Which one?" one of the soldiers asked from behind his mask.

"The d-" the guard moved closer to the soldier and whispered something in his ear. Nathaniel was sure that the soldier must have had a look of surprise hidden beneath his mask.

"Really? You got him? Right, well, of course, bring him in," said the soldier. "Gee, I didn't think Master Forredar was serious when he told us about his height." The soldiers unbolted the heavy gate and pushed each side of it back until it swung open before them. The guard in front of Nathaniel saluted with his halberd and beckoned Nathaniel to follow him. The trio walked in silence down the paved path, which allowed Nathaniel to hear the soldiers behind them expressing their excitement about his "capture".

"I wonder what they'll do with him?"

"Probably string him up in a day or two."

"Imagine the trouble they'd have putting him on the noose!"

"They could always just behead him, don't you think?"

"Nah, too bloody...the King hates that."

"You think they would stone him?"

"Again, too bloody."

"Maybe they'll let him rot in prison."

"Maybe they'll have him shot."

"Maybe they'll let one of our sorcerers have at him. It'd be fun to see what he's like as a toad."

"Right, but last time....." They reached the door to the palace, and Nathaniel couldn't hear the soldiers anymore due to their distance. He shivered, though, at the prospect at any of the listed punishments.

The guard in front of him knocked twice on the door. Within seconds, the door was pulled open and an old man dressed in a gray robe stood in the doorway. He was almost as tall as the guard, with a large bald spot in the middle of his head, surrounded by a circle of silvery white hair. The man appeared to be happy. Could he have already heard the news?

"Why, hello there," he said, strangely energetic. "What can I do for you today?"

"We have Dorf," said the guard. "He requests a meeting with the King. Is he in, at the moment?" The old man's smile did not falter.

"Oh, found him, have you? Good, very good indeed....bring him in, the King is at the throne." The old man held the door open as they walked into the palace. As Nathaniel passed him, he noticed that the old man was studying him as if he was an entirely foreign sort of person. Not being surprised at all, Nathaniel continued to follow the lead guard through the palace hall.

The hall was beautifully decorated with torches and tapestries hanging from every wall. Pillars similar to those in the city streets flanked their path and supported the at least three story-high ceiling. What Nathaniel thought was odd, though he had never been to a palace before, was that the hall was empty save for himself and the two guards. Did the King enjoy his privacy, or did members of the court simply not wait around the palace hall all day like Nathaniel suspected they did?

After climbing up a flight of stairs twice the size of his cottage back home, the two guards parted the way for Nathaniel and each stood next to a pillar on either side. Directly ahead of him was a middle-aged man sitting atop a large throne.

King Krellin sat in his tall chair, wearing extravagant clothing that included a purple buttoned shirt, a golden-colored vest, a golden crown, and two white gloves. The King had a large black beard and a kind face, but Nathaniel quavered slightly under his stare. True, the King kept his eyes fixed on Nathaniel for several moments before speaking.

"So, this is Nathaniel Dorf?" his mighty voice boomed around the throne room. "I figured you would be small. But, you surely understand that you are a wanted....well, for simplicity's sake, man?" Nathaniel nodded.

"Yes s-sire, I know that I'm wanted," he said, trying to sound brave. "But I am innocent, and I can explain everything!"

"You can? Well, please do!" said the King. Though he had rehearsed his account of the past events countless times in his head, it lunged from his mouth very quickly and nervously. Through ten minutes of stuttering and repeating his words, Nathaniel managed to give Krellin the full story of what had happened since the soldiers came into Kumaiyan. Throughout his story, he had taken care to emphasize that Forredar had been trying to kill him, had attacked him without any proof, and how he had turned three people to stone. At the end, Nathaniel felt very tired and had to catch his breath. Though he hadn't expected it, the King looked as if he believed every word he had spoken.

"So, you've been trying to get a message to me for the past week," he began, "and you say my trusted servant Forredar has been pursuing you? Well, your story definitely checks out, based on everything that has happened so far. There is nothing conflicting within anything you have told me."

"Thank you, sir," said Nathaniel. "And to top it off, I see you have your crown back." The King chuckled and tapped his head.

"Yes, Forredar recovered it a while ago. When he returned and said you had escaped, I didn't exactly believe him because I was occupied with the crown. But now, I don't think you ever had it. In fact, I believe that Forredar had it the whole time."

"But how-" Nathaniel was cut off as there was a loud bang and shouting from behind. Whirling around, Nathaniel saw an angry man dressed in all black running towards the throne room. His heart skipped when he realized that the man was none other than Forredar himself. Behind Forredar, two guards were sprawled on the ground, writhing uncontrollably and clutching their chests. When Forredar reached the stairs, the guards  that had escorted Nathaniel blocked his way.

"Excuse me, Master, but you'll have to expl-ahh!" screamed one of the guards as a jet of silver light struck him in the face. He froze, and was turned into a statue. The remaining guard swung his halberd at Forredar, who ducked under the blow. The wizard muttered something inaudible and a bolt of blue lightning shot from his fingers and blasted the guard backwards. The guard hit the stone wall forty feet behind him and dropped to the floor, unconscious. Krellin, who looked utterly startled, drew a silver dagger from his vest and grasped the blade between his thumb and forefinger just as Forredar grabbed Nathaniel and dug his fingers into his back.

Nathaniel felt as if he was on fire. The burning pain spread through his body and he fell. He saw spots and blackness before him, his vision obstructed with the intense agony. A second later, the pain lessened and he felt someone lift him up by the shoulders.

"Don't try it, my King," said Forredar darkly. "We'd both hate it if you dented my shield."

"Forredar, what are you doing?" asked Krellin worriedly. "Why are you doing this?"

"He warned you," said Forredar. "He told you what would happen to your reign of tyranny. Won't you ever learn? We have the power, and we won't hesitate to use it! Now, hand over the crown, or Dorf here gets cooked."

"Please, don't...you have nothing to gain, you know that! Forredar, please! He's using you, you should have figured that out by now! Put Nathaniel down, and everything will be all right," said Krellin. "You don't have to do this, Forredar."

"I'm warning you. Now, as your last chance. Give the crown to me or I kill him."

"You wouldn't dare," said the King. "You know what he could mean to all of us!"

"One more time: give me the crown, or else I kill him. I'm sure he's told you already how he's slipped through my grasp all the way from his little village. I'm now being generous. After all the times I have nearly finished him, I am giving him a chance to live. Are you going to get in the way of that?" The King looked desperately at Forredar, then sighed.

"All right," he said, resigned. He pulled the crown off his head when the throne room burst into chaos.

"Get behind me!" yelled a familiar voice. Nathaniel felt himself fly forward and landed at the King's feet. Without thinking, he drew his sword and stood facing Forredar.

Forredar was several feet to the left of where he had been, shouting incoherently and sending jets of fire swirling in every direction. Further down the hall, Nathaniel saw the old man at the door leading a group of four soldiers and pointing towards the throne room. They charged up the steps before Nathaniel could shout to warn them.

"Watch out, he's-"  he began. When the old man and the soldiers reached the top of the steps, Forredar struck.

"Gargoyle!" he yelled, aiming for the old man. The old man ducked promptly and the jet of silver light caught one of the soldiers in the chest, turning him to stone. "Trapped!" A net burst from the tip of Forredar's finger and latched itself around two of the soldiers, both of whom had not drawn their swords. The old man stepped back and whirled his  through the air.

He made his hand into a fist. A silver dagger similar to Krellin's appeared out of thin air and flew towards Forredar. It struck him in the leg, and he howled in pain.

"May your head be filled with the thoughts of hell!" he shouted, pointing at a soldier who was retreating. A blue spark of energy shot from Forredar's hand and struck him in the head. At once, the soldier fell to the ground, clutching his head and screaming. "And for you, burn!" A jet of fire shot towards the old man just as he flicked his wrist. The two spells collided and vanished. Forredar looked startled and hesitated, giving the old man an advantage.

"No!" yelled the old man. A powerful burst of water issued from his finger and struck Forredar's hand. Forredar clutched his hand in pain. The old man pointed at Forredar's leg. "Stop!"

There was a loud crack, and Forredar fell forward and hit the floor. He knelt near the old man, looking up at him and breathing heavily.

"You don't know what you're doing, old fool!" he spat. "You cannot stop us, you will not stop us! Justice will be served, whether you live to see it or not!" The old man shook his head.

"No, Forredar, I would say that you are the one who doesn't know the cause of his actions. What did he say he would do, anyway? I thought you liked it here. You have a family here, Forredar, and friends. Why throw it away to join a man who has repeatedly tried and failed to overthrow our King?" asked the old man.

"He is no man," said Forredar. "He is a god. And he's the only god strong enough to come to this world in human form. I have no family here, oh no I don't! My family is on my side, you people aren't! But you, you could be," he panted, the muscles in his face strained and tense. "Your assistance would be valued highly, Guera."

"After you called me an old fool?" asked Guera, feigning anger. "No, Forredar. But don't do this. You do not have to do this. This can all be forgotten if you let go of it." Forredar clutched at his injured leg and tried to pull the dagger out. It wouldn't budge. Just then, Forredar pointed at Guera, and the tip of his finger glowed silver.

"Forredar, calm down, calm down," said Guera. "You aren't going to do it, it's okay. Just cancel the spell, and no one has to get hurt. We'll heal you up and make sure you're safe...so, that's it, isn't it? Safe..."

"You don't know the half of it!" shouted Forredar. Then he pointed at his own chest. "Good-bye!" Then he vanished. Evidently, Guera saw something and dove at the spot where the wizard had been only a second ago, but crashed to the ground and cursed.

"Damn!" he said. He stood up and took a moment to examine his robes, then brushed them off and stamped at seemingly random spots on the floor. "Almost had him!"

"What happened?" asked Nathaniel. "Where did he go?"

"He did something dangerous, even for a wizard of his skill. He turned himself into a fly and is probably out of the palace by now."

"But I thought your spells stopped anyone from escape," said Krellin.

"They stopped anyone who can teleport from teleporting," said Guera. "I could not, however, prevent the use of morphing spells in the city. It isn't legal, and I don't think the spell would have held anyway. But that is very creative."

"Forredar was always good at escaping, we knew that," said Krellin. Guera nodded.

"Yes, it is a talent he must have practiced in private, and one that requires a lot of concentration. I don't think I could do it if I had a dagger in my leg and a broken bone. But as I recall, you were about to say something before he made off, weren't you?" he turned to Nathaniel. Nathaniel looked around for a moment, then realized he was being addressed.

"Oh, yes...I was going to warn you that he could do that. He turned into a dragon in the Maze," he said. "But how could he do that when he was badly injured?"

"Forredar is a very skilled wizard, always good with his studies," said Guera. "However, that is a matter we will discuss later. Right now, there are some people in need of my help." Nathaniel saw the unconscious soldier behind the throne, the soldier who was cursed twisting and turning, and the statue of the guard holding his halberd in front of him as he tried to stop Forredar. "Let's see....do I remember the incantation?" The old wizard walked to the statue and tapped it with his fingers.

"May the stone that was once flesh be returned to its original state," said the wizard, with a slight tune to it. The air around the statue rippled with waves of heat, then the statue began to shake. In a second, the stone slid away and dissolved on the floor to reveal the guard as he had been the moment Forredar cursed him. The guard looked down at his body in disbelief and dropped his weapon.

"What happened? I thought I blacked out!" he blurted as he tested his arms and legs as if to make sure he could move them properly.

"You have just spent a few minutes of your life as a statue," said Guera calmly.

"A few minutes? It seemed like a second!" exclaimed the guard. "Gods! Did he get away? What did he do?"

"Yes, Forredar escaped, but right now you should retire to your barracks and get some rest. It's a nasty experience, being turned to stone." The guard promptly shook his head.

"No, Master. I'm not leaving until I am sure everyone here is safe, and with someone as talented as Forredar out in the open, no one is safe." Guera chuckled and clapped his hands.

"Do not worry, sir. Don't forget, I am a master wizard! He will not come here as long as I or any other of the wizards are on alert! We are all safe, or am I not a master wizard?" The guard put his hands up in front of his chest.

"N-No, sir, you are a master wizard. I'll be on my way, then," he said hurriedly, picked up his halberd, and raced down the throne room stairs.

"Good, now I can attend to those plagued in the mind," said Guera. He knelt at the struggling and turning soldier's side and placed his open palm on his chest, whispering what must have been a magical incantation. After a few moments, the soldier stopped moving and fell still. "Ah, I see we have another stone case." Guera pointed at the statue of the soldier who had come with him to fight Forredar. He repeated his first incantation, and the soldier was returned to his original, human form, but collapsed. "Oh, he'll be fine. That happens some time. He'll recover within the hour."

There was a loud noise, and Nathaniel saw the palace door swing open. A very tall and muscular man entered, with dark brown skin and wearing leather pants and a thin leather cuirass. He had long tangles of dreadlocks falling beyond his shoulders which swung around wildly as he stormed into the throne room.

"My King," he said quickly, in a deep voice, "are you all right?"

"Of course I'm all right! It's these soldiers who have been attacked, everyone else is all right!" replied Krellin. The large man shook his head.

"No, my King, not everyone is all right. Three of my men are injured, and Bayard's stuck in the ground."

"Stuck?" asked the King.

"Yes, my King. It was a spell, something that made him sink into the ground up to his ankles. We aren't making any progress getting him out. And, my King, I take it that Dorf over there isn't wanted due to the change of events?" Nathaniel turned to the King, who nodded.

"Yes, Nathaniel here is no longer wanted. See to it that those wanted posters are taken down," he said, "and that new ones are posted with Forredar on it. Fetch Lauda to tend to them, she'll be able to heal them quickly enough. Do you think she knows how to get Bayard out of the ground?" He directed the question to Guera.

"I can't say," said Guera. "From what I know of her, she is capable in undoing curses, but I'm not sure if she can deal with this spell. I'll tend to him."

"Good, very good, why don't you do that now?" asked the King. Guera nodded. "Oh, and please take Dorf with you."

# The Hidden Power

The wizard Guera and Nathaniel departed from the palace hall to investigate the scene outside. On the neat path that led to the palace door was a circle of soldiers standing around three unconscious men. Kneeling over the men was the woman Nathaniel had met in the shop. When she saw him she waved and motioned for them to come closer.

"There you are! Master, can you help me with this? Bayard is stuck, and my attempts have failed thus far." The woman pointed to the right, where a man was standing up, looking completely normal. Then, as Nathaniel looked down, he saw an insect lying at his feet...but his feet weren't there. Instead, it looked as though his legs were sprouting from the ground. The man was fidgeting, his sweat showing through his red shirt and poring down his brow.

"Can't...get out, too weak...can't concentrate enough," panted the man stuck in the ground. "Used a tricky spell, he did." Guera shook his head.

"Bayard, you're the best war-wizard we have! How did he do this?" he asked.

"He caught me from behind," said Bayard. "He used nightmares on the guards, but since he knew I can undo them, he stuck me in the ground instead. Then he swept into the palace and we heard shouts and fighting in there. Did you capture him?"

"No, we did not," replied Guera while observing Bayard's legs. "He transformed himself and got away. I did break his leg, though, but it isn't anything he will have trouble mending."

"Did he...did he kill anyone?" Bayard asked rather reluctantly.

"No, he cursed some of our men, but I've set them right. He tried to take the crown again, using Dorf here as a hostage." As if seeing him for the first time, Bayard's eyes opened wide and he gasped.

"He's there! You got him!" he yelled energetically. "Wait...why isn't he in chains?"

"As I always expected, Nathaniel Dorf is innocent and has been cleared of all charges," said Guera. "My suspicion is that Forredar had the crown from the start. Now, this should do it." Guera took a step back from Bayard and pointed at his legs. He whispered something that Nathaniel could not decipher, and with a bang Bayard was tossed up and out of the ground, landing in a heap on the paved path. The ground where he had been was unscathed, and his feet were where they were supposed to be.

"Ah, that's better," said Bayard. He rubbed his legs, which Nathaniel imagined would be very sore. "What are we going to do about this? If Forredar has turned against us, we are in grave danger. And do you think he's really in league with our old enemy?" Guera nodded and put a finger to his lips.

"I have no doubt that they have joined forces," he stated. "And that means that the rest of the Ubeles will have banded together also. We knew that it was always their objective to take the crown, but it has been so long....."

"But if Talitenkus has indeed decided to attack us again, why doesn't he come here himself? Sure, maybe he's not quite as skilled as you, you taught him after all, but with Forredar on his side, they would be able to wreak much havoc throughout the city. Wouldn't it be so easy for him to get in here and just take it?" asked the woman, who Nathaniel reasoned must have been Lauda.

"Yes, but he knows that we're on alert for him," said Guera, "and that he cannot teleport once he has the crown. So if he managed to break through our defenses and reach the crown, he wouldn't be able to escape with it unless he brings an army, which we know he doesn't have. However, that is a good concern, Lauda. We are going to reinforce our security and station more watchmen in the city. I will also propose a guard just outside the city walls to serve as an extra scout." That reminded Nathaniel of Herbert and Jason. Were they all right? Had they managed to get away, or were they captured and in prison at the very moment?

"Excuse me, uh, Master?" he asked. He felt all eyes turn to him.

"Yes, Nathaniel?" asked Guera, looking down at him kindly.

"Do you mean the rebel leader Talitenkus?" Guera nodded.

"Yes, and I have long suspected something like this happening. And that reminds me. We have got to straighten a few things out. I'm sure you have many questions, Nathaniel, and I intend to answer as many of them as I can. If you'll excuse us, men, Lauda," he said, and he led Nathaniel back towards the palace.

"Let us walk," said Guera. "I know a great path around the palace." They headed towards the western wall of the palace and began to walk around it. "So, you traveled all the way here from Kumaiyan?"

"Yes, sir, I did," replied Nathaniel. "To meet with the King about what has been happening lately."

"Yes, of course. I must say, I'm surprised. You made it through the Maze in four days, and even more impressively with Forredar on your tail. Do you know how many people, such as criminals, have ever eluded his grasp?"

"No."

"Two, if you count what you accomplished this week. The only other person he failed to catch was a highly-trained thief who happens to be able to move like a sly fox. We are still looking for him, consequently. But back to the matter at hand. I know and you know that Forredar described you as dangerous for a few different reasons, and one of them was to have the guards use force on you. Do you know what the other could be?" Nathaniel knew very well what it was, and had wanted to ask the wizard a question about it anyway.

"Yes, I think I do. You see, over the past few weeks, I've been using this strange....I'm not sure what to call it, power?

And while I'm fighting, everything else seems to move very slowly, and I see a lot of green light. Isn't that why he says I'm dangerous?"

"Exactly!" said the old wizard. "Now, do you have any idea of what this power is?" Only one logical answer came to mind.

"Magic?" he asked. He was a little disappointed, but not very surprised, when Guera shook his head.

"No, Nathaniel, that is not magic. You possess a power which is unique to the Dwarven race. Dwarves are very in touch with their surroundings, so in touch with them that they can bend time itself to fit their needs. Yet I understand that you used this power by accident? When did you first use it?" Nathaniel explained to Guera how he had been challenged to a duel and defeated the soldier. Then he explained the other fights he had gotten into since then, and how the strange power had assisted him through them. All through his talk, Guera made no attempt to interrupt him, but nodded and listened intently to each word. When he was finished, Nathaniel asked the wizard if he knew anything else about it.

"I know a little about this power," said Guera. "It is a special ability that dwarves have to make up for their lack of height and strength. If a dwarf learns to do so, he or she may harness this power on the battlefield or in other situations similar to the ones you described. Of course, this power takes a great deal of practice and concentration when a dwarf purposefully applies it."

"Then how is it different from magic?" blurted Nathaniel before he thought through his words. "Isn't magic a special power, or a group of powers, that one uses by concentrating and directing their energy into a spell?" Guera sighed.

"To understand this, you will need to understand the basic teachings of magic. Don't worry, we have time," he added. "There are two sets of beliefs that wizards and sorceresses use today. One, which is used by most of us in the castle, is the set of Conservative laws. The other, a more modern concept, is the set of Reform laws.

"The Conservative laws state that magic is the process of editing the natural world, using both seen and unseen parts of it to do so. These laws define our hands as the "tools" that wizards use for editing, and that wizards are nothing more than artists who learn how to use their hands properly to change the world, or small pieces of it. What this means is that a wizard's ability to cast spells isn't dictated by his "power," but by his skill and creativity with spells.

"You have encountered spells before. A spell is made up of an object and a command. To cast a spell, each wizard has their own trigger, or multiple triggers, that they may use to manipulate the natural world. Personally, I enjoy flicking my wrist, but other wizards have been known to use other, more subtle motions, or even to use a battle cry.

"A curse, such as "Gargoyle," is a type of magic that inflicts a lasting effect on whom it is cast. Curses are generally incantations made up of at least one full sentence, but "Gargoyle" is an exception to this rule, which is why there has been much research and debating done on whether or not it is indeed a curse. For now, let's just say it is. So, if I wanted to curse somebody, I would focus my mind on my personal trigger and say what I wanted to happen, all the while pointing at my target. Curses are usually more difficult to perform than spells simply because they use many words, but the lack of a set formula allows the caster to create any effect he or she can imagine.

"Now, when a young man or woman is apprenticed as a wizard, very few are due to the general decrease of interest and regulations involved in the complex subject, he or she gets to choose to specialize in spells, incantations, or the combative magic, the training for those who hope to be war-wizards. Through learning about spells or incantations, students read over hundreds of documents on their subject and practice casting simple, effective spells, or longer blessings and curses. The third type of study, combative magic, was created two centuries ago, making it a fairly young area of learning.

Combative magic focuses on the use of spells meant to quickly inflict pain or defeat enemies, but also requires the user to be as physically fit as a soldier. War-wizards are trained in mind and body to be quick and prepared to take hits from unfriendly spells or non-magical attacks. Through the course of their studies, war-wizards will build immunities to moderate spells and learn how to avoid spells. Keep in mind, the only way to "block" another spell is to create a strong shield around yourself before the spell can hit you. Most spells are able to break through the shields, however.

"All of these methods of performing magic are taught under both Conservative and Reform instructors. However, Reform laws state that magic itself is a blessing, a divine power given to those who are able to exercise their minds properly. They do not believe solely in skill, but in power and capacity. Tell me, did Forredar question you about magic at all?"

"Yes, he did," said Nathaniel. "To tell you the truth, it was very annoying." Guera smiled.

"I expected him to. See, it is a fact that dwarves have this natural power within them to move faster than any other creature at certain times. Because the Reforms, such as Forredar, associate magic with divine powers, it was only expected that he believed you to be a "skilled" wizard, and I'm sure his attempts to defeat you have only strengthened his convictions. Though I have no doubt that you have the skill and aptitude for learning magic, you are not using it at the present moment.

"Now we can talk about the current dangers at hand. I know that Kumaiyan likes to keep itself out of the political situation of the Kingdom, so I do not expect you to know much about the events preceding the rebellion."

"You've been there before?" asked Nathaniel, a little surprised.

"Yes, a long time ago, I was there on the King's business. But never mind that. The leader of the Rebellion, Raulin Talitenkus, was apprenticed to me approximately ten years ago. He was the son of the Duke of Jerebno, a city far to the west of here. When I decided to take an apprentice, I surveyed the candidates for the position very carefully. But when I found out that Raulin, the son of a nobleman, wanted to take up the study of the magical arts, I was compelled to accept him. Not only was he royalty, but his mind was very quick, very sharp. He noticed things that many other people did not. He proved to be a quick learner, the quickest and easiest student I had ever taught.

"When the time came for him to select a specialty, Raulin's noble blood influenced him in his choice. He chose to become a war-wizard, mainly to assist the Duke or King in times of war. He said that he fully understood the danger that he was facing, and eagerly began his more vigorous training sessions with me. By chance, Bayard was in his apprenticeship at the same time, under a different master, of course. Though I specialized in spells during my study, over the years I had accumulated a great knowledge of combative magic and taught both boys what I knew.

"Bayard immediately proved to be a very naturally talented fighter. His aim was impeccable, and still is, and he could dodge and dive away from the most precise attacks, magical and non-magical. He and Raulin practiced with each other, though his master did not think it was a good idea because wizards swear an oath not to attack another wizard unless a just cause arises. Though they had both taken the oath, their fights were not dangerous by any means. The oath only applies to a hostile attack towards another wizard. Forredar for example, has broken that oath. If he does ever come back, he will need to serve his time and re-swear the oath if we feel we can trust him.

"Though I was impressed with Bayard's skill, Raulin was the better war-wizard. He moved not graciously like Bayard, but sharply in the blink of an eye. He drove much force in his attacks and built up a strong immunity to magic. He put a lot of effort into his practice of the summoning of shields. In fact, his summoned magical shield is strong enough to repel any non-magical and moderate magical attacks. When Raulin and

Bayard turned eighteen and began their careers, both were well on the way to surpassing any other wizard in history.

"Then, a month after Raulin completed his apprenticeship, his father died. He was here, at the capital, during that time, for he was an assistant to the King. He immediately teleported to Jerebno upon receiving the news. I think he was secretly glad to leave the palace; he was disappointed that he was merely being used as a servant to the King rather than as a real war-wizard.

"When he reached home, he was very saddened at the death of his father. His father was assassinated for increasing taxes in the city. It was one reckless man who took up the sword and charged through the castle, eventually killing Duke Talitenkus and was then captured by the city guard.

"Raulin Talitenkus inherited the throne, and as his first act ordered to speak with his father's killer. As soon as the guards brought the man to him, he asked why he had killed his father. The man began to insult the Duke Talitenkus, and Raulin exploded in a fit of rage, bringing a ball of fire into his hand and killing the man in one stroke. He burned with anger, but a new sense of power began to form in him.

"Over the next few months, I routinely visited him, asking how he was doing, if he was all right. He was still the young man who had been my apprentice, but he was definitely different. He rarely left his castle and spoke only when necessary. He continued to mourn his father, and would occasionally hide in his room or use magic to conceal himself for days on end.

"A half a year later, Raulin got over his father's death and became very active with the way Jerebno was being run. He changed the government in the city, and won the people's support in a fortnight. He soon went from being the recluse, the gloomy Duke, to being the most beloved man in the city. He began expressing more of his ideas and ways of freedom in letters to other cities, explaining to them how the people wanted their leaders to act. When he gave speeches, he was so persuasive that I doubt he needed his magic half of the time. Yes, he shifted the people's feelings towards him with a little help from magic, but his arguments and ideas were expressed with such vigor and enthusiasm that the people didn't give their allegiance a second thought. In a month, Raulin Talitenkus grew into the most popular politician in the west, east, and south. Only our King was, and is, more popular than he ever was.

"But Talitenkus challenged the King's visions, explaining to the people how things should be run in the capital. When he saw that the King did not approve of his ideas such as taxation based on a person's value, or the 'eye-for-an-eye' law, he asked his subjects who they thought would be a better king. His subjects responded that he would definitely be a better choice, for they were now fully under his spell. Talitenkus traveled to the capital and proposed a completely fair election to the King, outlining the rules and guidelines for the process. Our King declined the proposal, saying that this was not how power was passed down, and a breach of tradition would be uncalled for. Both Talitenkus and I happen to think that the King was merely afraid that he would lose to Talitenkus, so he decided to cut off any chances of him losing the throne.

"Talitenkus was enraged and denounced the King in the palace, calling him all sorts of variations of 'coward', and some other very rude words. He grew so angry that he lost his temper and threatened the King with his "power." Usually, Talitenkus did not publicly use magic to impress or threaten people, so this was an unexpected turn of events. Luckily, the King's personal guards rushed to Krellin's aid, and Talitenkus teleported back to Jerebno before they could apprehend him.

"Talitenkus wasted no time when he got back to his city. I have heard that within an hour of his arrival, he began gathering any soldiers, any militia men, and any citizens who would support him in battle. This is about the time he recruited the Ubeles, including Forredar, to fight for him." Nathaniel gasped.

"Forredar is one of them?"

"Yes, and they were immensely wealthy, something that they offered to Talitenkus without hesitation. Talitenkus' army grew in size rapidly as he recruited and gained volunteers from multiple western cities. Then he declared war on Arcoiris, which had not been done in many centuries.

"He knew that the best way to upset the King was to attack the area around the capital before going in for the kill. As you may or may not know, his army swept through the lands around Vikelad, mainly targeting smaller villages with little or no defenses. He accumulated many soldiers this way, offering the villages a choice to join him or die. A few of the first villages refused him, and his army burned them to the ground and massacred the people. Meanwhile, the King kept his army close to him, fearing what would happen if Talitenkus came any closer. But I knew that the wizard would not attack the capital until he was ready, and though many people thought he was, he wasn't.

"Talitenkus was always fascinated with weapons when he was my apprentice. War-wizards do carry other weapons and wear armor, and he spent almost as much time studying them as he did magic. He soon learned how valuable good weapons were to any militant group, and set out to collect as many of the best weapons as he could. I'm not talking about merely the best swords made by a master forger, or the strongest, most protective armor ever made. I mean magical weapons that gave him even more power over his subjects, and more ammunition for his campaign. This is where you and the crown come in."

"Me?" asked Nathaniel. "What do I have to do with all of this?"

"You are a dwarf, Nathaniel. Talitenkus knows that dwarves have power. For some time during his campaign, he searched for dwarves to aid him. Those he could find flat-out refused and were killed or forced to go into hiding. But he never found you until just a few weeks ago, which is truly impressive. You see, he thought that he could meld a dwarf into a supreme weapon, a force of destruction that he could use at his will. He would have tried to properly train you and allow you to harness your abilities, which you can do here, with myself and others. If he had you, the potentially strongest non-magical fighter on his side, he reasoned that he would be nearly invincible. But he never found you, so he did not attack the capital, even when his army approached it. I called his bluff. I organized all of our forces into action, and told him that we would defend ourselves. He teleported right before our army left the city gates. He fled because he did not know if his forces could defeat us. And he has been hiding ever since. A result of this has been the flight of many of his supporters, and a general dislike towards him, though some, like the Ubeles, who are also in hiding, support his ideas for a government.

"But now he has made another attempt to gain a valuable weapon, the crown. The crown is in fact an object that could give Talitenkus infinite power over those in Arcoiris. Hidden in the crown is an incantation that allows the reader to hold all of its subjects as if they were possessions, giving the reader their true allegiance and control. The reader would be able to magically enforce any decrees, use people any way he wanted, and make himself the undisputed master of the country. He would be powerful enough to rival a god, as much as I hate to say it. Fortunately for us, it is very difficult to unlock the incantation, which is probably why Forredar returned it to us. Talitenkus, however, has most likely given a lot of thought to the subject and knows which spells to use to unlock it. If he ever gets to hold the crown in his hands, we are all in danger not just of dying, but of being slaves to him for all eternity.

"So now you know why it is so important for us to keep you and the crown safe. True, there are other weapons out there that Talitenkus could get his hands on, but he either does not know of them or cannot even begin to look for them. If he gets you or the crown, everyone, including yourself, will be in danger. Now, do you have any questions?" It was so much information for him to comprehend. Never before had Nathaniel thought that he was something of concern in the larger world.

"Um, whoa," he said. "Sure. How come Forredar has been living here? I thought his family was part of the Rebellion."

"It's odd that you ask," said Guera. "Forredar fled his family estate once the rebellion became a series of massacres on small villages. He did not approve of the behavior, and it was only through the use of basic magic taught to him by Talitenkus that he escaped."

"Right, but then why did he attack you, and me, for that matter?" Guera looked grim upon answering.

"I believe that his family has found him and blackmailed him into service for Talitenkus. They knew he was close to the King, and putting him under pressure would give him no choice but to join them. He has been growing more, how can I say it, shut out from us in the past weeks. He's been very morose, and now I'm beginning to get an idea of why. I only hope that he'll make the right choice."

"Which would be?" asked Nathaniel.

"That he will fight for us when the time comes, that his fear of his family and Talitenkus will be cast out of his mind when it is his chance to act. The best that he can do at the moment is stay out of our way, not to be cruel. I feel a great deal of sympathy for what has happened to him."

"What you *think* happened to him," said Nathaniel. He wasn't ready to forgive Forredar just yet. "Maybe he just changed his mind and decided to help out his family." To his surprise, Guera shrugged.

"Maybe, but we may never know. Ah, I think someone is here to see you," he said, pointing forward. They had circled the palace completely, and in front of them was Jason, accompanied by Herbert who was flying beside him.

"Dorf!" yelled Herbert. "We've been looking all over for you! We thought they got you!" Jason and Herbert ran and flew to his side, the latter involving Herbert. Nathaniel was surprised to see that no guards were behind them.

"Herbert, Jason, what happened to you? How did you get here?" he asked.

"The horses led the guards on a nice long chase before turning around," said Jason. "So we decided to go after you. But the city was very crowded, so of course we had no idea which direction you went off in. Then we saw those wanted posters of us hanging all over the place, so we ducked into an alleyway and hid for a while before we could think of a plan."

"Yeah, but then we ran into this nice old lady who dropped her basket full of food," said Herbert. "And, being the gentleman that I am, I offered to assist her."

"Right, but I'm the only one who actually did anything," growled Jason. "You just flew around pretending to pick stuff up! Poor old woman didn't know what he was doing." Nathaniel failed to conceal a laugh.

"Anyway, she told us about some big event going on at the palace, that someone said a criminal was captured. We immediately thought of you, and asked her for directions to the palace. And after running all over the capital trying to find those gates, here we are now," finished Herbert proudly. He pointed to Guera as if he was not listening to their conversation. "So, did he say if he's able to put Ralf right?" Ralf! Nathaniel remembered another reason why he had traveled to the capital.

"Oh, Master Guera, this is Herbert," he said, pointing to Herbert. "And this is Jason." Guera extended his hand for Jason to shake.

"Charmed," he said. "What is this I'm supposed to do about a certain Ralf?"

"Yes, back in Kumaiyan, that wiz-Forredar turned a good friend of mine to stone. I've seen you undo the curse on others, so I'll just ask you: can you do the same for my friend? As a favor?" asked Nathaniel, pleading with the old wizard.

"Absolutely, I'll undo the curse whenever you would like. I could even do it now."

"Now? Right now? But how, it would take days to travel!" Guera wagged a finger over him.

"Do not forget, I have been to your town before. I can teleport there in an instant. I could take you with, if you would like. I am sure you want to see your friend again."

"You can? I thought only wizards could teleport!" said Nathaniel, astounded.

"I can take you with me. In fact, I could take you all with me, if you want." Herbert flew to his common perch on Nathaniel's shoulder.

"Take me with! I want to go!" he said, excitedly. Guera nodded and turned to Jason.

"No, not me," said Jason. "I'm not going anywhere, I've got to see what the King has to say about me house being burned down!"

"It was Forredar's doing," said Nathaniel, as a response to Guera's questioning look. "He destroyed his home in one of his attempts to kill me."

"Nathaniel, you should know by now that he wasn't really trying to kill you," said Guera gently. "He was trying to capture you, although that can hardly be described as better than being killed when we are talking about Talitenkus' men." The wizard looked at Jason. "Well, the palace is just behind us. Aren't you going to visit the King?"

"I will, I just want to see this teleportation thing work with them," said Jason, indicating Nathaniel and Herbert.

"Well, then," said Guera. "We shouldn't keep him waiting for a demonstration. Dorf, I want you to grab my arm and hold on very tightly." Nathaniel hesitated, then reached up and latched himself onto Guera's arm. "And you, parrot, clutch your friend  as if you were holding on to your life." Nathaniel winced with pain as he felt Herbert's claws sink in to his shoulder. "Good, good. Now, I want you, though it may not be necessary, to think of what it is like in Kumaiyan, where it is, whatever you can relate to it. I'll give you a few moments to do that."

Nathaniel closed his eyes and thought of his cottage, the town center, and everything he was familiar with in their small town. He thought of his friends and how they must be faring as of now. Then he thought of how he himself had recently changed in the town, such as his experience at the dueling competition last End Day.

"Good, you both seem to be concentrating very hard," said Guera. "Now, with keeping that information in mind, relax, and let me take over." Nathaniel had not put a lot of effort into his thoughts, but Herbert took a gulp of air and sighed deeply. "Now, Nathaniel, I want you to look at Jason." He turned to face Jason. "Good. Now say good-bye."

"Good-bye," said Nathaniel without conscious thought. Suddenly, there was a flash of purple light, a slight buzzing noise in his head, a feeling of being sucked into space, and the next thing he knew he was standing in the center of Kumaiyan.

## The Revival

Nathaniel blinked, hardly believing what he saw. He was standing next to Guera, he felt Herbert on his shoulder, but he was in the entirely incorrect place. Had they really managed to teleport to Kumaiyan, or was it simply an illusion? He saw people whom he knew begin to gather around him, some with looks of shock on their faces, some shaking their heads and folding their arms in disbelief. Nathaniel saw Varon walk into the town center and point directly at him, smiling and calling for others to join him.

"Dorf! You're back!" he yelled as he ran forward. He stopped when he came close to Guera. In a split second, he drew his sword. In a much sharper tone, he mentioned the old wizard. "Who is this? Tell me, we've had enough witchcraft in this town, and we don't need anymore!"

"It's okay, it's fine," said Herbert, in what Nathaniel assumed to be an effort to calm Varon down. "He's with us, he won't hurt you. He probably could, but he won't," added Herbert helpfully. Varon still did not lower his sword.

"Wizard, what do you have to say?" he asked with a hint of menace in his voice.

"I understand why you aren't so trusting of me," said Guera. "I know that one of my profession has inflicted much pain on your town, and I apologize on behalf of the King. But I assure you, I mean you know harm. In fact, I am here because of young Dorf. He informed me of one who needs my help. Please, you should put your weapon away, I am not going to attack anyone now." Varon squinted, as if trying to see past Guera's words, and lowered his sword to his waist.

"You mean Ralf? Yeah, he's a statue now. I suppose my blade could find its way into my sheath if you cured him," said Varon with a trickle of mischief sounding through his speech. "Follow me, and don't make any sudden movements." Varon turned his back to them and parted the crowd with a stroke of his sword. "Move, nothing to see!"

They followed Varon through the street and to the stone Ralf, not twenty-five yards from Nathaniel's cottage. They stopped walking in front of the statue, who was coincidentally pointing directly at Guera.

"Well?" asked Varon. "Can you set him straight?" Guera nodded.

"Of course I can," he said. With that, he tapped on the stone Ralf while reciting the incantation. "May the stone that was once flesh be returned to its original state." As before, the air around the statue rippled. Nathaniel felt the ground shiver slightly. There was a loud crack, and the stone seemed to melt off of Ralf. Their militia captain stood in a pose for a second, then collapsed. Varon dove to pick catch him, but Ralf was too heavy. They both hit the ground with a thud.

"Yes, well, as Nathaniel knows, that can happen sometimes," said Guera cheerfully. Varon glared at him from his place on the dirt. Ralf stirred feebly and blinked his eyes. "See, he isn't even completely unconscious!" Varon grunted.

"It'd be nice if he was standing up as well," he remarked sarcastically. He tried to push Ralf off of him, but it was no use. "Can you help me?" Guera snapped his fingers. Nathaniel felt a slight breeze against his neck. Ralf rose as if he was a leaf caught in the wind and gently drifted to the ground some five feet away from Varon. Varon gaped in disbelief and pushed himself off the ground. To Nathaniel's relief, he sheathed his sword.

"I guess you all aren't that bad," he said while looking at Guera. "Thanks."

"It was no trouble at all, a very simple spell," said Guera, shaking off Varon's response. "It was the least I could do to make up for what has happened to your town." That reminded Nathaniel of his original objective in his journey.

"Varon, have there been any attacks on us yet? I'm sure Master Guera here would have told me if there were any official attacks, such as those ordered by the King, but has Forredar been back at all?" he asked, basing his question off of Varon's rather glum manner.

"Maybe, since we've been dealing with the bears. A few strayed into here and began blindly clawing at people, but no one is really hurt except for Colin, who had some nasty bruises. We've repelled them and killed them, but when one dies it just disappeared into smoke. Could these bears be summoned creatures from that wizard?" he asked. Nathaniel nodded.

"We fought past him in our travels north," he replied. "I wonder why he didn't choose to show himself? He definitely could have done a lot more damage that way."

"Probably scared to show himself after what we did last time. Oh, the soldiers escaped yesterday. Managed to break through a wall. Noah and I pursued them into the Maze, and decided to let them go, though I'm still upset about what they did."

"Well, it was never the King's wish for any of this to happen to you. He was oblivious to it the whole time," said Guera evenly. "We'll explain it to you in a while, but now we should move this man. Is there anywhere we can take him that he can sit down and have some water?"

"Yeah, let's take him to Mit's," said Varon. "That'll be a good laugh." Guera looked at him, confused.

"Ralf's a bartender," explained Nathaniel, "of another bar." Guera chuckled.

"Ah, I see. Very well. I will support him, and lead the way, please." He pointed at Ralf. "Airhover!" Ralf rose to about Nathaniel's height, suspended in the air with his back to the ground.

Varon led them to Mit's inn. On the way there, they passed several townspeople who gasped and clapped at the floating body of Ralf, now back to its human (rather than its stone) form. By the time they reached the inn, Ralf was pretty much awake, though very tired.

They enter the Inn of the Full Moon and helped Guera fit Ralf into a chair. It was very difficult, seeing as Ralf wasn't entirely conscious and a little on the larger side. They pushed and heaved and tried as hard as they could for several minutes before Ralf fell into the chair and rested comfortably.

"What the hell do you think you're doing?" asked Mit. He was behind his counter, and had been watching their struggle with mild interest. "Oh, you got him. Hello Dorf, Varon, Herbert, strange wizard, Ralf. Hey, Dorf, weren't you supposed to be on a trip or something? What ever happened to that?"

"We came back to see Ralf," said Nathaniel. "I thought he'd want us to." Mit nodded.

"Yes, I understand that, but how did you get here so quick- oh never mind, the wizard, right. Of course, only need him to clap his hands and you can go anywhere," he said in a mocking tone. "Do you know what his people are like, Nathaniel? You know, one of them petrified Ralf. I'm not sure I'm too trusting of this one." Nathaniel sighed heavily as he climbed into a chair.

"Mit, not all of them are bad," he said. "In fact, Forredar was the only one who had anything to do with this. He organized the attacks, not the King or any other wizard."

"Yeah, well I still remember having to run when he blasted my door to smithereens!" he yelled defensively.

"Mit, you're door is fine. He never blasted it away," said Nathaniel. "Can't you just calm down and keep that in mind? This wizard, Master Guera, hasn't done anything wrong. On the contrary, he saved me not too long ago from Forredar." Mit took a step back and looked Guera over, squinting.

"A master, eh? Aren't you one of the King's puppets who trained for years just to wait by his side like a servant and assist him whenever his tea is too warm?" he asked. "Because I think it's a waste of talent," he added to everyone's surprise. Guera grinned.

"Well, I have been known to fix up the King's meals from time to time, but I wouldn't refer to myself as a puppet. My work mostly involves the security and well-being of not just the King, but of all others in the city. I can do anything from heating up tea to capturing dangerous criminals," he said. "Of course, I have been told that I am rather good at producing weapons with my hands, so I have many employers in addition to the King, although he is my primary concern. Most of the time I do not take orders from him. I simply use my skills to do whatever is necessary to the Kingdom, some of which the King himself doesn't know about. For example, he does not know of this impromptu visit to Kumaiyan, but I would say it has lessened hostilities towards us, wouldn't you?" Mit nodded.

"Yeah, I really don't want to bash anyone's head in right now," he said, bitterly. "But I think the King has been rather irresponsible lately, with what's been happening and all."

"How so?" asked Guera. Nathaniel thought that he wasn't being aggressive or daring Mit to challenge him, but curious instead, with a tiny sparkle in his eyes.

"Well, how could he not know of what has been happening? A wizard under his command comes down here, brining some of his soldiers and interrogating everyone in our village. Not only did they ask us questions, but they brutally beat some of our people even though they gave them straight answers. What's more, they attacked Dorf here without any proof and nearly killed him, then that wizard turned Ralf into stone! This was supposed to be for what, our King's crown? And all the while, our King is sitting on his throne growing fatter by the day, completely out of the picture. How did he not know about this?" A silence fell over all of them. Nathaniel would have assumed that Guera, as a high-ranking official in the King's eyes, would take offense to the Mit's torrent of insults, but he appeared to stay calm.

"What you must know is that the King trusts us wizards. He relies on us to send information to him if we are venturing out to other cities or towns. Forredar chose to send him no information or simply incorrect information, which resolves the point of being oblivious. There was no way for the King to know about what was going on at the time, and I'm sure he is very sorry for that. However, he has put on a considerable amount of weight," said Guera to the astonishment of everyone in the room. "I daresay you're right, he does eat quite a lot compared to how much he is out and about."

"I guess we're pretty luck that Dorf rode up to your capital city, then," said Mit, a little lightened by Guera's jokes. "At least we somehow got word to the King before our town could be demolished. But has that wizard been punished for his actions?"

"I would say yes," said Guera. "Dorf saw it, he knows what happened."

"Yeah," said Nathaniel. "He tried to attack me again and take the crown for himself, but Master Guera fought him off. In the end he fled, and now the people at the capital are looking for him." Mit snorted.

"That's not much of a punishment!" he said.

"Yeah, couldn't you have tried to execute him beforehand?" asked Varon from his seat. Nathaniel exchanged looks with Guera, who seemed to be mildly amused.

"I wouldn't say he fled without being punished," said Nathaniel. "I'd think a broken leg and a knife in the same is pretty painful, don't you?"

"What?" asked Mit. "I thought he got away!" Guera smile grew even wider.

"I just gave him a few parting gifts," he said. "But we will cross paths with him again, and we'll put our efforts into apprehending him and making him pay for his recent behavior. I have no doubt that he'll make more attempts at the crown, and I will be glad to assist in his arrest."

"Oh, yeah, nice," said Mit. "I'd help, if I wasn't afraid of fighting someone who can spew fire out of their hands by simply talking. And if I had some free time on my hands instead of having to cater to people every minute of the day." Varon waved his hand through the air.

"Come off it, Mit. We're you're first customers this week, and you haven't even given us water yet, and Ralf's recovering from being a statue. He needs water, right?" he asked Guera. The old man nodded.

"Yeah, right," said Mit. He turned around and rummaged behind the counter for glasses. Nathaniel thought he heard muffled swearing escaping from the bartender's mouth.

"So, Varon, other than the bears, how have things been around here? I'd really like to know, and it feels as if I've been away for a long time," he said. Varon leaned back in his chair and coughed slightly.

"Things were going badly enough already before the bears began attacking us. Everyone was very tense, very worried. We all thought that the King's army would be here within days, and hastily made to prepare ourselves for an invasion. We've been working on our defensive strategies for the past week and practicing vigorously for the onslaught. Noah and I have been leading the training of all of the men and a few women who decided to join up. Despite our best efforts, we cannot just create effective soldiers in four days," he said sadly just as Mit brought them glasses of water. Mit placed the glasses on the table and stood by them and held out his hand. Varon stared at him and reached into his pocket.

"Fine, I'll tip you for this," he said as he placed a coin in the innkeeper's hand, "but it's the last time." Mit pocketed the coin and hurried back to his counter. "As I was saying, we've had a pretty downcast mood here. Most people admit that they're simply not good fighters, but others blame each other for it. A lot of people have been fighting with each other, not physically, and viciously arguing amongst themselves. No one has really been speaking with anyone else for the past two days. As a result, many of them just stay inside instead of train, which I guess they won't need to do anymore.

"No one has been running your tavern, Nathaniel. The whole thing has shut down for a while. With you gone and Ralf incapacitated, there was no one left to take charge of it. Everyone else was just so busy preparing for battle. I offered to help out, but the militia training took priority. Just as it was when the soldiers first came, our regular lives kind of stopped for a while. No one followed their schedules anymore, you know? It was pretty much anyone who could fight went into training, and anyone else started formulating our plans for getting our women and children out of the town in time for the fighting. We have canceled the duels, as you may have guessed. Everything just got wiped out this week. I hope things will change now that the threat to our village has been averted," said Varon hopefully. Ralf coughed loudly, but he was still asleep. "Are we going to wake him up now?"

"Ah, yes, of course," said Guera. He grabbed a glass of water and spilled its contents on Ralf, who sat up immediately. He shook his head and wiped the water off of his face before becoming aware of where he was.

"What the heck happened to me?" he asked. "Just a minute ago I was outside." He looked towards a window, where the afternoon sunlight was clearly visible. "And it had been a lot darker. Does it have anything to that wizard casting one of them spells?" He looked from Nathaniel to Guera to Varon and then to Mit. Then he looked back towards Guera. "And who's that?"

"Ralf, you've been a statue for the past week," said Nathaniel. "Forredar hit you with a spell, and he revived you a short while ago." He gestured to Guera, who nodded. Ralf stared at him for a moment or two, then nodded as if he accepted the turn of events.

"I suppose it does explain how it's light out now," he grumbled, "and why I feel a little stiff. But he attacked you, Nathaniel! And you're all right! How is this?"

"He teleported after he got you," said Nathaniel, "and just before I charged him. He attacked me during my trip through the Maze also."

"The Maze?" asked Ralf. "Dorf, when was this? Why have you been off traveling places?"

"When Forredar escaped, we reasoned that he would rally the King's army into action to fight us," he said. "We decided to send a messenger to tell the King what really happened to us, for he really did not know what Forredar was doing here. I was.....elected," he said with a sideways glance at Varon, "into making the journey, and the only way was to go through the Maze. For the past four days Herbert and I have been trekking up north, and just this afternoon we reached Vikelad. Don't worry, we got everything straightened out with the King, he was very nice about it. But then Forredar attempted to steal the crown, and was overpowered and fled. I informed

Master Guera here about your situation, and we teleported here to revive you."

"He teleported all three of you?" asked Ralf. "Odd. Herbert's been really quiet." Nathaniel noticed that Herbert was fast asleep, though still perched on his shoulder. The parrot was snoring as usual.

"Yeah, It's pretty peaceful, isn't it? I'd prefer it if he slept more often. Anyway, I'm glad to see that you're all right, Ralf. Mit, could you bring us some mead? Yes, I'll pay for it," he added when Mit grunted in an excessively loud tone.

Mit brought several glasses of mead to their table and eventually joined them in their drinking. They celebrated their good fortune, Ralf's revival, and the future for their town now that the militia didn't have to prepare for an assault. They toasted Nathaniel's success in his mission and to the King. For what seemed like hours they drank and sang, giddy with laughter and song. Guera contributed to the celebrations by creating sparks and refilling glasses with incantations.

As the afternoon light dwindled away into the evening darkness, more people entered the inn and joined the small festival. Their differences aside, Nathaniel and Varon were both pleased to see that no one held any grudges long into the celebration. People who Nathaniel knew to not get along well were arm in arm, clapping each other on the back or talking happily. But most of all, everyone wanted to see Nathaniel and Ralf. Nathaniel was congratulated and toasted to many times as was Ralf. Ralf was wished a speedy recovery, which seemed to already have taken place.

The next time Nathaniel checked his watch, it was nine o'clock and Mit's inn was completely full. Though upset with being disturbed "all afternoon," Mit eagerly accepted handfuls of coins and stowed them in his second-story room. Many townspeople became involved in the celebration, and it seemed as if the stories Varon told of them had never happened. Nathaniel was glad that something he had contributed to had helped the town repair itself. Just as he was about to pour more mead into his glass, he was abruptly jerked out the door and into the street. In his foggy, slightly inebriated state, he barely noticed the action until he hit the ground.

"What is it?" he asked, groggy. He looked up to see Guera pointing a finger in his face.

"The cloud will be lifted from your mind," sang the wizard. At once, the fogginess from his head disappeared. He suddenly felt very attentive.

"Yeah, what is it?" he asked again. "Why did you take me out here?" Guera produced a small, glowing orb from his robe. As Nathaniel watched, it pulsated with color and wisps of steam wrapped around it.

"The capital is in need of our assistance," he said gravely. Nathaniel eyed the orb curiously. "This crystal ball will send a message from another wizard to me. The intensity of the pulse is a measure of the estimated danger that wizard beliefs himself to be in."

"Wait, our assistance?" asked Nathaniel. "Like, you, me, and Herbert?" Guera nodded.

"Yes, you have been personally requested. But there's no time for the parrot. We'll leave him behind, you'll see him later."

"No, I'm not leaving my friend," said Nathaniel. "I'm bringing him out here before you say anything else." With that, he marched into the inn and searched for Herbert. He eventually found the parrot trying to snatch a glass from an unsuspecting Noah, and pulled him away before the latter could turn to look. Nathaniel carried Herbert outside and allowed him to rest on his shoulder.

"Huh, no, party's in there," moaned Herbert. With a short spell from Guera, he was brought into a semi-attentive state. "What do you want, Dorf?"

"Now that everyone's bird is here," said Guera, "we have to get back to Vikelad. I received an urgent message in this crystal ball, and its pulse is growing stronger each second. "

"So, they need our help. Did they say why?" asked Nathaniel. Guera shook his head.

"No, such details cannot be described in a crystal ball unless a true master of it does so. But they managed to say that you have been specified in this, and you should come with me. Yes, Herbert, you may come too." Herbert jumped.

"It's fine with me, let's move!" he yelled. Evidently the spell Guera had used on Nathaniel didn't have quite the same effect on Herbert.

"How imminent do you think the danger is?" asked Nathaniel. Just then, the crystal ball burst into shards. Guera surveyed it and spoke softly.

"Pretty damn imminent, if you ask me," he said. "Now, grab my arm, and we'll be off." Nathaniel grabbed the wizard's arm, and Herbert dug his claws into his shoulder. There was a flash of purple light, and Nathaniel once again found himself at the southern gate to Vikelad.

## The Master and Servant

"Master Guera! There you are!" shouted a nearby guard as soon as they arrived at the gate. "The King needs to see you and Mister Dorf immediately!" Guera tugged on Nathaniel's shirt.

"Let's go, Dorf," he said, and Nathaniel got the impression he was slightly worried. The guards held the gate open for them and they ran through the city streets which were now strangely empty. Guards lined the streets, standing in front of doors with their weapons held in front of them. The remaining citizens frantically rushed into whatever interior was closest to them.

"Master Guera, what is going on?" asked Nathaniel. "Why is everyone so worried?"

"I'm not entirely sure, but I think that someone is going to invade us soon," said Guera. Herbert snorted loudly.

"Would this be that Forredar wizard who's been chasing us up and down the country? Or someone else not fit enough to take us down?" he asked. Guera shook his head as they ran.

"No, much worse, much worse indeed," he said. "But I may be wrong, as unlikely as it seems."

"I'll keep my fingers crossed," said Herbert. "Oh, wait, I don't have any!"

They reached the palace gates, where a circle of six guards stood around a massive figure, blocking it from view. Nathaniel wouldn't have been able to see what they were hiding even if he was a human. Each guard looked a little scared, some of them trembling slightly.

"Sir," said one of the braver guards, addressing Guera, "he claims that he has to talk with Dorf over here."

"Me?" asked Nathaniel. Who would need to talk with him so badly that this much unrest had been caused. Guera stepped forward.

"Well, then, if it's this important, then allow us to see him!" he ordered. "Now!" The circle of guards parted to reveal the large but slightly hunched figure standing behind them. Nathaniel recognized the tangled braids, the gray, bumpy skin, and knew who the figure was; Brutus the troll had ran to the capital in search of his friend.

"Brutus?" said Nathaniel, shocked. Guera's surprise was mirrored in his eyes. "What are you doing here?"

"It has a name?" asked one of the guards. Brutus grunted.

"Of course I have name!" he bellowed. "But I need to warn little-dwarf-man of danger."

"Danger, what danger? What is happening, Brutus?"

"I saw them, tall, dressed with black, men gliding through forest. Both held sticks in hand and were shooting stars from them into forest. One shorter man with all black cloak and hood over face was laughing, other man look very angry. I heard one say words about dwarf, and little man, so I ran here fast to warn you." Guera audibly gasped. Nathaniel turned to face him.

"Who do you think he is talking about?" he asked. "Forredar isn't really coming back here, is he?"

"It fits this description perfectly. From what the tr-Brutus, says, Forredar and Talitenkus are on the way to steal the crown, and possibly capture you while they're at it. You there!" Guera pointed to a guard. "Go alert Everard that two intruders are on the way or are already in the palace. Have him send soldiers out into the street and have them search every alley and every street for two men dressed in all black, probably with cloaks and staffs. Go!" The guard sprinted towards the palace and crossed the yard in seconds. "Troll, I would like you to go and guard the gate you arrived at. Do not allow anyone through. Treat it as if it was your bridge." Brutus hesitated, then waved to Nathaniel and lumbered off towards the gate, dragging his large club with him. Nathaniel could not help but be amused at the comical scene.

"Have you seen that troll before?" he asked the wizard. Guera shook his head.

"No, but I know quite a lot about them, how they think, what they were born to do," he said. "We just have to use what we can to our advantage. Am I correct in saying that this troll will protect you if necessary?" Nathaniel shrugged.

"I guess, we only briefly met before, we had to solve his riddles. I guess Herbert, Jason and I are his only friends, so yeah, he would guard us," he said. Despite being very tolerant of others, Nathaniel still didn't believe that he could be associated with a troll in such a friendly manner. Guera seemed to understand, and patted him on his non-Herbert shoulder.

"It's okay, but one can never have too many friends. Such people are valuable assets and loyal allies in times of trouble. But as much as I would like to continue this discussion with you, we have a serious problem on our hands. Forredar and Talitenkus could already be in our city!"

"Well, what can we do to help?" asked Herbert. "By we, I mean you, me, and Dorf."

"We'll just have to assist the guards and send a few men back to the crown's vault," said Guera. "It's located deep inside the palace, towards the King's quarters. Of course, you wouldn't know where that is." Just then, the large dark-skinned man who had spoken with the King hours earlier appeared at Guera's side, clutching a long two-handed sword in his hands.

"Master, I have sent my men on their orders," he said in the same deep voice. "What do you wish me to do now?"

"Everard, thank you for your quick response," said Guera. "For now, I would like you to head back to where the crown is kept, and guard it. I will be sending another wizard along with you in a minute or two."

"But don't you think the gate is of greater importance?" asked Everard. "If we stop them there, we can stop them from ever reaching the palace!"

"I have sent a tr- someone else to guard the gate along with a contingent of others," said Guera calmly. "Your assistance will be needed back in the palace, I'm afraid. Go on, we don't have much time." Everard stared hard at the wizard for a moment, then turned towards the palace. Suddenly, there was a loud bang and a wave of heat flew through the air.

Two men stood before the palace gates. One of them was indeed Forredar, dressed in his all black attire. He looked utterly enraged, as if he couldn't wait to push past anyone who stood in his way.

The other man was almost a foot shorter than Forredar. He was covered in a large black cloak that concealed his entire body except for his right hand, which glowed red. This wizard must be the one named Talitenkus.

"I'll get the crown," rasped Talitenkus. The gates exploded and dirt and stone were kicked up and sent flying in every direction. Nathaniel saw Everard thrown backwards from the force of the explosion. Nathaniel ducked and held his hands over his head in an effort to block the flying debris. Finally, the chunks of earth settled and the dust floated gently to the ground. Talitenkus was gone, but Forredar was running forward as if trying to break through some sort of invisible barrier. Nathaniel saw Guera pointing at the younger wizard and muttering under his breath.

"Dorf, get out of here!" he yelled. He clenched his fist and punched forward in the same stroke. "Run!" Forredar ducked, and the flames soared over his head and incinerated a nearby statue. Silver light burst from Forredar's fingertips, and Guera spun off to the left to dodge it, all the while bringing his fists around to deliver a spell to his target. A conjured net shot towards Forredar, but the wizard was too quick. He brought his hand over his head in an arc, lighting the net on fire and disintegrating it entirely. "Go, Dorf!"

Nathaniel turned towards the palace, Herbert miraculously still perched on his shoulder, and ran as fast as he could in that direction when he saw Everard running up the palace steps. He must be chasing Talitenkus! Picking up his speed, Nathaniel followed him through the doors and into the palace hall. And into the half a dozen bears.

Everard stopped also. In the hall, blocking their path, were six fully grown black bears bearing their claws and roaring. Though he was sure he was in mortal peril, Nathaniel could not help but notice how out of place they were and what the people in Kumaiyan would think when he told them of this. Herbert flew off of his shoulder and higher, towards the ceiling, and to safety. Nathaniel drew his sword and braced himself to fight the bears. He caught a glimpse of Everard readying himself into a fighting stance, holding his sword in front of him with its tip pointing right at a bear's head. Nathaniel knew that they were going to need some kind of a miracle when the first three bears charged. And then it happened.

Nathaniel felt the world slow down around him, but much more than it ever had done before. He saw the bears in front of him almost come to a complete stop with their arms in the air and their teeth bared in rage. His hands glowed with green light and felt more energized than he had ever felt in his life. And yet he felt a strange calm, a confidence pulse through him as he brought his sword up for the fight. He could be invincible at this very moment.

He jumped forward and swung at the bear directly in front of him. As the blade neatly cut through the creature's neck, the bear gave a low, drawn out groan and vanished with a puff of smoke. Nathaniel landed some five feet behind the two advancing bears. He quickly charged the one on the left and stabbed its back. The bear vanished as the first one had. When Nathaniel turned to the third bear, he saw that it was slowly turning to face him. Wasting no time, he ran at the bear and sliced its legs out from under it and miraculously brought his sword around to cut through the summoned creature's chest. The bear fell, then vanished. Nathaniel ran to Everard, who had only begun to charge the remaining beasts. Nathaniel suddenly felt tired, as if drained of energy. He breathed deeply, and at the same time the world was brought up to speed.

Everard impaled one bear with his sword after crossing their distance in two strides. He pulled his sword away from the creature just as it vanished. Another bear to the right of him ran at him, but Everard brought his sword in front of him just in time. He was knocked back by the force of the soldier and landed fifteen feet away. As the bear advanced on him, he brought his sword up high. The bear swung its massive arms down at Everard just as he struck.

The bear was momentarily cleaved in two, then vanished into nothingness with a yelp of pain. Everard pulled himself up and ducked a tackle from the remaining bear. It overshot him and crashed into a pillar. As it struggled to stand, Everard hacked at its neck and killed it. The bear disappeared and the palace hall was now silent.

"Dorf, are you all right?" asked Everard. "That was amazing! You moved faster then I've seen anyone move before! How did you do it?"

"I'm a dwarf," said Nathaniel. "But never mind that right now. We've got to stop Talitenkus! Where was he headed?" Everard pointed to a wooden doorway off to the left of the throne room.

"He's gone after the crown, to its hiding place," he said. "Parrot, you fly behind us," he added to Herbert, who had flown back down to Nathaniel's height. "Follow me!" He waved his sword towards the door and ran to it. Nathaniel followed and they burst through the door and into an extravagant hallway. Unfortunately, he had no time to observe it closely as he was having a hard time keeping up with Everard.

They ran through the seemingly endless hallway, brushing past several horrified attendants and passing many guards, some of which who followed them. The hallways were full of sculptures, paintings, lit torches, and beautiful stone carvings etched into the walls. Every door they passed was shut, and Nathaniel noticed that a good number of them had thick iron bolts across them.

Everard didn't stop for anything, which was a good aid to Nathaniel. He easily pushed past any lingering stewards and cleared the way for Nathaniel and the few guards who had joined them. No one dared stand in front of them too long for fear of being trampled. For now, that was quite all right with him.

At last they reached a widened part of the hallway. It had a circular shape but looked similar to the palace hallways they had been through. Three doors, one to the left, one to the right, and one straight ahead of them, were located forty feet away. They came to a halt.

"Which one do we go through?" asked Nathaniel. Everard pointed his sword towards the right.

"We go there, but prepare yourself! There will probably be more enemies that way. Talitenkus always likes to leave something to watch his back," he said grimly. "Charge!" He took off for the door on the right. As he reached it, the door swung open and a sea of black shapes poured out of it.

They looked as if they were shadows. The black figures were the shape of soldiers, holding shields and swords, but were entirely black. They had no detail in them whatsoever, just an outline filled with darkness. Each was roughly twice Nathaniel's size, in other words, the size of the average human being.

Without hesitating, Everard slew the first two enemies in one stroke. Their bodies dissolved into what looked like black liquid and fell to the floor. Nathaniel and the other guards quickly joined in the fight. The dark soldiers were not very good fighters, but each one was able to hold its own for a few minutes before being brought down. Nathaniel easily surprised them from hacking at their legs or stabbing at them from underneath. Each time one of them lost a limb, the severed limb would dissolve and spread its death throughout the entire soldier. The whole thing would dissolve as the result of a missing limb.

They fought against the dark soldiers, pushing them back through the doorway. But they were innumerable and filled every inch of space in between Nathaniel's sword and the doorway. He slew scores of them, but when one fell, another one was there to take its place. He saw Everard cutting them down at incredible speeds, moving with graceful and fluid motions. The man was clearly a very strong and experienced swordsman. He didn't flinch when the dark soldiers surrounded him, he merely planted his feet and brought his blade through them. He roared and his dreadlocks whipped around savagely, but the dark soldiers did not respond any differently to his behavior. What would have surely demoralized any living creature didn't faze them.

The endless horde continued to put up a struggle, but Nathaniel knew that they were making progress, no matter how slow it was. None of the guards had fallen, Everard was hacking at the enemies with increased enthusiasm and strength, and Herbert flew above the dark soldiers, clawing their heads and cutting them in order to make them dissolve. Though they did not make any noises, Nathaniel could've sword he saw a dark soldier fall and clutch his neck before dissolving into a pool of darkness. After fighting them for several minutes, Nathaniel realized that he did not have any clue as to what they were.

"What are these things?" he yelled over the shouts and grunts of the combating guards.

"They're shadowlings," said Everard. "Not much when you fight them, really," he said as he knocked at least ten over with a hard swipe. "But they're easy to make, if you're a wizard." Nathaniel spun at that moment, de-legging two shadowlings in the process. They tripped and dissolved before hitting the ground.

"Is there a way to make them stop coming?" he asked. "Someone has to be summoning them!"

"There is, but it's behind them," said Everard. He beheaded six shadowlings and put his back to Nathaniel. "The one summoning them has a nice barrier blocking us. Our only chance is to kill enough of them to make Talitenkus give up. Or, we could try to push through them, though I'm not sure what good that'll do." The swordsman brought his sword spinning in a full circle two feet above Nathaniel's head, taking several arms from the shadowlings' ranks. "Despite their poor fighting skills, they are rather good at getting in the way." Nathaniel agreed wholeheartedly with the opinion as he cut the legs out from under a nearby shadowling. It fell towards Nathaniel, and he put his arms up to block it. The dark shape enclosed him...and passed right through. There had been no weight or force put on him at all! Once the shadowlings were given a fatal blow, they lost all solid properties.

"Everard! I have an idea!" said Nathaniel.

"Good, can you get across?" he heard Everard ask. "No real time for explaining, so just do what you're going to do!" Nathaniel nodded, though he doubted he could be seen. He took a deep breath and ran straight towards the doorway, hacking and slashing at the shadowlings' legs as he went. He had planned to use his height, or lack of it, to take the shadowlings by surprise and kill them without being buried in a pile of bodies. Their strange properties allowed Nathaniel to become enveloped in their darkness, but no worse for wear when he emerged into a small clearing and resumed to cutting down more of them. They had no idea where he was, and they fell instantly. His plan working, he cut a pathway through the darkness and ran through the doorway, which led to another hallway. But this one was empty.

It was lined with stones, with rows of torches hanging from each side. Other than that, it was blank and undecorated. Nathaniel looked back towards the fighting, where he could only see a black mass moving and pulsating with the struggle. He briefly hesitated, torn between helping those behind and continuing forward to stop Talitenkus. He turned away from the battle a little reluctantly, but knew he was doing the right thing. He sprinted the length of the hallway and ran into yet another wooden door. He turned the shiny golden knob, and it fell open to reveal a large, circular room.

This room was larger than the throne room. It's ceiling was nearly as high as the palace hall's, and it formed a dome over the room. The room was brightly lit, the source of it being a short rectangular podium in the very center. On top of the podium was the crown, untouched and secure, with a bright blue magical shield protecting it. But something with red sparks and flames was clashing with the shield. With a jolt, Nathaniel saw who else was in the room.

The cloaked Talitenkus stood over the podium with his hands held over the crown and could be heard muttering quickly through incantations. A continuing jet of flame assaulted the shield, but it showed no signs of damage yet. Then, remembering that Forredar had managed to steal the crown, Nathaniel realized that the shield wouldn't be much of a match for Talitenkus. Guera had described him as very skilled, probably more skilled than Forredar.

There were no other obstacles to hide behind, so Nathaniel quickly hid behind the door as Talitenkus turned towards him. Evidently, he was not seen, and Talitenkus went back to his magical work. Nathaniel exhaled deeply, relieved. But he had made it this far. What was he going to do now? He hadn't fought all this way just to hide from some wizard. No, he had the intent of stopping him and denying the wizard the possession of the crown. But how?

He still did not know how to slow down time voluntarily, and didn't think he'd be able to take down Talitenkus. Maybe he could hold him off for a while, talk to him, or run around the enormous room in circles while the wizard tried to incinerate him, but he would need reinforcements to finish him off. Nathaniel looked down at his hands, wishing they would glow and he could move faster than anyone else. Of course, they did not respond to his wants, his needs. They would act of their own accord when they saw fit. Damn dwarf powers. Never knew when they could help him out.

He would have to keep the wizard at bay, or at least break his assault to get to the crown. Taking a deep breath, he strode into the large room. Talitenkus was still furiously reciting whatever spells or incantations he was using. Nathaniel, almost hating himself for doing it, loudly cleared his throat. Talitenkus' head whipped around and he saw Nathaniel.

"Dorf," he said, slowly, "Dorf! So, you made it back here! Very good, very good! You have already begun to harness your true powers, no?" Though he did not attack Nathaniel, Talitenkus brought his hands away from the podium and held them in front of him. Nathaniel's heart skipped. He had broken the flow of incantations! "I asked, have you been using your powers?"

"Yes, yes I have," said Nathaniel, "but I really don't know how to control it." Suddenly, Talitenkus threw back his hood and Nathaniel could properly see his face for the first time.

He had a very handsome face, Nathaniel would give him that. His skin was tan with a dark beard nicely cut around his cheeks and around his mouth. His eyebrows were dark and thick. His hair, the same dark color, was neatly parted down the middle and hung down to his neck. Everything about Talitenkus' face was hard and intense. Nathaniel could see why he was a very popular politician, or why he had been. He looked as if he was the strongest, most confident man in the world! And in his eyes burned such intelligence and knowing that Nathaniel would gladly learn anything from him....

"You do not know how to control your powers," said Talitenkus, smiling slightly. "Good, good, I assume you had no way of learning, did you?"

"No, sir, I did not," said Nathaniel. "It just....it just happened to me one day. I'm not even sure how." He tried to change his expression to that of confusion, and it seemed to work. Talitenkus nodded keenly.

"Do you know that I have studied your Dwarven powers for some time?" he asked. Nathaniel shook his head. "Yes, I hadn't thought so. For the past few years, I have been searching for you, for someone just like you. Do you know the potential of your gift?"

"No, I don't," said Nathaniel. "It really doesn't seem to do much for me, to be honest. I just become very dizzy and my vision becomes blurry. I'm not sure I would exactly call it a gift."

"Ah, you say that solely because you have not been taught to use it well! Have you ever wondered why, or how, you came into possession of this gift, this power if you will?"

"Not really. I haven't thought about it much," said Nathaniel, scratching his head. He was trying to play dumb, but had the feeling that Talitenkus was beginning to manipulate him as well.

"Your race has been given the power because it is closely connected to this world. When you move, it responds and moves with you. It will truly make you one with the earth you stand on, the air you breath, the water you drink, and the body you inhabit. The power in you is what countless sorcerers and men of all kinds have been trying to harness for centuries.

"Dorf, I can offer you this now, I can offer you a very exclusive opportunity. Come, stand by my side, join my cause. I can teach you everything you want to know. I can help you unlock your powers to the fullest extent. I can make you invincible, one to rival the gods themselves! I can teach you how to not just manipulate your body and those around you, but how to manipulate the very fabric of this world we live in. You will be a renowned warrior, a hero, one of high accomplishment and honor! All you need to do is give me your allegiance." Nathaniel was startled to find his mouth opening, but a voice inside his head stopped him before he could accept the proposal.

*Stop! This is what he wants you to think! Don't give in!*

If I don't, he'll surely kill me and abscond with the crown!

*If you do join him, what do you think he is going to do first? He will snatch the crown and take you away, profiting twice from his burglary!*

Nathaniel thought hard between his options. He could not let the wizard use the crown, Guera had told him that much. Talitenkus was awaiting his response patiently, not showing any emotions but pure contempt on his face. Nathaniel saw his hand lazily drift back to the podium, and knew that he had to act.

"Why else should I join you?" he asked. "What do you plan to do once you have that over there?" He pointed to the crown. Talitenkus brought his hand up to point at himself, taking it away from the crown.

"What I am going to do is of paramount importance to our country," he began. "Once my work here is complete, I can focus my efforts on making a better world. Imagine a world with no crime, no war, no injustices. I can create such a world once I have used this crown to claim my power in Arcoiris. You see, I know that my views cannot be expressed before the King. He simply will not listen to what I have to say. I have made many propositions to change our laws to prevent crime and wars, but they have been dismissed with the wave of a hand.

"We cannot rely on the King and his advisors to help our country anymore. It is time that we, the people, take matters into our own hands and prevent the problems that plague our cities. Wouldn't you rather have our King elected rather than inherited? Wouldn't you prefer a military that only comes into action when our safety is threatened? I have learned that if I do not do this, it is not going to get done. Though there are many others who agree with my ideas, few of them are willing to stand up to our King.

"But I will not back down from such a challenge. I have been leading a fight against him for five years, and I intend to keep fighting until he is defeated! What I need from you, is your courage and skill. Though your powers have yet to manifest in such an ideally controllable way, your skills and bravery are indeed superior to those of others. You have been a very brave man throughout your journey, Nathaniel Dorf. I need help from good people such as yourself." Nathaniel felt himself go slightly pink. Though Talitenkus was certainly his enemy, he felt a strong sense of pride swell up inside him as he spoke the words. He had been brave, he had gone against the odds to make it here. And yet.....

It was a ploy. For all he knew, Talitenkus didn't care at all about which traits he exhibited. He was lying to him, using his words to sway him. All the wizard wanted was a truly powerful weapon. Tonight, he was very close to getting two. But Nathaniel remembered that Talitenkus would not be able to immediately escape with the crown after breaking through the shield. No, he could not teleport from the palace room, there were spells against it. Or could he? Though he still had only scraps of knowledge pertaining to magic, he reasoned that Guera was a skilled enough wizard to hold such spells against enemies. Talitenkus would need to take Nathaniel and the crown if he hoped to escape successfully. It was double or nothing for the rebellious sorcerer.

"Well, Nathaniel? Will you help me?" Talitenkus strode towards Nathaniel slowly as he spoke. "I can do much for our world, for you. All I need is your word that you will be at my side...." The wizard now stood over Nathaniel, only taller than him by about three feet. He was still an imposing figure anyway.

Oh, how he wanted to say yes. Nathaniel yearned to give up his facade, to join Talitenkus. He felt as if all his troubles would end. But it was not the right thing. Talitenkus was spilling lies to him, and Nathaniel wouldn't be helping anybody except him if he joined Talitenkus. He knew that the wizard would use any newfound powers to devastate the Kingdom, that he would spread destruction until he was proclaimed King. Nathaniel looked down at his shoes, as if they had the answer. Summoning his courage, he cleared his throat to speak.

"No," he said in a faint voice.

"What did you say?" asked Talitenkus, suddenly stern.

"No," said Nathaniel, with a little more volume added to his voice.

"Choose your words carefully, Dorf, or you'll end up amongst the dead," said Talitenkus. Nathaniel swiftly brought his head up to look the wizard straight in the face.

"No," he said firmly. "I won't join your rebellion. I was happy with the Kingdom until you started causing trouble a few weeks ago. I know what you plan to do, and I won't let it happen." Talitenkus frowned and his voice lost all warmth.

"Well, then, you are going to stop me?" he asked. "How will that hurt me? You're a dwarf who cannot even control the power he has been given, let alone a powerful wizard. I will push you out of my way if you try to stand in it. You see, the others learned, they did. The villages surrounding our capital knew how to save their lives instead of wasting them for what they believed to be noble causes. Now, I'll give you one more chance. What do you have to say to me?"

"No," said Nathaniel. "I'll never back down." He tried to be strong, but it didn't help that Talitenkus towered over him. His voice quavered as he trembled.

"This is how many of your kind went, dwarf," sneered Talitenkus. "I had hoped that at least one of you would have a brain larger than a bird's! But no, you're not going to 'back down' from me. I'll have to kill you - " a thought seemed to strike him as he said it. "No, not kill you....I can, *enslave* you to do my bidding....yes, that will work quite well....just a simple incantation and off you go.." Nathaniel had the impression that the wizard was talking to himself more than to him. Then, Talitenkus pointed at Nathaniel and opened his mouth to speak when there was a loud bang accompanied by shouts from behind. Talitenkus looked up and Nathaniel whirled around.

Forredar was sprinting down the hallway at full speed, pointing his right hand behind him as he sent jets of fire into the wall of shadowlings behind him. Forredar reached them and stopped.

"Master, we'll have to leave, quickly!" he said, out of breath. Talitenkus looked slightly annoyed.

"And why is that, Mister Ubele?" asked Talitenkus. "Has something gone wrong?" Forredar nodded his head quickly.

"Y-yes, sorry sir," he said quickly. "But Guera is on the way with reinforcements. They're using a troll!"

"Guera?" yelled Talitenkus, enraged. "He is not dead? I thought you would have taken care of him by now! Do you realize that the only way out is where they are, fool?" Forredar flinched at his words, a sight Nathaniel thoroughly enjoyed.

"Came on too strong, master. He's got about a dozen men and the troll with him, they'll be past the shadowlings soon."

"And how are the shadowlings holding up, Forredar?"

"It's a stalemate," said Forredar. "None of their guards have been killed, though I did manage to use the gargoyle curse on one of them, but they're providing us with a good wall of cover. Oh, the guards also have a parrot assisting them, master.

"A parrot?" yelled Talitenkus. "But what do you mean, helping?" So Herbert was still in the thick of the fight. Nathaniel was glad to hear that he had not been harmed.

"Its claws can c-cut through the shadowlings, master," said Forredar. "It's attacking them from above, causing them to dissolve from the head. None of our shadowlings can seem to bring it down."

"How far behind was Guera?" asked Talitenkus, his voice quickening. "How far?"

"I barely esc – no less than a hundred feet or so, master." Talitenkus swore loudly.

"I haven't even gotten the crown! You! Guard Dorf, and keep watch on the hallway! I will do this myself!" Talitenkus kicked Nathaniel in the chest, sending him flying towards Forredar. He then strode to the podium with the crown on it.

Flames burst from the tip of his fingers and began to eat away at the magical field protecting the crown. The fire could be heard whirling through his hands and into the shield, moving at speeds that could not be reached by lightning. Nathaniel felt the room grow slightly warmer. He tried to stand up to see what Talitenkus was doing, but Forredar planted a foot on his chest and held him down.

This could not be how it was supposed to happen. As he lay there, amidst the growing heat, the roar of the flames, the clanging of weapons behind him, and the weight holding him down, Nathaniel felt as if everything had fallen apart. He had been thrown into this mess when Forredar had shown up in Kumaiyan. He had traveled many miles just to clear his name, facing challenges and attacks on the way. And now he lay in the palace safe room, surely dying, watching helplessly as Talitenkus made his way to take the very thing he himself had been accused of stealing. It simply wasn't fair.

Nathaniel began to feel the weight on his chest increasing, his ability to breath weakening. He coughed loudly and flailed his arms, noticing a glimpse of silver as they went....

His sword. He had held onto his sword. He did not know how, had not even thought about it, but his sword was still in his right hand, ready to be used. Slowly, he let his right arm go limp, then quickly swung towards Forredar's leg.

"A-Ha!" His sword, inches away from making contact, was blasted up and away over Nathaniel's head. Nathaniel saw Forredar pointing at his face and glaring down at him. "Don't try anything else, dwarf." His last sliver of hope lost, Nathaniel closed his eyes and waited for it to happen. He did not want to see Talitenkus when he decided to kill him.

Nathaniel did find it odd that at this moment, he found himself to be...calm, or at rest. He no longer worried about stopping Talitenkus, he didn't think about Forredar, Guera, or Brutus. It was peaceful for him, and the feeling warmed his insides as he smiled.

"Shield's down!" he heard Talitenkus yell. He heard what sounded like shattering glass, and white lines of light spread through the air. It was as if a hundred white lightning bolts had shot through the sky at the same time and vanished in seconds. "Yes! It's mine!" Had Talitenkus broken the crown's shield?

"That's him, there he is!" he heard someone yell from behind. "Get him!" He heard a loud cry and Forredar jumped off him and landed several feet to his right. Nathaniel leapt to his feet and rolled out of the way just as a group of soldiers charged into the room, swords drawn.

The wall of shadowlings was failing. As Nathaniel watched, they dissolved before his eyes, leaving a long shadow on the floor. He saw Everard push a few remaining shadowlings out of his way as he ran into the safe room holding his sword above his head and followed by three other guards.

The soldiers who had ran into the room were forming around Forredar and Talitenkus, trying to surround them. The wizards disrupted the formations by sending flames or silver light their way. The soldiers moved out of the way, diving and shouting their way past the spells.

Talitenkus was spinning as he recited his spells, but the ten soldiers were closing in on him. With a loud scream, he summoned three shadowlings out of thin air. Nathaniel noticed that these shadowlings were taller and wider than the others had been. The bigger shadowlings pushed the soldiers back away from their master.

Forredar was moving faster than Talitenkus, waving his hands in wide arcs or complex patterns and dodging attacks from the soldiers. Two soldiers around him had fallen, one with a black mark on his leg and the other clutching his chest. Forredar not only used his magic, but used his arms to block attacks or knock his enemies down. The soldiers around him ran in circles, holding their sword tips towards the wizard but not daring to approach him any further.

Everard charged at Forredar and swung his sword. Forredar ducked and kicked at Everard's middle. He connected, and Everard staggered back, but he regained his footing easily. He ran at Forredar again and hacked at him, but a quickly created jet of fire blocked the sword from ever coming down. It seemed that Everard was strong enough not to let his weapon fly out of his grip from the attack.

Forredar dove to the right and spun in a whirl on the ground. He rose with a silver sword, one of the soldier's, in his left. He exchanged blows with Everard while the other soldiers formed a small circle around them, readying their weapons but keeping their distance. Everard knocked Forredar's sword aside easily enough, but would end up having to duck or dodge a spell from the wizard before he could deliver a killing blow. The combatants were locked in deadly battle.

Nathaniel looked back to Talitenkus, who was keeping his opponents away from him with a purple ball of light that surrounded him. Like the shield Nathaniel had seen Forredar use in Kumaiyan, it blocked the soldiers from getting at him or striking him. Then Nathaniel saw that the crown lying on its podium, outside of Talitenkus' shield.

"Dorf!" yelled a familiar voice from behind. Nathaniel turned to see Herbert fly over him and drop something into his arms. It was his sword. He quickly placed it in his right hand and held it in front of him. "There you go!"

"Herbert! Is Guera on the way?" he asked, his heart leaping. The parrot flew to his shoulder.

"Yep, he was right behind me. Helped us out a lot by blasting through those dark-lings or whatever they're called. He should be here at any moment!" Nathaniel nodded and knew what he had to do then and there. He took off towards the crown, dodging errant jets of fire and fallen soldiers as he went. He ran past Everard and Forredar, still locked in combat, then stopped to watch for a moment.

There was no way Everard could win. Forredar kept using his magic when his sword failed. Whenever Everard did get a good hit on his enemy, he would be pushed out of the way or forced to dodge an attack, giving Forredar time to quickly mend a cut or wound.

Suddenly, as Nathaniel watched, Everard was struck with a blue bolt of lightning that shot from Forredar's hand. He flew backwards, slamming into another soldier and sending them both to the ground. Forredar walked towards Nathaniel, pointing at him.

"Go, Herbert!" yelled Nathaniel. He felt the parrot leave his shoulder just as Forredar shouted. The jet of fire went right over his head. Nathaniel threw his sword at Forredar, but the wizard pounded it out of the air with his own. Nathaniel backed away from Forredar as he advanced and shot silver lights at him. Nathaniel dodged and ducked away from them, but knew he would run out of space eventually. After taking a few more steps back, he charged Forredar.

"Gargoyle!" yelled Forredar as Nathaniel jumped as high as he could and swung his fist forward. The beam of silver light struck Nathaniel's fist while in motion. Nathaniel's punch hit Forredar half a second later, catching him in the face. As Nathaniel landed, he saw Forredar grow rigid. Now only as high as his waist, Nathaniel looked up at Forredar's face, expecting to see him cursing or saying an incantation. His face, however, was perfectly still and the color of gray stone...

Forredar was now a statue, standing over Nathaniel, his mouth open as he had cast his spell. His sword was still in his left hand and hanging down at his waist.

A few soldiers cheered, and Talitenkus cursed loudly and a wave of heat swept across the room. Nathaniel turned to the purple shield in time to see the surrounding guards thrown backwards by a rush of air. Talitenkus shouted a command, and the shield around him vanished into thin air. He strode to snatch the crown from its podium when something green flew over it and picked it up and took it high towards the ceiling.

"Good job, Herbert!" cried Nathaniel as he watched his friend soar above the furious Talitenkus, clutching the crown in his claws. Talitenkus aimed at Herbert and yelled.

"Die!" The spell missed by a foot and struck the ceiling, leaving a scorch mark. Just as he began to cast another spell, something whizzed through the air and struck him in the side. Talitenkus ripped the arrow out of his left shoulder and tapped it with his thin fingers, healing it in a second. He then turned to his attacker, and so did Nathaniel.

Jason stood at the front of the hallway, leaning in close to the safe room. He held his bow in his left hand and had an arrow readied in his right. His quiver was slung over his shoulder, and it was full of arrows. Behind him was Guera, holding a tall wooden staff in his right hand and a golden shield in his left. He ran into the center of the room and stopped ten feet from Talitenkus.

"You had better give up, Raulin," he said. "You're surrounded, and you know you can't teleport out of this one!"

"Quite right, quite right," said Talitenkus. "But I don't plan on giving up, master. I think I'm going to fight and defeat you in a way which you cannot win." A silver light came to life around him, which soon formed a curved black and gold sword that rested in his hand. He brought the sword over his head. "And now, a shield!" A black square shield burst to life in his left hand and bound itself to Talitenkus' arm. "Your sword, Guera?"

Guera nodded and whispered a command. His staff morphed into a sword, but his was straight and the blade was completely white. The blade shone brightly against the blue light.

Talitenkus ran at Guera not five seconds later and swung his sword. Talitenkus parried the blow easily with his own sword and spun, knocking Talitenkus back with his shield. Guera made to attack Talitenkus, but his sword was blocked instantly by his former student's shield.

The two wizards were both fighting very well, attacking and defending with skilled movements, but Talitenkus was clearly the better swordsman. He moved faster than Guera and had no trouble blocking each and every one of his attacks before he could even follow through with his swing. Nathaniel didn't think that Guera could fend him off for much longer, but also didn't think he'd be able to help. He would just get in the way.

Talitenkus was winning, and soon began to dominate the match as it wore on. He showed no signs of tiring, yet Guera was moving slower with each attack, as if he could barely summon the strength to parry one blow. He resorted to using his shield to block nearly all of Talitenkus' blows, and made little effort to cut him down.

At last, Talitenkus spun and thrust his sword at Guera. The old wizard blocked the attack with his shield, but was pushed backwards by the force of the attack. He stumbled and fell to the floor, his shield laying at his side and his right arm splayed out with his sword still in it. He didn't seem to have the strength to lift his arm when Talitenkus approached him.

"Master, that was too easy," he said. "Seeing that I was your student, but wait a moment! Right, I was the one who became a war-wizard, and look where that's gotten me! Wasting all your time away with simple spells rather than the use of combative magic.....no wonder you couldn't even defeat the Ubele boy." Talitenkus' shield disappeared into smoke and he grabbed the hilt of his sword with both hands, ready to plunge it down.

"Raulin, what will you accomplish?" said Guera weakly. "As soon as you have killed me, the others will bring you down." Talitenkus laughed, and a glint of madness shone in his eyes.

"I will have accomplished something that no one else has even dreamed of," he said. "I have killed the 'great' Master Guera." He brought his sword down, but Guera moved with astonishing speed. He rolled away from the thrust just before the sword slammed into the ground. Talitenkus swore and brought his sword up to kill Guera, but the old man bested him again.

Guera's sword slid neatly into Talitenkus' shoulder. The younger wizard screamed, and Guera's blade glowed with yellow light.

"May you be expelled from this place!" yelled Guera. A flame leapt from the hilt of his sword and struck Talitenkus. He froze, his eyes wide open, his former master's sword in his arm, and an unheard cry caught in his open mouth. A second later, there was a loud bang and he vanished.

The surrounding soldiers and guards stood for a moment, then broke into applause and cheers. A slight mist hung over the spot where Talitenkus had been just seconds ago. Guera twisted his wrist and his sword was transformed back into a staff. His golden shield dropped to the floor. Nathaniel was shocked to see that Guera was looking directly at him, smiling.

"I want you to escort Nathaniel to one of the palace's guest suites," he said to no one in particular. "He's earned the right to stay here at the very least. Then I would like a few of you to come with me to see the King. It's been a tough night, and it will be over soon." Nathaniel looked at his watch. It was around eleven o'clock. Herbert fluttered over to his shoulder and dropped something onto the floor. The King's crown lay at Nathaniel's feet, now safe. And Nathaniel began to feel the same.

# Entering the Tunnel

Nathaniel awoke the next morning in the most extravagantly furnished room he could have imagined. First of all, it was about twice the size of his cottage, and had an entire sitting area with royal cushions and wooden armchairs. The curtains covering the large windows were purple with a golden lace around their edges. The bed he was lying in was big enough to hold at least four humans, so he had a lot of room to spread out while he was sleeping. Herbert was nestled at the foot of the bed, fast asleep and snoring. His bed also happened to have pillows nearly as large as he was.

It had been a long night, even after the fight in the safe room was over. He had been escorted by a few guards through the palace and into what would become his temporary room. While walking with the guards, he had been asked many questions about what happened once he reached the safe room.

"Is it true that you faced him alone?"

"Did you fight him off?"

"What did he try to do before we arrived?"

"How can your parrot talk?" He had done his best to answer the guards' questions and grew even more tired as he had drawn nearer to his room. Finally, at about midnight, he was allowed a reprieve from the barrage of questions and promptly fell asleep.

But when he awoke, he did not feel tired at all. He felt well rested yet very curious as to exactly what had happened the previous night. He still did not know how Forredar had been turned to stone, or how Talitenkus had vanished, and he knew only one person who would know the answers.

Nathaniel had been told, minutes before he fell asleep, that when he awoke he may go to the King's throne room to discuss his "situation." As he pulled himself out of bed, he wondered if he should wear some better clothing other than his plain, tarnished outfit. He walked to a washbasin in the corner and splashed water on his face and made an effort to make his hair neat and tidy. When he reached for a cloth to dry himself, he found a set of elegant clothing resting on a stool. He changed into the red and purple tunic and pulled a pair of black cloth pants over his old ones. The clothing seemed to be made to fit him perfectly, which it probably had been.

He walked to the room's mirror, which was located to the left of the bed. He looked himself over. Nathaniel thought he looked rather comical wearing such royal clothing, but accepted the change in attire without any complaints. At least he would be able to present himself in front of the King properly. He saw that his hair was combed over to the side, the result of his random swipes of his hands and splashes of water.

He went back to the bed and collected his watch and sword from the foot of it. He strapped his watch to his left wrist and sheathed his sword at his side. Nathaniel heard a movement of air behind him, and the next thing he knew Herbert was perched on his right shoulder.

"Dorf! Dorf! Go to the mirror!" the parrot shouted.

"I was just there, why?" asked Nathaniel.

"Yeah, but you haven't seen what you look like now!" Nathaniel sighed and reluctantly went back to the mirror. He looked exactly the same, except his fancy watch was now on his wrist, Herbert was on his shoulder, and his sword was at his side. He chuckled, thinking that he kind of looked like a –

"Pirate!" yelled Herbert. "See? With the jewelry, the sword, and your own parrot! I thought you'd be amused." Nathaniel really was, and he imagined what the crowd in the throne room would think when he showed up there. "Well, Captain Dorf, don't you have something to say?"

"Uh, I look like a pirate?" he said tentatively. Herbert shook his head. "Uh, you were right?" Herbert shook his head again.

"No, *Captain* Dorf, I thought you would like to address the crew!"

"Oh! Uh, argh!" he said, contorting his face to look menacing. Herbert nodded.

"Good, just had to see what you would look like if you did that," he said. "Now, let's go downstairs, we shouldn't keep the King waiting.

They left the guest suite and made their way down a few flights of stairs and through a very long hallway which led to the throne room. The palace seemed to be oddly quiet, yet Nathaniel's watch read nine o'clock. Where was everybody?

When they reached the throne room, they found it to be empty save for the King and Guera, standing in the center of the room, apparently engaged in a conversation. Upon his entrance, Nathaniel saw them both turn to him.

"Ah, Dorf!" boomed Krellin. "I trust you slept well! You certainly had enough time!"

"Yes, sir, it was very comfortable," said Nathaniel. "It was the best I've slept in weeks."

"Excellent, perfect!" said Krellin. "Now, Dorf, I believe I owe you my thanks. From what Master Guera says, you helped my men fight the shadowlings, and even kept Talitenkus distracted long enough for him to arrive and defeat him!" Nathaniel felt himself go red.

"Well, yes, sir, I did. I just thought it was the most important thing to do at the time," he said as Guera nodded and smiled. "And to be fair, Herbert helped a lot also. He's the one who risked his life to snatch the crown from Talitenkus, and was nearly incinerated had it not been for Master Guera. I deserve no more thanks than they do." The King threw back his head and laughed.

"Of course, of course, so modest! Yes, parrot, I heard of your bravery and actions too. You have my thanks, and if you have any requests, I would be more than happy to fulfill them for you."

"Well," said Herbert, "I would like to be knighted." The King chuckled.

"Very well, then. Mister Herbert, please fly to me and I will knight you. Master Guera, a sword please." Guera gave the command, and a silver sword appeared in Krellin's right hand. Herbert flew to the King and hovered in the air at his side. "This day, I dub thee Sir Herbert. May you carry your new title well and work to demonstrate your heart's true courage." Herbert flew back to Nathaniel's shoulder, looking very impressed and pleased with himself. "Now, Dorf, I wish for you to be knighted also. I mean, if I do it to a bird I might as well do it to you."

Nathaniel walked to the King. When a human was knighted, he would kneel at the King's feet. In this case, Nathaniel merely stood as the King tapped the top of his head with the sword and repeated the ritual. Nathaniel took a few steps back from the King, who was smiling broadly.

"I am please to announce that two knights have been added to our ranks today," he said to them. "This is a very high honor for both of you. Sir Dorf, with all you've been through the past weeks and with all of your contributions to our society, you have proved yourself above many men, even if you are still shorter than they are. And Sir Herbert, you have got to be the highest ranked bird in all of existence. You both should be very proud of yourselves."

"Thank you, sir," said Nathaniel. "I am." Herbert gave a small squeak indicating his pride.

"Excellent! Now, I believe Master Guera would like to talk with you both," said Krellin.

"Yes, that's right," said Guera. "And in private, if you please."

"Ha! Master Guera, though the most respected wizard here, this is still my throne room we're talking about," said Krellin. "But you may go into a hallway if you wish for your conversation to be private." Guera nodded.

"Nathaniel, come with me," he said, and he walked to the hallway in which Nathaniel had come from. Nathaniel followed the wizard and stopped once they were in an intersection of the hallways. Up close, he saw that Guera looked very worn and tired.

"Nathaniel, what you did yesterday was not only helpful, but it was brave," he said. "The only other people who would dare be in Talitenkus' presence by themselves would be his henchmen or one or two wizards from this city. I am impressed with your courage and would like to be the second person to congratulate you and Herbert for your services. We are still in debt to both of you."

"Thank you, Master Guera," said Nathaniel, dumbfounded. "But master, what happened to Forredar?"

"What do you mean?" asked Guera. Nathaniel thought he was missing something.

"He was turned to stone!"

"Oh, yes, wasn't he hit by a stray gargoyle spell from Talitenkus? That's what I assumed had happened."

"No, master, that isn't what happened," said Nathaniel. "He tried to turn me to stone as I leapt at him, and the spell sort of bounced off of my fist and spread through him. Wasn't I supposed to be turned to stone once I was hit by the spell?" Guera seemed to think hard about this, bringing his hand up to his chin and frowning.

"Nathaniel, the full extent of your powers is unknown to me, but I do know that dwarves have an ancient resistance to magic. Because your power is indeed a power, you are able to ignore or counteract magic, which is not technically a power. When you punched Forredar, I believe that you subconsciously activated your power, which knocked the spell away from you and back at its caster."

"Talitenkus told me that he could instruct me to harness my power," said Nathaniel. "Is that possible?" Guera nodded reluctantly.

"Yes, Nathaniel, Raulin has researched dwarves for a large part of his life, even before he became a politician. I am sure that he knows the proper training techniques and forms to turn you into a very dangerous, yet highly useful, weapon."

"Master, could someone here teach me how to use my powers properly? I would like to learn how, but I definitely don't want to have to sign up with Talitenkus to do so." The question had been on the tip of his tongue ever since he had fallen asleep, and he was glad when Guera answered.

"Yes, absolutely. I know a fair bit about instructing dwarves, but Everard is the best person for the job. I can teach you how to activate your powers at will, but sadly not how to use them. Everard, however, is the most skilled swordsman we have and can teach you how to fight properly with your powers. Of course, I can also help you build up an even stronger immunity to magic, which will undoubtedly help you on the road ahead."

"Wait, what do you mean, 'the road ahead'?" asked Herbert. "What happens next? I thought we won!" Guera shook his head sadly.

"No, Sir Herbert, I am afraid that we have not won yet. We have merely halted Talitenkus' progress temporarily. I know, and many others agree, that he is going to continue his campaign until he rules this country."

"How did you make him vanish?" asked Nathaniel. "Did he go somewhere else?"

"The incantation I used creates a magical barrier that affects only Talitenkus," said Guera. "As long as the curse is active, he will not be able to enter Vikelad ever again. When I expelled him, he was transported to the closest place away from here. By now, he has probably fled to the mountains, or to Jerebno to regroup and accumulate more troops."

"If you expelled him, then how can he continue his campaign?" asked Nathaniel. "I mean, he doesn't pose a threat to us, now does he?"

"He himself cannot enter here, so we are safe from him," said Guera. "However, he can send in anyone else to do his bidding or attack our city. He can also do what he did a few years ago, and attack the surrounding area and searching for any powerful weapons, two of which are safe now. He poses a threat to everywhere in the Kingdom except the capital."

"There are other weapons? I thought that the crown and myself were the only ones."

"No, Nathaniel, there are others he can choose to seek out, though they are far more difficult to actually find. There is a strong staff, a book filled with evil incantations, and a few other scrolls he wouldn't mind having in his possession. But the people in his service are the main threat to us. Mr. and Mrs. Ubele have both been trained as wizards, and he has other dangerous men and women on his side such as assassins and strong fighters. He is also capable of summoning shadowlings, but he also knows where they naturally occur, and will undoubtedly put them in his ranks. You also saw that his shadowlings are a bit stronger than normal."

"Master, when you actually expelled him, how did you do it? You weren't holding a staff, but a sword!"

"One of the most uncommon magical laws is that a wizard or sorceress may channel his or her magic through any object. Of course, we use staffs most of the time because they are simple and easy to use. A wizard can point a staff in one direction, thus allowing his spoken command to form a spell which travels in the direction away from the caster. For example, if I tried to channel my magic through you, then I would get negative or no results. You do not have a specific point or two sides. I am sure that Talitenkus was as surprised as anyone else when I expelled him."

"Master, what am I supposed to do now?" asked Nathaniel.

"What do you mean, Nathaniel? I thought you wanted to learn about your powers."

"Yes, I do, but how can I help the Kingdom now that Talitenkus is making another bid for the throne? I do not want to simply watch the war continue, especially after I thought it was over."

"Many others thought the war was over," said Guera, "but Talitenkus never gave up. He just fled from one battle and went off in search of even more powerful weapons to use in his assault on the capital. What he wasn't counting on was our tremendous victory over his army once he left. So, naturally, many people in the Kingdom thought he had given up. They were wrong. He has changed his style of warfare, and is now seeking other methods of taking over besides an open *military* campaign. I believe that he plans to demonstrate the use of his powerful weapons to rally others to his cause."

"But he doesn't have those weapons yet."

"And that is why it is so important that we find him and put an end to his campaign very soon. If we can cut off the potential sources of his power, we can end the war. As for what you will be doing, Nathaniel, it is up to you and Herbert. You have already contributed to our cause greatly, and there is nothing saying that you must help us."

"So, I could choose to stay here and train, if I wanted?" asked Nathaniel.

"Yes, Nathaniel, but why do you want to train? To become a great swordsman?"

"Yes, and to fight Talitenkus' forces. I believe that he is right, in one case. I could be a deadly weapon, but I choose to work for the Kingdom. I believe that if properly instructed, I could inflict a lot of damage on his campaign. I also accept that no where else but the capital will be secure, and that Talitenkus has probably linked me with Kumaiyan. If I learn how to fight well, I want to help defend my hometown from his forces. We have skilled fighters in Kumaiyan, but not nearly enough."

"Yes, Nathaniel, and you do not need to give me a decision just yet. Though we must move quickly, I will have time to train you and so will Everard. Most of the work that is being done now is being done by our scouts and Bayard, all of whom are keeping an eye out for Talitenkus and leading our mission to find him. I know that you have been away from home for some time, and it is a tough choice to make. I will always be around the palace if you want to stop by and give me your answer. Now, do you have any other questions?"

"Yes, master. What are you going to do with Forredar right now? He's still in the safe room." Guera chuckled lightly.

"Forredar? Why, I plan to leave him there for the moment. It's better than placing him in prison, where he could find a way to escape, but he is utterly trapped in stone. Besides, I think it's a rather ornate feature to the room, don't you? I think it gives people an example of what happens if they try to break in!"

"Or what happens when you mess with Captain Dorf over here," said Herbert. "Remind me never to be on the wrong side of your fist."

"I hope that answers all of your questions," said Guera. But a question had just popped into his head.

"Do you know why Herbert can talk?" he asked. "Because I've never figured it out, and Herbert says that he's been talking for his whole life." He was not surprised to see Guera shake his head.

"No, Nathaniel, it is a mystery that I thought over while you had your little celebration in your town. At first I thought that some other wizard had placed a blessing on him that allowed him to do so, but Herbert surely would have said something about that, and you say that you have never encountered wizards before. Next, I thought that he was a human transformed into a parrot with a morphing spell, but from what you've said that's not it, either. All I can deduce is that he is either part of an undiscovered race of talking parrots, or an anomaly crafted by magic or by the gods. I'm afraid I don't have any explanation for it."

"Yeah, and I don't think there needs to be an explanation!" said Herbert. "I'm a talking parrot, and it was about time I was knighted for it!"

"Sir Herbert, you were knighted because you stopped Talitenkus from reaching the crown."

"Yep, that too," interrupted Herbert. "And I've been talking for as long as I can remember."

"Okay, then, Master Guera," said Nathaniel. "I have no more questions for you. Thank you for your time." The old wizard put up his hand.

"No, Nathaniel, thank *you* for your time and assistance, it was of great help to us. I plan to see you later today." Guera swung his hand down for Nathaniel to shake, and he took it. "And you, Herbert, I will be seeing you also." He broke the handshake with Nathaniel. "Sorry, but I don't think I can shake your hand, or claws."

"It's no trouble," said Herbert. "Good-bye, wizard-man."

"Good-bye," said Nathaniel. Master Guera nodded and headed back to the throne room. As the sound of his steps grew fainter, Nathaniel wondered what he was going to do next.

Nathaniel and Herbert set off back to their room, up the staircases and through the hallways. Once they were back in the suite, Nathaniel found that his bag and bow and quiver full of arrows were on top of his bed. When he moved closer to look through his bag, he found a note lying amidst his possessions.

*Dorf-*

*I'm glad that you and Herbert are okay. I was happy to assist you in the defense against those two wizards. I'm sorry that I won't be able to formally say good-bye to you, but a few of the King's men and I left early this morning, along with Brutus, to inspect my inn and plan out the rebuilding of it. Because of my assistance, the King has agreed to pay for the construction of a newer, larger, inn for me. So, if you're heading through the Maze in a couple of weeks or so, you can feel free to stop by. Also, tell Herbert that he owes me, and I could use a new bow sometime soon. Yours truly – Jason.*

"What does it say, what does it say?" asked Herbert as Nathaniel silently read it. He reiterated the letter to Herbert, who laughed. "Oh, so I'm supposed to buy him a new bow? Well, I did win all of that money when you beat that soldier in the duel...." That reminded Nathaniel of how much had happened in the past two weeks. It seemed as if it had been a year since he had faced the soldier down in the duel, but only a week had passed. Suddenly, he remembered something else he needed to do, something he hadn't had a chance to do for the past few days.

He rummaged through his back and found his journal, a closed bottle of ink, and a quill. He propped himself up on his pillow and opened a blank page in the thin book.

"Dorf, what are you doing?" asked Herbert.

"I have a story to tell, Herbert," said Nathaniel, and he dipped his quill in the bottle of ink and began to record the events of the last week. As he thought about how much he would need to cover, his wrist pained in warning not to over do it.

## Journal Entry Number Three

*Date:4254, 20, First Day*                                    *Nathaniel Dorf*

*The events of the past week have been truly amazing and have taught me much about our country. I have not been able to keep this up to date because I've been off fighting bears, bandits, talking my way past a troll (which helped in more ways than one), and battling two evil wizards instead. And all of this was because I was wrongly accused of a crime.*

*Herbert has been a great help to me throughout my journey. He has been by my side in battle and has been the best friend I could ever ask for, even though he's a parrot. I'm just happy that he decided to come along, because this adventure would have been a lot harder, and certainly less exotic, without him.*

*Though I took away a lot from my valuable experience, I can't help but think that my life would have been a lot simpler and easier if I hadn't undertook this journey. Before magic and politics became a part of my life, I was happy and undisturbed. Now, I have been thrust into the larger world, the world of magic and politics, I feel as if I'm in way over my head.*

*I am planning to stay in Vikelad to train myself and my powers. I know that it will be hard, I know that getting involved in the war against the Rebellion will put me in danger, but I wouldn't be able to sleep at night if I stood by and watched it happen. If I do not use my powers to help the country, then I am allowing Talitenkus to attack more places and progress even* further with his campaign. If I allow him to continue this, I am as good as helping him by not getting in his way. So, I plan to fight him, because it will affect me and those around me if I don't. I'll face it, if Talitenkus wins the war and takes over Arcoiris, I won't live much longer. I would rather die fighting him and knowing that I am standing in the way of injustice rather than die begging for mercy at the wizard's hands. I'm pretty sure I know what the right way to die is, and I'm not willing to live in a world where he is in control. If he takes over, I will fight him to the death.

I am preparing to begin training, but I would like to stop back home first, most likely with some 'help' from Master Guera, and see my friends. They probably have not heard the news yet, and I am eager to tell them of what happened only hours after I had left Mit's inn.

I also would like to ask some of my friends such as Varon and Noah, if they would like to join the military ranks at the capital. Though Kumaiyan doesn't get involved in politics or wars, we are about to. If Talitenkus has been told of where I'm from, he will most likely invade it, search for me, and decide to burn or take the village for himself. With the help of others, I would like to lessen the chances of that. This is our country's war, our people's war, and those who can must do what they can to help.

I have been thrust into a more complicated world, I know that. But I have learned so much. Note: the formula for a spell is an object and a command (impress townspeople with knowledge?). I have learned the true value of a good friend, the importance of standing up for what I believe in, and that someone cannot be judged by their looks, including myself. Though it may seem as if I am limited in my actions because of being a dwarf, I learned that I have a power that most humans would desperately wish for. I also learned that if I am confident and believe in myself, that I have a greater chance of succeeding.

I learned about Brutus, the troll, and that he should not be feared or hunted because of his size and race. He is in fact a gentle creature who was vital in stopping Talitenkus from making off with the crown. I feel privileged to know him, and that much more enlightened now that I have met him.

Whatever the future has in store for me, I would like to think that I am ready for it. I will not back down from a challenge, no matter how tough training may be, no matter how strong the enemy army is, no matter how battered and bruised I become along the way, and no matter how much suffering I endure. Some people may think that the easiest thing to do now is to side with the winning army. I think that the best thing to do is to help make our army into a winning one.

# The Storm

While Nathaniel Dorf was writing in his journal, three
people were in the palace throne room, two standing and one

sitting. King Krellin sat in his throne, and Master Guera and Bayard stood in front of him. The King was very tired, and found it hard to stay awake in his massive chair.

"So, what can we do now?" he asked his advising wizards gloomily. "He's escaped again, and could start terrorizing the other cities and villages with his forces in days. What do you suggest we do to combat the threat?"

"I'm afraid there's not much we can do, my King," said Guera. "We have sent men out to look for him, yes, but none of them have been to the Ubeles' estate before. Of course, if one of our scouts happened to find it, their fortifications are great. However, Talitenkus may have moved the Rebellion headquarters over the past three years, in his search for his weapons."

"He's going to start looking for them again?" asked the King. Guera shook his head.

"No, my King, he will *continue* to look for them. That's what he's been doing these past years, not just hiding. He's been after the crown for sometime, researching it and learning how to unlock its spells. I am sure that he has also been practicing his magical skill a lot too. He is not restarting his campaign, but merely continuing it with a different approach." The King groaned.

"But what can I do now? I told the people the war was over, we believed it to be over! Do I just have to tell everybody that the rebels are a threat again? Do you know what that could do to me?" asked Krellin.

"If you ask me, sir," said Bayard, "I think you have a better chance of raising a large army if you tell everyone. First of all, you would be raising awareness to the threat, and the would compel many people to join the army in seconds. If they think that they are threatened and their security is at stake, they will be eager to put a stop to the rebellion. Also, you would prove yourself to be an honest King who simply made the same mistake everyone else did. Believe me, as long as you aren't the threat, there's nothing wrong with telling someone they're threatened."

"But that'd be the second time I fouled up. I was wrong about Dorf, wasn't I?"

"That was misinformation, my King. Forredar knew you trusted all of us with your life, and used it to his advantage. That was not your fault, and if you hadn't agreed to see him, Talitenkus might already be in control. No lasting harm has been done because of that, even if it was your fault."

"Speaking of Dorf, what are we going to do about him?" the King asked, looking at Guera. "What did he say?"

"I think that Nathaniel will go through the training we have planned for him," said Guera. "Everard would be more than happy to help him with his swordsmanship, and I can teach him to access his powers with ease." Krellin nodded.

"How much of a help will he be to us?" he asked. "Is it worth the time and effort to try to make him into a warrior?"

"Yes, I believe it is," said Guera. "He already has skills, he has already used his power. I have seen the results of it, and Everard has informed me of how he did last night. Did you know that he slew three summoned bears by himself before proceeding to assist them with the shadowling? Did you know that it was through his ingenuity that he ended up in the safe room with Talitenkus? And I'm sure you know that he withstood Talitenkus and Forredar on his own. I have no doubt that he is a valuable ally in such times."

"What happened between Dorf and Talitenkus before the battle broke out in the safe room?" asked the King. "How did he get away?"

"Talitenkus tried to get Nathaniel on his side. Because Nathaniel is a dwarf, Talitenkus has been searching for him for the past few years, and is prepared to instruct him in his powers. Nathaniel refused his offers, a feat that cannot go unnoticed due to Talitenkus' persuasive personality. I am sure that Nathaniel kept him talking until help arrived. He also stood up to Forredar without holding a weapon in his hands. In fact, that's the reason he's a statue now. Forredar's spell bounced off of Nathaniel's fist and turned him into stone. Nathaniel did not try to escape, my King. He either knew that we were coming, or swore to himself that no matter what, he would not join Talitenkus' forces. Either way, it was crucial to our success." Krellin nodded and shifted back in his seat.

"Do you think Talitenkus will go for Dorf's hometown? It seems that they are in mortal peril now that he has shown himself to be on our side. Talitenkus could blackmail Dorf into joining him by threat of wiping out Kumaiyan." A thin smile curled on Guera's lips.

"Talitenkus isn't ready to invade Kumaiyan yet, he would be making a grave mistake. I believe that Dorf will choose to visit his hometown before beginning his training, and Talitenkus would be a fool to attack while he is around. I plan to teleport Dorf to Kumaiyan with me to help rally their local militia to join up with us. Yes, they have a rather well-trained militia force in Kumaiyan. That's how they got rid of Forredar after he attacked Nathaniel Dorf. Talitenkus doesn't have enough troops to attack it just yet."

"Very well, then. But is it possible that Talitenkus could come back here? I know you placed a curse on him, but is there any possibility of him breaking it?" Guera shook his head again.

"No, Talitenkus cannot lift the curse. There are only two ways that he will allowed to walk into Vikelad again."

"And those are?"

"I would have to voluntarily lift the curse, or I would have to die. It is likely that he will be sending assassins after me sooner or later, similar to opening the gates from the inside."

"How do you think it is going to happen, Master Guera? Surely he will not wait for you to die!"

"Only time will tell what he plans to do," said Guera. "Though I am a skilled wizard, I cannot look into the future."

"Then this meeting is over. But Master Guera, I need you to do something."

"Which is?"

"Watch over Dorf, and do your best to instruct him. I expect great things from him." Guera smiled and his eyes lit up.

"So do I." Guera and Bayard turned away from the King and began to walk down the palace hall. Guera sighed deeply.

"What is it, Master?" asked Bayard.

"Oh, nothing too worrisome. I just remember a time when magic wasn't used for fighting and warfare, a time when it was unheard of for a wizard to strike anyone with a jet of fire or a gargoyle curse. You were too young, you wouldn't remember, but our world has become a much more violent place than it was half of a century ago. Wizards used to only use their skills for the benefit of mankind, creating food and water, repelling beasts away from the settlements, or healing the injured and curing the infirm. But that has now changed to some degree, and I fear that staffs and wizards' hands are becoming more like weapons than tools," said Guera.

"Do you think there will ever be a time when magic will no longer be used for violence?" asked Bayard.

"No, Bayard, I do not. There are too many evils in this world to allow that to happen. But we can hope that one day wizards and sorcerers and even witches will stop fighting with each other."

"Master, isn't Talitenkus the cause of a lot of this? He was the first wizard to break the law in a very, very long time."

"Yes, Bayard, but what point are you trying to make?"

"If we can defeat him, if we can put an end to the rebellion, don't you think the other wizards will not need to use violence?" Guera noticed a sort of longing, a hopeful note, in the young man's voice.

"There's a possibility that we will use violent magic a lot less often, but our spell books and scrolls have already been marred by it. Unless we completely reform our teachings, there is no way to separate violence from magic, just as it is somehow impossible to separate everyone and everything in our world from it. Though it is a terrible, terrible thing, it has become a part of our society and our world. No, Bayard, even when this war is over, our world will not be perfectly peaceful."

"Master, when we instruct Dorf, how do you plan to use him? Does he know of his resistance to magical energies?" Guera nodded.

"Yes, he does, and I believe that he can be used as a powerful weapon, but I have to give him some freedoms. I'm glad he came to us first because I think he's the only one left." Bayard looked confused.

"The only what left?"

"The only dwarf left. I don't know where his parents are, and the Dorf family has been the last line of known dwarves for a century. He could very well be the only dwarf, which gives us an advantage over the rebels." Bayard's eyes widened as he remembered a question to ask the master.

"Master, what about the parrot? What do you make of him?"

"I have given much thought to it, and I have not come up with a logical answer. It does seem very strange, very strange, and I intend to research it more over the course of the next months. Besides from being capable of speech, Herbert has other talents. He is clearly highly intelligent, and brave, for that matter. You heard about what he did. He snatched the crown right out from under Talitenkus' grasp. And what parrot asks to be knighted?"

The two wizards had reached the palace yard. The sun shone brilliantly overhead, with not a cloud in the sky. They had tried to end their conversation on a light-hearted note. But both wizards knew deep down, that a storm was coming.

## -The End-

Cover Art by Shakeil Greeley

Dorf by David White, Copyright 2007

## About the Author

David White is a student at Moorestown Friends School in Moorestown, New Jersey. He has been thinking of writing a novel for some time, and was glad to finally get Dorf out of his head and into the world.

## About the Artist

Shakeil Greeley is too a student at Moorestown Friends School, and resides in Delran, New Jersey, where he enjoys art and music.

www.ingramcontent.com/pod-product-compliance
Lightning Source LLC
Chambersburg PA
CBHW031105030726
4749.6CB00002BA/398